Horatio Stevens White

Selections for German Prose Composition

With Notes and a Complete Vocabulary

Horatio Stevens White

Selections for German Prose Composition
With Notes and a Complete Vocabulary

ISBN/EAN: 9783337401429

Printed in Europe, USA, Canada, Australia, Japan

Cover: Foto ©Andreas Hilbeck / pixelio.de

More available books at **www.hansebooks.com**

SELECTIONS

FOR

GERMAN PROSE COMPOSITION

With Notes

AND A COMPLETE VOCABULARY

BY

HORATIO S. WHITE

PROFESSOR OF THE GERMAN LANGUAGE AND LITERATURE
IN CORNELL UNIVERSITY

Boston
ALLYN AND BACON
1891

University Press:

JOHN WILSON AND SON, CAMBRIDGE.

PREFACE.

———◆———

THIS manual may be used by students of German who have finished the grammar, and have had some preliminary practice in translating German into English and English into German. In other words, it has been planned for students who have completed about one year of study in school or college, as well as for those who have reached a more advanced stage of preparation.

The editor has had some hesitation in launching a book of this kind, which was originally undertaken — before the appearance of the excellent " Selections " of Professor Harris and Mr. Fasnacht, or the announcement of Professor von Jagemann's forthcoming manual — with the design of partially filling what was then an apparent lacuna. Even now it may at least represent another variety of treatment of the subject. He desires, therefore, to anticipate if not entirely to meet some probable inquiries or objections.

The selections have been made with the view of interesting the student in their substance, and accordingly contain many references to German literature and life. The number of selections is small, from the belief that the student will be as much attracted to his work by following a connected narrative as by dealing with isolated sentences, whose difficulty is perhaps not diminished by such isolation.

Authors have been chosen whose style is simple and fresh, rather than formal or elaborate. The eighth extract, however, affords an opportunity for reproducing the structure of involved German periods; while the ninth selection may be satisfactory to those who prefer broken sentences and the staccato manner. The tenth extract, which with a brief introduction would form a little drama by itself, was chosen, in spite of its age, for practice in dialogue; and the eleventh and twelfth selections present specimens of an admirable and natural epistolary style.

The vocabulary has been made as comprehensive as possible, and is supplemented by a variety of renderings and suggestions in the notes. The chief stress is thus laid upon practice in framing properly German sentences, and the acquisition of a vocabulary has been subordinated to accuracy of syntax. It has seemed to the editor unnecessary to include any grammatical references, as many of the difficult points in translation are solved by the notes and vocabulary. Among the principal perplexities which students meet may be mentioned the choice of the proper prepositions to use with verbs or with nouns, the position of the verb (auxiliary, infinitive, participle, etc.) in relation to its subject, and the order and arrangement of words in the phrase or clause, and of phrase or clause in the sentence or period. It is the office of the teacher to explain and illustrate these usages, an office which could only partially be fulfilled by even the bulkiest commentary; and in prose composition more depends, after all, upon the skill and training of the instructor than in almost any other branch of language teaching.

The vocabulary has been derived from several sources. The editor has made a translation of the whole work, and has utilized whatever other translations of special selections were available, in order that the vocabulary might be not only fairly complete, but accurate and varied. Valuable assistance has also been received from Dr. Martin Krummacher of Cassel, a descendant of the well-known fabulist, and himself the author of numerous skillful and elegant translations from English into German. By his hand was furnished the principal part of the vocabulary for Nos. I., III., VIII., XI. v. and VI., and XII. I., and he has contributed various felicitous suggestions to the notes, which he has kindly examined.

Some hints to teachers in the form of a short bibliography of helps for instruction or for self preparation will be found at the beginning of the notes.

For the privilege of using selections from various copyright editions, the publishers and editor desire to express their obligations to Messrs. Charles Scribner's Sons for No. VII., to Messrs. Henry Holt & Co. for No. IX., to Mr. Charles Dudley Warner for Nos. I. and III., to Dr. Oliver Wendell Holmes for No. VIII., and to the executors of John Lothrop Motley for No. XI. The passages from the " Life and Letters of Bayard Taylor" are used by special arrangement with Messrs. Houghton, Mifflin & Co.

HORATIO S. WHITE.

ITHACA, N. Y.
August, 1891.

SELECTIONS

FOR

GERMAN PROSE COMPOSITION.

SELECTIONS FOR

GERMAN PROSE COMPOSITION.

_____

I.

HEIDELBERG.

I F you come to Heidelberg, you will never want to go
away. To arrive here is to come into a peaceful
state of rest and content. The great hills out of which
the Neckar flows infold the town in a sweet security; and
yet there is no sense of imprisonment, for the view is 5
always wide open to the great plains where the Neckar
goes to join the Rhine, and where the Rhine runs for
many a league through a rich and smiling land. One
could settle down here to study, without a desire to go
farther, nor any wish to change the dingy, shabby old 10
buildings of the university for anything newer and smarter.
What the students can find to fight their little duels about
I cannot see; but fight they do, as many a scarred cheek
attests. The students give life to the town. / They go
about in little caps of red, green, and blue, many of them 15
embroidered in gold, and stuck so far on the forehead
that they require an elastic, like that worn by ladies,

under the back hair, to keep them on ; and they are also distinguished by colored ribbons across the breast.] The majority of them are well-behaved young gentlemen, who carry switch canes, and try to keep near the fashions, like
5 students at home. Some like to swagger about in their little skull-caps, and now and then one is attended by a bull-dog./

I write in a room which opens out upon a balcony. Below it is a garden, below that foliage, and farther down
10 the town with its old speckled roofs, spires, and queer little squares. Beyond is the Neckar, with the bridge and white statues on it, and an old city gate at this end, with pointed towers. Beyond that is a white road with a wall on one side, along which I see peasant women
15 walking with large baskets balanced on their heads. \ The road runs down the river to Neuenheim. Above it on the steep hillside are vineyards ; and a winding path goes up to the Philosopher's Walk, which runs along for a mile or more, giving delightful views of the castle and the
20 glorious woods and the hills back of it. Above it is the mountain of Heiligenberg, from the other side of which one looks off towards Darmstadt and the famous road, the Bergstrasse. / If I look down the stream, I see the narrow town, and the Neckar flowing out of it into the
25 vast level plain, rich with grain and trees and grass, with many spires and villages ; Mannheim to the northward, shining when the sun is low ; the Rhine gleaming here and there near the horizon ; and the Vosges Mountains, purple in the last distance ;] on my right, and so near that
30 I could throw a stone into them, the ruined tower and

battlements of the northwest corner of the castle, half
hidden in foliage, with statues framed in ivy, and the
garden terrace, built for Elizabeth Stuart when she came
here the bride of the Elector Frederick, where giant trees
grow. Under the walls a steep path goes down into the 5
town, along which little houses cling to the hillside. High
above the castle rises the noble Königsstuhl, whence the
whole of this part of Germany is visible, and, in a clear
day, Strasburg Minster, ninety miles away.

I have only to go a few steps up a narrow, steep street, 10
lined with the queerest houses, where is an ever-running
pipe of good water, to which all the neighborhood resorts,
and I am within the grounds of the castle. I scarcely
know where to take you ; for I never know where to go
myself, and seldom do go where I intend when I set 15
forth. We have been here several days ; and I have not
yet seen the Great Tun, nor the inside of the show-rooms,
nor scarcely anything that is set down as a "sight." I
do not know whether to wander on through the extensive
grounds, with splendid trees, bits of old ruin, overgrown, 20
cosy nooks, and seats where, through the foliage, distant
prospects open into quiet retreats that lead to winding
walks up the terraced hill, round to the open terrace overlooking the Neckar, and giving the best general view of
the great mass of ruins. If we do, we shall be likely to 25
sit in some delicious place, listening to the band playing
in the "Restauration," and to the nightingales, till the
moon comes up. Or shall we turn into the garden
through the lovely Arch of the Princess Elizabeth, with
its stone columns cut to resemble tree trunks twined with 30

ivy? Or go rather through the great archway, and under
the teeth of the portcullis, into the irregular quadrangle,
whose buildings mark the changing style and fortune of
successive centuries, from 1300 down to the seventeenth
5 century? There is probably no richer quadrangle in
Europe; there is certainly no other ruin so vast, so impressive, so ornamented with carving, except the Alhambra. And from here we pass out upon the broad terrace
of masonry, with a splendid flanking octagon tower, its
10 base hidden in trees, a rich façade for a background, and
below the town, the river, and beyond the plain and
floods of golden sunlight. What shall we do? Sit and
dream in the Rent Tower under the lindens that grow on
its top? The day passes while one is deciding how to
15 spend it, and the sun over Heiligenberg goes down on
his purpose.

From *Saunterings,* by
CHARLES DUDLEY WARNER.

II.

A BEER–SCANDAL.

O N their way homeward, Flemming and the Baron
passed through a narrow lane, in which was a well-
known Studenten-Kneipe. At the door stood a young
man, whom the Baron at once recognized as his friend
Von Kleist. He was a student ; and universally acknowl- 5
edged, among his young acquaintance, as a " devilish
handsome fellow," . ¨ ¨thstanding a tremendous scar on
his cheek, and a cream-colored mustache as soft as the
silk of Indian corn. In short, he was a renowner, and a
duellist.   10

"What are you doing here, Von Kleist ? "

" Ah, my dear Baron ? Is it you ? Come in ; come
in. You shall see some sport. A Fox-Commerce is on
foot, and a regular Beer-Scandal."

"Shall we go in, Flemming ? "   15

" Certainly. I should like to see how these things are
managed in Heidelberg. You are a baron and I am a
stranger. It is of no consequence what you and I do, as
the king's fool Angeli said to the poet Bautru, urging him
to put on his hat at the royal dinner-table."   20

William Lilly, the Astrologer, says in his Autobiography,
that, when he was committed to the guard-room in White-

hall, he thought himself in hell ; for "some were sleeping,
others swearing, others smoking tobacco ; and in the chimney of the room there were two bushels of broken tobacco-
pipes, and almost half a load of ashes." What he would
5 have thought, if he had peeped into this Heidelberg Studenten-Kneipe, I know not. He certainly would not
have thought himself in heaven ; unless it were a Scandinavian heaven. The windows were open ; and yet so
dense was the atmosphere with the smoke of tobacco and
10 the fumes of beer, that the tallow candles burned but
dimly. A crowd of students were sitting at three long
tables, in the large hall ; a medley of fellows, known at
German universities under the cant names of Old-Ones,
Mossy-Heads, Princes of Twilight, and Pomatum-Stallions.
15 They were smoking, drinking, singing, screaming, and
discussing the great Laws of the Broad-Stone and
the Gutter. They had a great deal to say, likewise, about Besens, and Zobels, and Poussades ; and,
if they had been charged for the noise they made,
20 as travellers used to be in the old Dutch taverns, they
would have a longer bill to pay for that than for their
beer.

In a large arm-chair, upon the middle table, sat one
of those distinguished individuals known among Ger-
25 man students as a Senior, or Leader of a Landsmannschaft. He was booted and spurred, and wore a
very small crimson cap, and a very tight blue jacket,
and very long hair, and a very dirty shirt. He was
President of the night ; and, as Flemming entered the
30 hall with the Baron and his friend, striking upon the

table with a mighty broadsword, he cried in a loud
voice : —

" Silentium ! "

At the same moment, a door at the end of the hall was
thrown open, and a procession of new-comers, or Nasty- 5
Foxes, as they are called in the college dialect, entered
two by two, looking wild, and green, and foolish. As
they came forward, they were obliged to pass under a
pair of naked swords, held crosswise by two Old-Ones,
who, with pieces of burnt cork, made an enormous pair 10
of mustaches on the smooth rosy cheeks of each, as
he passed beneath this arch of triumph. While the
procession was entering the hall, the President lifted
up his voice again, and began to sing the well-known
Fox-song, in the chorus of which all present joined 15
lustily. . . .

At length the song was finished. Meanwhile large tufts
and strips of paper had been twisted into the hair of the
Branders, as those are called who have been already one
term at the University, and then at a given signal were 20
set on fire, and the Branders rode round the table on
chairs amid roars of laughter. When this ceremony was
completed, the President rose, and in a solemn voice pro-
nounced a long discourse, in which old college jokes were
mingled with much parental advice to young men on en- 25
tering life, and the whole was profusely garnished with
select passages from the Old Testament. Then they all
seated themselves at the table and the heavy beer-drinking set in, as among the Gods and Heroes of the old
Northern mythology. 30

"Brander! Brander!" screamed a youth whose face
was hot and flushed with supper and with beer; "Brander,
I say! Thou art a Doctor! No, — a Pope; — thou art
a Pope, by — !"

5   These words were addressed to a pale, quiet-looking
person, who sat opposite, and was busy in making a
wretched shaved poodle sit on his hind legs in a chair,
by his master's side, and hold a short clay pipe in his
mouth, — a performance to which the poodle seemed
10 nowise inclined.

"Thou art challenged!" replied the pale student,
turning from his dog, who dropped the pipe from his
mouth, and leaped under the table.

Seconds were chosen on the spot; and the arms or-
15 dered; namely, six mighty goblets or Bassgläser, filled
to the brim with foaming beer. Three were placed before
each duellist.

"Take your weapons!" cried one of the seconds,
and each of the combatants seized a goblet in his
20 hand.

"Strike!"

And the glasses rang, with a salutation like the crossing
of swords.

"Set to!"

25 Each set the goblet to his lips.

"Out!"

And each poured the contents down his throat, as if he
were pouring them through a tunnel into a beer-barrel.
The other two glasses followed in quick succession, hardly
30 a long breath drawn between. The pale student was vic-

torious. He was first to drain the third goblet. He held
it for a moment inverted, to let the last drops fall out,
and then, placing it quietly on the table, looked his antagonist in the face, and said,—

"Hit!" 5

Then, with the greatest coolness, looking under the table,
he whistled for his dog. His antagonist stopped midway in his third glass. Every vein in his forehead
seemed bursting; his eyes were wild and bloodshot,
his hand gradually loosened its hold upon the table, 10
and he sank and rolled together like a sheet of lead.
He was drunk.

At this moment a majestic figure came stalking down
the table, ghost-like, through the dim, smoky atmosphere.
His coat was off, his neck bare, his hair wild, his eyes 15
wide open, and looking straight before him, as if he saw
some beckoning hand in the air, that others could not
see. His left hand was upon his hip, and in his right
he held a drawn sword extended, and pointing downward. Regardless of every one, erect, and with a martial 20
stride, he marched directly along the centre of the table,
crushing glasses and overthrowing bottles at every step.
The students shrank back at his approach; till at length
one more intoxicated, or more courageous, than the rest,
dashed a glass full of beer into his face. A general tu- 25
mult ensued, and the student with the sword leaped to
the floor. It was Von Kleist. He was renowning it. In
the midst of the uproar could be distinguished the offensive words : —

"Arrogant! Absurd! Impertinent! Dummer Junge!" 30

Von Kleist went home that night with no less than six duels on his hands.   He fought them all out in as many days ; and came off with only a gash through his upper lip and another through his right eyelid from a dexterous
5 Suabian Schläger.

From *Hyperion*, by
HENRY WADSWORTH LONGFELLOW.

III.

THE MAN WHO SPEAKS ENGLISH.

I T was eleven o'clock at night when we reached Sion,
a dirty little town at the end of the Rhone-Valley
Railway, and got into the omnibus , for the hotel ; and it
was also dark and rainy. They speak German in this part
of Switzerland, or what is called German. There were 5
two very pleasant Americans who spoke American, going
on in the diligence at half past five in the morning, on
their way over the Simplon. One of them was accustomed to speak good, broad English very distinctly to all
races ; and he seemed to expect that he must be under- 10
stood if he repeated his observations in a louder tone, as ℞
he always did. I think he would force all this country to
speak English in two months. We all desired to secure
places in the diligence, which was likely to be full, as is
usually the case when a railway discharges itself into a 15
postroad.

We were scarcely in the omnibus when the gentleman
said to the conductor, —

" I want two places in the coupé of the diligence in the
morning. Can I have them ? "   20

" Yah," replied the good-natured German, who did n't
understand a word.

"Two places, diligence, coupé, morning.   Is it full?"

"Yah," replied the accommodating fellow.   "Hotel man spik English."

I suggested the banquette as desirable, if it could be obtained, and the German was equally willing to give it to us.   Descending from the omnibus at the hotel, in a drizzling rain, and amidst a crowd of porters and postilions and runners, the "man who spoke English" immediately presented himself; and upon him the American pounced with a torrent of questions.   He was a willing lively little waiter, with his moony face on the top of his head; and he jumped round in the rain like a parching pea, rolling his head about in the funniest manner.

The American steadied the little man by the collar, and began, —

"I want to secure two seats in the coupé of the diligence in the morning."

"Yaas," jumping round, and looking from one to another.   "Diligence, coupé, morning."

"I — want — two seats — in — coupé.   If I can't get them, two — in — banquette."

"Yaas — banquette, coupé, — yaas, diligence."

"Do you understand?   Two seats, diligence, Simplon, morning.   Will you get them?"

"Oh yaas, morning, diligence.   Yaas, sirr."

"Hang the fellow!   Where is the office?"   And the gentleman left the spry little waiter bobbing about in the middle of the street, speaking English, but probably comprehending nothing that was said to him.   I inquired the way to the office of the conductor: it was closed, but would

soon be open, and I waited ; and at length the official, a
stout Frenchman, appeared, and I secured places in the in-
terior, the only ones to be had to Visp. I had seen a diligence at the door with three places in the coupé and one
perched behind ; no banquette. The office is brightly 5
lighted ; people are waiting to secure places ; there is the
usual crowd of loafers, men and women, and the Frenchman sits at his desk. Enter the American.

" I want two places in coupé, in the morning. Or
banquette. Two places, diligence." The official waves 10
him off and says something.

" What does he say ? "

" He tells you to sit down on that bench till he is
ready."

Soon the Frenchman has run over his big way-bills, 15
and turns to us.

" I want two places in the diligence, coupé," etc., says
the American.

This remark being lost on the official, I explain to him
as well as I can what is wanted, — at first, two places in 20
the coupé.

" One is taken," is his reply.

" The gentleman will take two, " I said, having in mind
the diligence in the yard, with three places in the coupé.

" One is taken," he repeats. 25

. " Then the gentleman will take the other two."

" One is taken," he cries, jumping up and smiting the
table, — " one is taken, I tell you."

" How many are there in the coupé ? "

" Two." 30

"Oh, then the gentleman will take the one remaining
in the coupé, and the one on top."

So it is arranged. When I come back to the hotel,
the Americans are explaining to the lively waiter "who
5 speaks English" that they are to go in the diligence at
half-past five, and that they are to be called at half-past
four and have breakfast. He knows all about it, — "Diligence, half-past four, breakfast. Oh, yaas!" While I
have been at the diligence office, my companions have
10 secured rooms and gone to them; and I ask the waiter
to show me to my room. First, however, I tell him that
we three, two ladies and myself, who came together, are
going in the diligence at half-past five, and want to be
called and have breakfast. Did he comprehend?

15 "Yaas," rolling his face about on the top of his head
violently. "You three gentlemen want breakfast. What
you have?"

I had told him before what we would have, and now I
gave up all hope of keeping our party separate in his
20 mind; so I said, —

"Five persons want breakfast at five o'clock. Five
persons, five hours. Call all of them at half-past four."
And I repeated it, and made him repeat it in English and
French. He then insisted on putting me into the room
25 of one of the American gentlemen; and then he knocked
at the door of a lady, who cried out in indignation at
being disturbed; and, finally, I found my room. At the
door I reiterated the instructions for the morning; and
he cheerfully bade me good-night. But he almost im-
30 mediately came back, and poked in his head with, —

"Is you go by de diligence?"

"Yes, you stupid."

In the morning one of our party was called at half-past three, and saved the rest of us from a like fate ; and we were not aroused at all, but woke time enough to get 5 down and find the diligence nearly ready, and no break· fast, but "the man who spoke English" as lively as ever. And we had a breakfast brought out, so filthy in all respects that nobody could eat it. Fortunately, there was not time to seriously try ; but we paid for it and de- 10 parted. The two American gentlemen sat in front of the house waiting. The lively waiter had called them at half-past three, — for the railway train, instead of the diligence ; and they had their wretched breakfast early. They will remember the funny adventure with "the man 15 who speaks English," and, no doubt, unite with us in warmly commending the Hotel d'Or at Sion as the nastiest inn in Switzerland.

From *Saunterings*, by
CHARLES DUDLEY WARNER.

2

IV.

MARTIN LUTHER.

NO man has ever arisen in the German nation, or in any other nation, who was able to speak to his whole people with such weight as Luther. Never has a writer attained so great and so direct results with his 5 writings as Luther. Never has a professor so thoroughly renounced any pedantic superiority as Luther. The doctor of theology called into existence the German public school. The exalted peasant's son put into the hands of the peasantry the divine sources of truth. The monk 10 destroyed monkery, praised the blessings of marriage, and founded the evangelical parsonage. The priest restored its public dignity to his much derided order. The servant of the Church encompassed with warm love the nation from which he had proceeded, and said : " For 15 my Germans I was born. It is they whom I will serve." That in spite of school, university, cloister, and pulpit, he remained at heart a man of the people, — this made him the people's hero. The natural impulse of the whole nation was to follow him and to break away from Rome. 20 Whether his act be glorified or condemned, no one can deny that his people stood behind him. Those regions in which the preaching of the gospel was not initiated, or

in which it was suppressed, remained for a long time cut
off from the great development of our intellectual life and
of our literature. Without religious stimulus, without the
pastors as educators of the people, there was no internal
progress. As long as Luther lived he was the centre of 5
Germany. Toward Wittenberg from every quarter in
which German was spoken, streamed scholars who filled
the world with the reform spirit. When Luther died, the
German Protestants lost their unity; Melanchthon did not
show the firmness of which there was need; and the 10
University of Luther never again regained its commanding
position. His memory, however, remained sacred to all
Protestants. Comprehensive editions of his works appeared; his table-talk, his letters, were collected; and
his life was written in an admirable and truly popular 15
style. But Luther's preponderating authority was not
entirely a blessing for his church. It became also a
weapon of intolerance and a source of discord. Yet the
after effects of the might of his.spirit extended far beyond
those who considered themselves his legitimate heirs. 20

Translated from WILHELM SCHERER'S
Geschichte der deutschen Litteratur.

V.

LESSING.

N O German can utter the name of Lessing without an
echo more or less strong becoming audible in his
own breast. Since Luther, Germany has produced no
greater or better man than Gotthold Ephraim Lessing.
5 These twain are our pride and our joy.

Like Luther, Lessing's influence consisted not only in a
definite deed, but in exciting the German people to its
very depths, and producing by his criticisms and his
polemics a wholesome intellectual agitation. He was the
10 incarnate criticism of his day, and his whole life was a
polemic. This criticism made itself felt in the widest
domain of thought and feeling, — in religion, in science,
and in art. His polemics overcame every opponent, and
gained strength after every victory. It is comprehensible
15 that such a contentious champion caused no little stir in
Germany. All trembled at Lessing's sword. No head
was safe from him. Yea, many a cranium he smote off
from mere wantonness, and was moreover so malicious as
to pick it up and show the public that it was hollow in-
20 side. Those whom his sword could not reach, he slew
with the arrows of his wit. His friends admired the
motley feathers of these arrows; his foes felt the barbs
in their hearts.

It is noteworthy that Lessing, who was the wittiest man in Germany, was also the most honest. There is nothing like his love of truth. He could do everything for the truth except lie for it.

His style in writing is quite like his character, — true, 5 firm, unadorned, beautiful and imposing through its indwelling strength. His style is quite the style of Roman architecture ; the greatest solidity with the greatest simplicity.

Heartrending is it to read in his biography how fate 10 refused this man every joy, and how it did not even vouchsafe to him after his daily struggles, to refresh himself in the family circle. Only once Fortune seemed willing to favor him ; she gave him a beloved wife, a child, — but this happiness was like the sunbeam gilding the pinion 15 of a fleeting bird, and as swiftly vanishing.

Translated from HEINRICH HEINE'S
Über Deutschland.

VI.

GOETHE.

WHAT most interested our travellers in the ancient city of Frankfort was neither the opera, nor the Ariadne of Dannecker, but the house in which Goethe was born, and the scenes he frequented in his childhood and remembered in his old age. Such, for example, are the walks around the city, outside the moat; the bridge over the Main, with the golden cock on the cross, which the poet beheld and marvelled at when a boy; the cloister of the Barefooted Friars, through which he stole with mysterious awe to sit by the oilcloth-covered table of old Rector Albrecht; and the garden in which his grandfather walked up and down among fruit-trees and rose-bushes, in long morning-gown, black velvet cap, and the antique leather gloves, which he annually received as Mayor on Pipers-Doomsday. Thus, O Genius! are thy footprints hallowed; and the star shines for ever over the place of thy nativity.

"Your English critics may rail as they list," said the Baron, while he and Flemming were returning from a stroll in the leafy gardens outside the moat; "but, after all, Goethe was a magnificent old fellow. Only think of his life; his youth of passion, alternately aspiring and desponding, stormy, impetuous, headlong; — his romantic

manhood, in which passion assumes the form of strength; ·
assiduous, careful, toiling, without haste, without rest; —
and his sublime old age,— the age of serene and classic repose, where he stands like Atlas, as Claudian has painted
him in the Battle of the Giants, holding the world aloft 5
upon his head, the ocean-streams hard frozen in his
hoary locks." . . .

"Have you read Menzel's attack upon him?" said
Flemming.

"It is truly ferocious. The Silesian hews into him 10
lustily. I hope you do not take sides with him."

"By no means. He goes too far. He blames the
poet for not being a politician. He might as well blame
him for not being a missionary to the Sandwich Islands."

"And what do you think of Eckermann?" 15

"I think he is a kind of German Boswell. Goethe
knew he was drawing his portrait, and sat for it accordingly. He works very hard to make a Saint Peter out
of an old Jupiter, as the Catholics did at Rome."

"Well, call him Old Humbug, or Old Heathen, or 20
what you please; I maintain, that, with all his errors and
shortcomings, he was a glorious specimen of a man."

"He certainly was. Did it ever occur to you that he
was in some points like Ben Franklin, — a kind of
rhymed Ben Franklin? The practical tendency of his 25
mind was the same; his love of science was the same;
his benignant, philosophic spirit was the same; and a vast
number of his little poetic maxims and soothsayings seem
nothing more than the worldly wisdom of Poor Richard,
versified." 30

"What most offends me is, that now every German
jackass must have a kick at the dead lion."

"And every one who passes through Weimar must
throw a book upon his grave, as travellers did of old a
5 stone upon the grave of Manfredi, at Benevento. But, of
all that has been said or sung, what most pleases me is
Heine's Apologetic, if I may so call it ; in which he says,
that ' the minor poets, who flourished under the imperial
reign of Goethe, resemble a young forest, where the trees
10 first show their own magnitude after the oak of a hundred
years, whose branches had towered above and overshadowed them, has fallen.] There was not wanting an
opposition that strove against Goethe, this majestic tree.
Men of the most warring opinions united themselves for
15 the contest. The adherents of the old faith, the orthodox,
were vexed that in the trunk of the vast tree no niche
with its holy image was to be found ; nay, that even the
naked Dryads of paganism were permitted to play their
witchery there ; and gladly, with consecrated axe, would
20 they have imitated the holy Boniface, and levelled the
enchanted oak to the ground. ⌊ The followers of the new
faith, the apostles of Liberalism, were vexed, on the other
hand, that the tree could not serve as a Liberty Tree, or,
at any rate, as a barricade. In fact the tree was too high ;
25 no one could plant the red cap upon its summit, or
dance the Carmagnole beneath its branches. The multitude, however, venerated this tree for the very reason
that it reared itself with such independent grandeur,
and so graciously filled the world with its odor, while its
30 branches streaming magnificently toward heaven made it

appear as if the stars were only the golden fruit of its wondrous limbs.' Do you not think that beautiful?" -

" Yes, very beautiful. And I am glad to see that you can find something to admire in my favorite author, notwithstanding his frailties; or, to use an old German 5 saying, that you can drive the hens out of the garden without trampling down the beds."

" Here is the old gentleman himself!" exclaimed Flemming.

" Where?" cried the Baron, as if for the moment he 10 expected to see the living figure of the poet walking before them.

" Here at the window, — that full-length cast. Excellent, — is it not? He is dressed, as usual, in his long yellow nankeen surtout, with a white cravat crossed in 15 front. What a magnificent head! and what a posture! He stands like a tower of strength. . And, by Heavens! he was nearly eighty years old when that was made."

" How do you know?"

" You can see by the date on the pedestal." 20

" You are right. And yet how erect he stands, with his square shoulders braced back, and his hands behind him! He looks as if he were standing before the fire. I feel tempted to put a live coal into his hand, it lies so invitingly half-open. Gleim's description of him, soon 25 after he went to Weimar, is very different from this. Do you recollect it?"

" No, I do not."

" It is a story which good old Father Gleim used to tell with great delight. He was one evening reading the 30

Göttingen Musen-Almanach in a select society at Weimar,
when a young man came in, dressed in a short, green
shooting-jacket, booted and spurred, and having a pair of
brilliant, black, Italian eyes. He, in turn, offered to read;
5 but finding, probably, the poetry of the Musen-Almanach
of that year rather too insipid for him, he soon began to
improvise the wildest and most fantastic poems imaginable,
and in all possible forms and measures, pretending all the
while to read from the book. | 'That is either Goethe or
10 the Devil,' said good old father Gleim to Wieland, who
sat near him. To which the Great I of Ossmannstedt replied, — 'It is both, for he has the Devil in him to-night;
and at such times he is like a wanton colt, that flings out
before and behind, and you will do well not to go too
15 near him!'"

"Very good!"⌋

"And now that noble figure is but mould. | Only a
few months ago, those majestic eyes looked for the last
time on the light of a pleasant spring morning. Calm,
20 like a god, the old man sat; and with a smile seemed to
bid farewell to the light of day, on which he had gazed for
more than eighty years. Books were near him, and the
pen, which had just dropped, as it were, from his dying
fingers. — Open the shutters, and let in more light! were
25 the last words that came from those lips. Slowly
stretching forth his hand, he seemed to write in the air;
and, as it sank down again and was motionless, the spirit
of the old man departed."

From *Hyperion*, by
HENRY WADSWORTH LONGFELLOW.

VII.

COLLEGE.

SCHOOLMATES slip out of sight and knowledge, and
are forgotten; or if you meet them, they bear
another character; the boy is not there. It is a new
acquaintance that you make, with nothing of your fellow
upon the benches but the name. Though the eye and 5
face cleave to your memory, and you meet them afterward, and think you have met a friend, the voice or the
action will break down the charm, and you find only
another man.

But with your classmates in that later school where 10
form and character were both nearer ripeness, and where
knowledge, labored for together, bred the first manly
sympathies, it is different. And as you meet them, or
hear of them, the thought of their advance makes a
measure of your own, it makes a measure of the NOW. 15

You judge of your happiness by theirs, of your progress
by theirs, and of your prospects by theirs. If one is happy,
you seek to trace out the way by which he has wrought
his happiness; you consider how it differs from your own;
and you think, with sighs, how you might possibly have 20
wrought the same, but now it has escaped. ✓

If another has won some honorable distinction, you fall
to thinking how the man, your old equal, as you thought,

upon the college benches, has outrun you. | It pricks to
effort, and teaches the difference between now and then.
Life, with all its duties and hopes, gathers upon your
Present like a great weight, or like a storm ready to burst.
5 It is met anew; ,it pleads more strongly, and the action
that has been neglected rises before you, a giant of
remorse. J

Stop not, loiter not, look not backward, if you would be
among the foremost ! The great NOW, so quick, so broad,
10 so fleeting, is yours; in an hour it will belong to the
Eternity of the Past. The temper of Life is to be made
good by big honest blows; stop striking, and you will do
nothing; strike feebly, and you will do almost as little.
Success rides on every hour, — grapple it and you may win;
15 but without a grapple, it will never go with you. Work is
the weapon of honor, and who lacks the weapon will never
triumph.J

There were some seventy of us — all scattered now.
I meet one here and there at wide distances apart; and
20 we talk together of old days, and of our present work and
life, and separate. Just so ships at sea, in murky weather,
will shift their course to come within hailing distance,
and compare their longitude, and part. One I have met
wandering in southern Italy, dreaming, as I was dreaming,
25 over the tomb of Virgil, by the dark grotto of Pausilippo. J
It seemed strange to talk of our old readings in Tacitus
there upon classic ground, but we did ; and ran on to talk
of our lives. And sitting down upon the promontory of
Baiæ, looking off upon that blue sea, as clear as the
30 classics, we told each other our respective stories. And

two nights after, upon the quay, in sight of Vesuvius, which shed a lurid glow upon the sky, that was reflected from the white walls of the Hotel de Russie, and from the broad lava pavements, we parted, he to wander among the isles of the Ægean, and I to turn northward. ⌣ 5

Another time, as I was wandering among those mysterious figures that crowd the *foyer* of the French opera upon a night of the Masked Ball, I saw a familiar face : I followed it with my eye until I became convinced. He did not know me until I named his old seat upon 10 the bench of the Division Room, and the hard-faced tutor G——. Then we talked of the old rivalries, and Christmas jollities, and of this and that one whom we had come upon in our wayward tracks ; while the black-robed grisettes stared through their velvet masks. Nor did we 15 tire of comparing the old memories with the unearthly gayety of the scene about us, until daylight broke.]

In a quiet mountain town of New England I came not long since upon another. He was hale and hearty, and pushing his lawyer-work with just the same nervous en- 20 ergy with which he used to recite a theorem of Euclid. He was father, too, to a couple of stout curly-pated boys ; and his good woman, as he called her, appeared a sensible, honest, good-natured lady. I must say that I envied him the possession of his wife much more than I 25 had envied my companion of the opera his Domino.

I happened only a little while ago to drop into the college chapel of a Sunday. There were the same hard oak benches below ; and the lucky fellows who enjoyed a corner seat were leaning back upon the rail after the old 30

fashion. The tutors were perched up in their side boxes, looking as prim and serious, and important as ever. The same stout Doctor read the hymn in the same rhythmical way, and he prayed the same prayer for (I thought) the
5 same old sort of sinners. As I shut my eyes to listen, it seemed as if the intermediate years had all gone out, and that I was on my own pew bench, and thinking out those little schemes for excuses, or for effort, which were to relieve me or to advance me in my college world. |

10 There was a pleasure, like the pleasure of dreaming about forgotten joys, in listening to the Doctor's sermon : he began in the same half embarrassed, half awkward way, and fumbled at his Bible leaves and the poor pinched cushion, as he did long before. But as he went on with
15 his rusty and polemic vigor, the poetry within him would now and then warm his soul into a burst of fervid eloquence, and his face would glow and his hand tremble, and the cushion and the Bible leaves be all forgot in the glow of his thought, until, with a half cough, and a pinch
20 at the cushion, he fell back into his strong but tread-mill argumentation.|

In the corner above was the stately, white-haired professor, wearing the old dignity of carriage, and a smile as bland as if the years had been all playthings ; and had
25 I seen him in his lecture-room, I dare say I should have found the same suavity of address, the same marvellous currency of talk, and the same infinite composure over the exploding retorts.

Near him was the silver-haired old gentleman, with a
30 very astute expression, who used to have an odd habit of

tightening his cloak about his nether limbs. I could not
see that his eye was any the less bright, nor did he seem any
the less eager to catch at the handle of some witticism or
bit of satire, to the poor student's cost. I remember my
old awe of him, I must say, with something of a grudge ; 5
but I had got fairly over it now. There are sharper griefs
in life than a professor's talk.

Farther on I saw the long-faced, dark-haired man, who
looked as if he were always near some explosive electric
battery, or upon an insulated stool. I He was, I believe, a 10
man of fine feelings ; but he had a way of reducing all
action to dry, hard, mathematical system, with a very little
poetry about it. I know there was not much poetry in
his problems in Physics, and still less in his half-yearly
examinations. But I do not dread them now.   15

Over opposite I was glad to see still the aged head of
the kind and generous old man, who in my day presided
over the college ; and who carried with him the affection
of each succeeding class, added to their respect for his
learning. I This seems a higher triumph to me now than it 20
seemed then. A strong mind, or a cultivated mind, may
challenge respect ; but there is needed a noble one to
win affection.

A new man now filled his place in the president's seat ;
but he was one whom I had known and had been proud 25
to know. His figure was bent and thin ; the very figure
that an old Flemish master would have chosen for a
scholar. I His eye had a kind of piercing lustre as if it
had long been fixed on books ; and his expression — when
unrelieved by his affable smile — was that of hard, mid- 30

night toil. With all his polish of mind, he was a gentleman at heart ; and treated us always with a manly courtesy
that is not forgotten.

But of all the faces that used to be ranged below, four
5 hundred men and boys, there was not one with whom
to join hands, and live back again. | Their griefs, joys, and
toils, were chaining them to their labor of life, — each
one in his thought coursing over a world as wide as my
own ; how many thousand worlds of thought upon this
10 world of ours.

I stepped dreamily through the corridors of the old
Athenæum, thinking of that first fearful step, when the
faces were new, and the stern tutor was strange, and the
prolix Livy so hard. | I went up at night and skulked
15 around the buildings, when the lights were blazing from all
the windows, and they were busy with their tasks, — plain
tasks, and easy tasks, because they were certain tasks.
Happy fellows, thought I, who have only to do what is
set before you to be done.   But the time is coming, and
20 very fast, when you must not only do but know what to
do.   The time is coming when in place of your one master, you will have a thousand masters, — masters of duty,
of business, of pleasure, and of grief, — giving you harder
lessons, each one of them, than any of your Fluxions.
25   Morning will pass and the noon will come, hot and
scorching. |

From *Reveries of a Bachelor,*
by " IK MARVEL."

VIII.

THE YOUNG AMERICAN.

A YOUNG fellow, born of good stock, in one of the more thoroughly civilized portions of these United States of America, bred in good principles, inheriting a social position which makes him at his ease everywhere, means sufficient to educate him thoroughly without taking 5 away the stimulus to vigorous exertion, and with a good opening in some honorable path of labor, is the finest sight our private satellite has had the opportunity of inspecting on the planet to which she belongs. In some respects it was better to be a young Greek. If we may 10 trust the old marbles, — my friend with his arm outstretched over my head, above there (in plaster of Paris), or the discobolus, whom one may see at the principal sculpture gallery of this metropolis, — those Greek young men were of supreme beauty. Their close curls, their 15 elegantly set heads, column-like necks, straight noses, short curled lips, firm chins, deep chests, light flanks, large muscles, small joints, were finer than anything we ever see. It may well be questioned whether any human shape will ever present itself again in a race of such per- 20 fect symmetry. But the life of the youthful Greek was local, not planetary, like that of the young American.

He had a string of legends in place of our Gospels.
He had no printed books, no newspapers, no steam cara-
vans, no forks, no soap, none of the thousand cheap con-
veniences which have become matters of necessity to our
5 modern civilization.| Above all things, if he aspired to
know as well as to enjoy, he found knowledge not
diffused everywhere about him, so that a day's labor
would buy him more wisdom than a year could master,
but held in private hands, hoarded in precious manu-
10 scripts, to be sought for only as gold is sought, in narrow
fissures and in the beds of brawling streams. Never,
since man came into this atmosphere of oxygen and azote,
was there anything like the condition of the young American of the nineteenth century. ❘ Having in possession or
15 in prospect the best part of half a world, with all its climates and soils to choose from ; equipped with wings of
fire and smoke that fly with him day and night, so that he
counts his journey not in miles, but in degrees, and sees
the seasons change as the wild-fowl sees them in his annual
20 flights ; with huge leviathans always ready to take him on
their broad backs and push behind them with their pectoral
or caudal fins the waters that seam the continent or separate the hemispheres ; heir of all old civilizations, founder
of that new one which, if all the prophecies of the human
25 heart are not lies, is to be the noblest, as it is the last ; ·
isolated in space from the races that are governed by dy-
nasties whose divine right grows out of human wrong, yet
knit into the most absolute solidarity with mankind of all
times and places by the one great thought he inherits
30 as his national birthright ;❘ free to form and express his

opinions on almost any subject, and assured that he will soon acquire the last franchise which men withhold from man, — that of stating the laws of his spiritual being and the beliefs he accepts without hindrance except from clearer views of truth, — he seems to want nothing for a 5 large, wholesome, noble, beneficent life. In fact, the chief danger is that he will think the whole planet is made for him, and forget that there are some possibilities left in the debris of the Old-World civilization which deserve a certain respectful consideration at his hands.   10

The combing and clipping of this shaggy, wild continent are in some measure done for him by those who have gone before. Society has subdivided itself enough to have a place for every form of talent. Thus, if a man show the least sign of ability as a sculptor or a painter, for 15 instance, he finds the means of education and a demand for his services. Even a man who knows nothing but science will be provided for, if he does not think it necessary to hang about his birthplace all his days, — which is a most un-American weakness. The apron strings of 20 an American mother are made of India-rubber. Her boy belongs where he is wanted ; and that young Marylander of ours spoke for all our young men when he said that his home was wherever the stars and stripes blew over his head.

From the *Professor at the Breakfast Table*, by
OLIVER WENDELL HOLMES.

IX.

A GALLOP OF THREE.

W^E were off, we Three on our Gallop to save and to slay.

Pumps and Fulano took fire at once. They were ready to burst into their top speed, and go off in a frenzy.

5 "Steady, steady," cried Brent. "Now we'll keep this long easy lope for a while, and I'll tell you my plan."

"They have gone to the southward, — those two men. They could not get away in any other direction. I have heard Murker say he knows all the country between here 10 and the Arkansaw. Thank Heaven! so do I, foot by foot."

I recalled the sound of galloping hoofs I had heard in the night to the southward.

"I heard them, then," said I, "in my watch after 15 Fulano's lariat was cut. The wind lulled, and there came a sound of horses, and another sound, which I then thought a fevered fancy of my own, a far-away scream of a woman."

Brent had been quite unimpassioned in his manner 20 until now. He groaned, as I spoke of the scream.

"O Wade! O Richard!" he said, "why did you not know the voice? It was she. They have terrible hours the start."

He was silent a moment, looking sternly forward. Then he began again, and, as he spoke, his iron-gray edged on with a looser rein.

" It is well you heard them ; it makes their course un-mistakable. We know we are on their track. Seven or eight full hours ! It is long odds of a start. But they are not mounted as we are mounted. They did not ride as we shall ride. They had a woman to carry, and their mules to drive. They will fear pursuit, and push on without stopping. But we shall catch them ; we shall catch them before night, so help us God ! "

" You are aiming for the mountains? " I asked.

" For Luggernel Alley," he said.

I remembered how, in our very first interview, a thousand miles away at the Fulano mine, he had spoken of this spot. All the conversation then, all the talk about my horse, came back to me like a Delphic prophecy suddenly fulfilled. I made a good omen of this remembrance.

" For Luggernel Alley," said Brent. " Do you recollect my pointing out a notch in the Sierra, yesterday, when I said I would like to spend a honeymoon there, if I could find a woman brave enough for this plain's life? "

He grew very white as he spoke, and again Pumps led off by a neck, we ranging up instantly.

It was a vast desert level where we were riding.

Behind was the rolling region where the Great Trail passes ; before and far away, the faint blue of the Sierra. Not a bird sang in the hot noon ; not a cricket chirped. No sound except the beat of our horses' hoofs on the

pavement. We rode side by side, taking our strides
together. It was a waiting race. The horses travelled
easily. They learned, as a horse with a self-possessed
rider will, that they were not to waste strength in rushes.
5 "Spend, but waste not," — not a step, not a breath, in
that gallop for life ! This must be our motto.

So we galloped three abreast, neck and neck, hoof
with hoof, steadily quickening our pace over the sere
width of desert. We must make the most of the levels.
10 Rougher work, cruel obstacles were before. All the wild,
triumphant music I had ever heard came and sang in my
ears to the flinging cadence of the resonant feet, tramping
on hollow arches of the volcanic rock, over great, vacant
chasms underneath. Sweet and soft around us melted
15 the hazy air of October, and its warm, flickering currents
shook like a veil of gauzy gold, between us and the blue
bloom of the mountains far away, but nearing now and
lifting step by step.

On we galloped, the avenger, the friend, the lover, on
20 our errand, to save and to slay.

It came afternoon, as we rode on steadily. The
country grew rougher. The horses never flinched, but
they sweated freely, and foam from their nostrils flecked
their shoulders. By and by, with little pleasant admoni-
25 tory puffs, a breeze drew down from the glimmering
frosty edges of the Sierra and cooled us. Horses and
men were cheered and freshened, and lifted anew to
their work.

We held steadily for that notch in the blue Sierra.
30 The mountain lines grew sharper ; the country where we

travelled, rougher, every stride. We came upon a wide tract covered with wild-sage bushes.

A little pathway suddenly opened before me, as a lane rifts in the press of hurrying legions 'mid the crush of a city thoroughfare. I dashed on a hundred yards in ad- 5 vance of my comrades.

What was this? The bushes trampled and broken down, just as we in our passage were trampling and breaking them. What?

Hoof-marks in the dust !   10

" The trail ! " I cried, " the trail ! "

They sprang toward me. Brent followed the line with his eye. He galloped forward, with a look of triumph.

Suddenly, I saw him fling himself half out of his sad- dle, and clutch at some object. Still going at speed, 15 and holding on by one leg alone, after the Indian fashion for sport or shelter against an arrow or a shot, he picked up something from the bushes, regained his seat, and waved his treasure to us. We ranged up and rode beside him over a gap in the sage.   20

A lady's glove ! — that was what he had stooped to recover. An old buckskin riding gauntlet, neatly stitched about the wrist, and pinked on the wristlet. A pretty glove, strangely, almost tragically, feminine in this des- olation. A well-worn glove, that had seen better days, 25 like its mistress, but never any day so good as this, when it proved to us that we were on the sure path of rescue.

" I take up the gauntlet," said Brent. " Gare à qui le touche ! "   30

We said nothing more; for this unconscious token, this silent cry for help, made the danger seem more closely imminent. We pressed on. No flinching in any of the horses. Where we could, we were going at speed. 5 Where they could, the horses kept side by side, nerving each other. Companionship sustained them in that terrible ride.

And now in front the purple Sierra was growing brown, and rising up a distinct wall, cleft visibly with dell, gully, 10 ravine, and cañon. The saw-teeth of the ridge defined themselves sharply into peak and pinnacle. Broad fields of cool snow gleamed upon the summits.

Brent's unerring judgment had divined the course aright. On he led, charging along the trail, as if he were 15 trampling already on the carcasses of the pursued. On he led and we followed, drawing nearer, nearer to our goal.

The brown Sierra here was close at hand. Its glittering, icy summits, above the dark and sheeny walls, far 20 above the black phalanxes of clambering pines, stooped forward and hung over us as we rode. We were now at the foot of the range, where it dipped suddenly down upon the plain. The gap, our goal all day, opened before us, grand and terrible.

25 "Here we are," said Brent, speaking hardly above his breath. "This is Luggernel Alley at last, thank God! In an hour, if the horses hold out, we shall be at the Springs; that is, if we can go through this breakneck gorge at the same pace. My horse began to flinch a little before the 30 water. Perhaps that will set him up. How are yours?"

"Fulano asserts that he has not begun to show himself yet. I may have to carry you *en croupe*, before we are done."

Armstrong said nothing, but pointed impatiently down the defile. The gaunt white horse moved on quicker at this gesture. He seemed a tireless machine, not flesh and blood, — a being like his master living and acting by the force of a purpose alone.

Our chief led the way into the cañon.

Terrible riding it was ! A pavement of slippery sheeny rock ; great beds of loose stones ; barricades of mighty boulders, where a cliff had fallen an æon ago, before the days of the road-maker race ; crevices where an unwary foot might catch ; wide rifts where a shaky horse might fall, or a timid horseman drag him down. Terrible riding ! A pass where a calm traveller would go quietly picking his steps, thankful if each hour counted him a safe mile.

Terrible riding ! Madness to go as we went ! Horse and man, any moment either might shatter every limb. But man and horse neither can know what he can do, until he has dared and done. On we went, with the old frenzy growing tenser. Heart almost broken with eagerness.

No whipping or spurring. Our horses were a part of ourselves. While we could go, they would go. Since the water, they were full of leap again. Down in the shady Alley, too, evening had come before its time. Noon's packing of hot air had been dislodged by a mountain breeze drawing through. Horses and men were braced and cheered to their work ; and in such riding as

that, the man and the horse must think together and move together, — eye and hand of the rider must choose and command, as bravely as the horse executes. The blue sky was overhead, the red sun upon the castellated walls
5 a thousand feet above us, the purpling chasm opened before. It was late, these were the last moments. But we should save the lady yet.

"Yes," our hearts shouted to us, "we shall save her yet."

10 An arroyo, the channel of a dry torrent, followed the pass. It had made its way as water does, not straightway, but by that potent feminine method of passing under the frowning front of an obstacle, and leaving the dull rock staring there, while the wild creature it would have
15 held is gliding away down the valley. This zigzag channel baffled us ; we must leap it without check wherever it crossed our path. Every second now was worth a century. Here was the sign of horses, passed but now. We could not choose ground. We must take our leaps on
20 that cruel rock wherever they offered.

Poor Pumps !

He had carried his master so nobly ! There were so few miles to do ! He had chased so well ; he merited to be in at the death.

25 Brent lifted him at a leap across the arroyo.

Poor Pumps !

His hind feet slipped on the time-smoothed rock. He fell short. He plunged down a dozen feet among the rough boulders of the torrent bed. Brent was out of
30 the saddle almost before he struck, raising him.

No, he would never rise again. Both his fore legs were broken at the knee. He rested there, kneeling on the rocks where he fell.

Brent groaned. The horse screamed horribly, horribly, — there is no more agonized sound, — and the scream went echoing high up the cliffs where the red sunlight rested.

It costs a loving master much to butcher his brave and trusty horse, the half of his knightly self; but it costs him more to hear him shriek in such misery. Brent drew his pistol to put poor Pumps out of pain.

Armstrong sprang down and caught his hand.

"Stop!" he said in his hoarse whisper.

He had hardly spoken since we started. My nerves were so strained, that this mere ghost of a sound rang through me like a death yell, a grisly cry of merciless and exultant vengeance. I seemed to hear its echoes, rising up and swelling in a flood of thick uproar, until they burst over the summit of the pass and were wasted in the crannies of the towering mountain-flanks above.

"Stop!" whispered Armstrong. "No shooting! They'll hear. The knife!"

He held out his knife to my friend.

Brent hesitated one heart-beat. Could he stain his hand with his faithful servant's blood?

Pumps screamed again.

Armstrong snatched the knife and drew it across the throat of the crippled horse.

Poor Pumps! He sank and died without a moan. Noble martyr in the old, heroic cause.

I caught the knife from Armstrong.   I cut the thong
of my girth.   The heavy California saddle, with its
macheers and roll of blankets, fell to the ground.   I cut
off my spurs.   They had never yet touched Fulano's flanks.
5 He stood beside me quiet, but trembling to be off.

" Now Brent ! up behind me ! " I whispered, — for the
awe of death was upon us.

I mounted.   Brent sprang up behind.   I ride light for
a tall man.   Brent is the slightest body of an athlete I
10 ever saw.

Fulano stood steady till we were firm in our seats.

Then he tore down the defile.

Here was that vast reserve of power ; here the tireless
spirit ; here the hoof striking true as a thunderbolt, where
15 the brave eye saw footing ; here that writhing agony of
speed ; here the great promise fulfilled, the great heart
thrilling to mine, the grand body living to the beating
heart.   Noble Fulano !

I rode with a snaffle.   I left it hanging loose.   I did
20 not check or guide him.   He saw all.   He knew all.   All
was his doing.

We sat firm, clinging as we could, as we must.   Fulano
dashed along the resounding pass.

Armstrong pressed after, — the gaunt white horse
25 struggled to emulate his leader.   Presently we lost them
behind the curves of the Alley.   No other horse that ever
lived could have held with the black in that headlong
gallop to save.

Over the slippery rocks, over the sheeny pavement,
30 plunging through the loose stones, staggering over the

barricades, leaping the arroyo, down, up, on, always
on, — on went the horse, we clinging as we might.

It seemed one 'beat of time, it seemed an eternity,
when between the ring of the hoofs I heard Brent whisper
in my ear. 5

" We are there."

The crags flung apart, right and left. I saw a sylvan
glade. I saw the gleam of gushing water.

Fulano dashed on, uncontrollable !

There they were, — the Murderers. 10

Arrived but one moment !

The lady still bound to that pack-mule branded A. & A.

Murker just beginning to unsaddle.

Larrap not dismounted, in chase of the other animals
as they strayed to graze. 15

The men heard the tramp and saw us, as we sprang
into the glade.

Both my hands were at the bridle.

Brent, grasping my waist with one arm, was awkward
with his pistol. 20

Murker saw us first. He snatched his six-shooter and
fired.

Brent shook with a spasm. His pistol arm dropped.

Before the murderer could cock again, Fulano was upon
him ! 25

He was ridden down. • He was beaten, trampled down
upon the grass, — crushed, abolished.

We disentangled ourselves from the *mêlée*.

Where was the other?

The coward, without firing a shot, was spurring Arm- 30

strong's Flathead horse blindly up the cañon, whence we had issued.

We turned to Murker.

Fulano was up again, and stood there shuddering.   But
5 the man?

A hoof had battered in the top of his skull; blood was gushing from his mouth; his ribs were broken; all his body was a trodden, massacred carcass.

He breathed once, as we lifted him.

10   Then a tranquil, childlike look stole over his face, — that well-known look of the weary body, thankful that the turbulent soul has gone.   Murker was dead.

Fulano and not we, had been executioner.   *His* was the stain of blood.

From *John Brent*,
by THEODORE WINTHROP.

X.

THE LADY OF LYONS.

ACT V.

[Two years and a half from the date of Act IV.]

SCENE I. — *A street in Lyons.*

[*Enter* CAPT. GERVAIS, LIEUT. DUPONT, *and* MAJ. DESMOULINS, L.]

CAPT. GERVAIS. This Lyons is a fine city ! your birth- 5
place, I think?

LIEUT. D. Yes ; it is just two years and a half since I
left it under the command of the brave General Damas ;
here we are returned, he a general, I a lieutenant.

MAJOR D. Ay, promotion is rapid in the French army. 10
Now the war in Italy is over, I hope he will find employment for our regiment elsewhere.

CAPT. GERVAIS. Well, I hope so, too. Here comes the
General.

[*Enter* GENERAL DAMAS, L.]   15

DAMAS. Good day, gentlemen, good day ; so here we
are in Lyons, improved since we left it. It is a pleasure
to grow old when the years that bring decay to ourselves
ripen the prosperity of our country.

CAPT. GERVAIS. And cover our gray hairs with the 20
laurel wreath, General.

DAMAS. I hope you will amuse yourselves during our stay at Lyons.

CAPT. GERVAIS. I shall make the best use of my time, General; but I have little appetite for sight-seeing with-
5 out Morier; his fine taste and extensive information qualify him for a professional cicerone; by the way, General, this is the anniversary of the glorious day in which the Colonel so distinguished himself.

DAMAS. Ah, poor Morier! he deserves all his honors.
10 LIEUT. D. That he does, indeed, General. Pray, can you tell us who this Morier really is?

DAMAS. Is! why a colonel in the French army.

MAJOR D. True. But what was he at first?

DAMAS. At first? Why a baby in long clothes, I sup-
15 pose.

CAPT. GERVAIS. Ha, ha! Ever facetious, General. Who were his parents? Who were his ancestors?

DAMAS. Brave deeds are the ancestors of brave men.
20 LIEUT. D. The General is sore upon this point; you will only chafe him. Any commands, General?

DAMAS. None. Good day to you.

[*Exeunt* MAJOR DESMOULINS *and* LIEUT. DUPONT, R.]

DAMAS. Our comrades are very inquisitive. Poor Morier
25 is the subject of a vast deal of curiosity.

CAPT. GERVAIS. Say interest, rather, General. His constant melancholy, the loneliness of his habits, his daring valor, his brilliant rise in the profession, your friendship, and the favors of the commander-in-chief,
30 — all tend to make him as much the matter of gossip as

of admiration. But where is he, General? I have
missed him all the morning.

DAMAS. Why, Captain, I 'll let you into a secret. My
young friend has come with me to Lyons in hopes of
finding a miracle. 5

CAPT. GERVAIS. A miracle !

DAMAS. Yes, a miracle ! In other words, a constant
woman.

CAPT. GERVAIS. Oh, an affair of love !

DAMAS. Exactly so. No sooner did he enter Lyons 10
than he waved his hand to me, threw himself from his
horse, and is now, I warrant, asking every one who can
know anything about the matter, whether a certain lady
is still true to a certain gentleman !

CAPT. GERVAIS. Success to him ! and of that success 15
there can be no doubt. The gallant Colonel Morier, the
hero of Lodi, might make his choice out of the proudest
families in France.

DAMAS. Oh, if pride be a recommendation, the lady
and her mother are most handsomely endowed. By the 20
way, Captain, if you should chance to meet with Morier,
tell him he will find me at the hotel.

CAPT. GERVAIS. I will, General. [*Exit* R.]

DAMAS. Now will I go to the Deschappelles, and make
a report to my young Colonel. Ha ! by Mars, Bacchus, 25
Apollo, Virorum — here comes Monsieur Beauseant !
[*enter* BEAUSANT, R.] Good morrow, Monsieur Beauseant !
How fares it with you?

BEAU. [*aside*] Damas ! that is unfortunate. If the
Italian campaign should have filled his pockets, he may 30

seek to baffle me in the moment of my victory. [*aloud*] Your servant, General — for such, I think, is your new distinction ! Just arrived in Lyons?

DAMAS. Not an hour ago. Well, how go on the
5 Deschappelles? Have they forgiven you in that affair of young Melnotte? You had some hand in that notable device, eh?

BEAU. Why, less than you think for ! The fellow imposed upon me. I have set it all right now. What
10 has become of him? He could not have joined the army, after all. There is no such name in the books.

DAMAS. I know nothing about Melnotte. As you say, I never heard the name in the Grand Army.

BEAU. Hem ! You are not married, General?
15 DAMAS. Do I look like a married man, sir? No, thank Heaven ! My profession is to make widows, not wives.

BEAU. You must have gained much booty in Italy ! Pauline will be your heiress, eh?

DAMAS. Booty ! Not I. Heiress to what? Two trunks
20 and a portmanteau, four horses, three swords, two suits of regimentals, and six pairs of white leather inexpressibles ! ⋅ A pretty fortune for a young lady !

BEAU. [*aside*] Then all is safe ! [*aloud*] Ha ! ha ! Is that really all your capital, General Damas? Why, I
25 thought Italy had been a second Mexico to you soldiers.

DAMAS. All a toss-up, sir. I was not one of the lucky ones ! My friend, Morier, indeed, saved something handsome. But our commander-in-chief took care of him,
30 and Morier is a thrifty, economical dog, not like the rest

of us soldiers, who spend our money as carelessly as if it were our blood.

BEAU. Well, it is no matter! I do not want fortune with Pauline. And you must know, General Damas, that your fair cousin has at length consented to reward my 5 long and ardent attachment.

DAMAS. You! — the devil! Why, she is already married! There is no divorce!

BEAU. True; but this very day she is formally to authorize the necessary proceedings, this very day she 10 is to sign the contract that is to make her mine within one week from the day on which her present illegal marriage is annulled.

DAMAS. You tell me wonders! — Wonders! No; I · believe anything of women! 15

BEAU. I must wish you good morning!

[*as he is going,* L., *enter* DESCHAPPELLES, R.]

M. DESCHAP. Oh, Beauseant! well met. Let us come to the notary at once.

DAMAS. [*to* DESCHAPPELLES] Why, cousin? 20

M. DESCHAP. Damas, welcome to Lyons! Pray call on us; my wife will be delighted to see you.

DAMAS. Your wife be — blessed for her condescension! But [*taking him aside*] what do I hear? Is it possible that your daughter has consented to a divorce? — that 25 she will marry Monsieur Beauseant?

M. DESCHAP. Certainly! What have you to say against it? A gentleman of birth, fortune, character. We are not so proud as we were; even my wife has had enough of nobility and princes! 30

DAMAS. But Pauline loved that young man so tenderly !

M. DESCHAP. [*taking snuff*] That was two years and a
half ago !

5   DAMAS. Very true. Poor Melnotte !

M. DESCHAP. But do not talk of that impostor ; I hope
he is dead or has left the country. Nay, even were he
in Lyons at this moment, he ought to rejoice that, in an
honorable and suitable alliance, my daughter may forget
10 her sufferings and his crime.

DAMAS. Nay, if it be all settled, I have no more to say.
Monsieur Beauseant informs me that the contract is to be
signed this very day.

M. DESCHAP. It is ; at one o'clock precisely. Will
15 you be one of the witnesses?

DAMAS. I ? No ; that is to say, yes, certainly ! At one
o'clock I will wait on you.

M. DESCHAP. Till then adieu — come, Beauseant.

[*Exeunt* BEAUSEANT *and* DESCHAPPELES, L]

20   DAMAS. The man who sets his heart upon a woman
Is a chameleon, and doth feed on air ;
From air he takes his colors — holds his life, —
Changes with every wind, — grows lean or fat,
Rosy with hope, or green with jealousy,
25 Or pallid with despair — just as the gale
Varies from north to south — from heat to cold !
Oh, woman ! woman ! thou shouldst have few sins
Of thine own to answer for ! Thou art the author
Of such a book of follies in a man,
30 That it would need the tears of all the angels

To blot the record out !

[*Enter* MELNOTTE, *pale and agitated,* R.]

I need not tell thee !   Thou hast heard —

MEL.   The worst !

I have !   [*crosses,* L.] 5

DAMAS.   Be cheer'd ; others are fair as she is !

MEL.   Others !   The world is crumbled at my feet !

She *was* my world ; fill'd up the whole of being —

Smiled in the sunshine — walk'd the glorious earth —

Sate in my heart — was the sweet life of life.   10

The past was hers ; I dreamt not of a Future

That did not wear her shape !   Mem'ry and Hope

Alike are gone.   Pauline is faithless !

DAMAS.   Hope yet.

MEL.   Hope, yes ! — one hope is left me still — 15

A soldier's grave !

[*after a pause*]   — But am I not deceived ?

I went but by the rumor of the town ;

Rumor is false, — I was too hasty !   Damas,

Whom hast thou seen ?   20

DAMAS.   Thy rival and her father.

Arm thyself for the truth.   He heeds not —

MEL.   She

Will never know how deeply she was loved !

DAMAS.   Be a man ! 25

MEL.   I am a man ! — it is the sting of woe

Like mine that tells us we are men !

DAMAS. .   The false one

Did not deserve thee.

MEL.   Hush ! — No word against her ! 30

Why should she keep, through years and silent absence,
The holy tablets of her virgin faith
True to a traitor's name !   Oh, blame her not ;
It were a sharper grief to think her worthless
5 Than to be what I am !   To-day, — to-day !
They said " To-day ! "   This day, so wildly welcomed —
This day, my soul had singled out of time
And mark'd for bliss !   This day ! oh, could I see her,
See her once more unknown ; but hear her voice.
10   DAMAS.   Easily done ! come with me to her house ;
Your dress — your cloak — moustache — the bronzed hues
Of time and toil — the name you bear — belief
In your absence, all will ward away suspicion.
Keep in the shade.   Ay, I would have you come.
15 There may be hope !   Pauline is yet so young,
They may have forced her to these second bridals,
Out of mistaken love.

MEL.   No, bid me hope not !
Bid me not hope !   I could not bear again
20 To fall from such a heaven !   Oh, Damas,
There 's no such thing as courage in a man ;
The veriest slave that ever crawled from danger
Might spurn me now.   When first I lost her, Damas,
I bore it, did I not ?   I still had hope,
25 And now I — I —   [bursts into an agony of grief.]
DAMAS.   What, comrade ! all the women
That ever smiled destruction on brave hearts
Were not worth tears like these !

MEL.   [crossing to R.]   'T is past ; forget it.
30 I am prepared ; life has no further ills !

DAMAS. Come, Melnotte, rouse thyself;
One effort more. Again thou 'lt see her.
MEL.   See her !
DAMAS. Time wanes ; — come, ere yet it be too late.
MEL.   *" Too late ! "*   5
Lead on. One last look more and then —
DAMAS.   Forget her !
MEL. Forget her ! yes. — For death remembers not.   .

                          [*Exeunt,* L.]

SCENE 2. — *A room in the house of* MONSIEUR DESCHAP-   10
PELLES ; *not so richly furnished as in the First Act.*   ·
PAULINE *seated in great dejection at a table,* R.

PAULINE. It is so, then. I must be false to Love,
Or sacrifice a father ! Oh, my Claude,
My lover, and my husband ! Have I lived   15
To pray that thou mayest find some fairer boon
Than the deep faith of this devoted heart, —
Nourish'd till now — now broken?

        [*Enter* MONSIEUR DESCHAPPELLES, L.]

M. DESCHAP.   My dear child,   20
How shall I thank — how bless thee? Thou hast saved
I will not say my fortune — I could bear
Reverse, and shrink not ; but that prouder wealth
Which merchants value most : my name, my credit —
The hard-won honors of a toilsome life —   25
These thou hast saved, my child !   .
PAULINE.   Is there no hope?
No hope but this?   ·

M. Deschap.   None. If without the sum
Which Beauseant offers for thy hand, this day
Sinks to the west, to-morrow brings our ruin !
And hundreds, mingled in that ruin, curse
5 The bankrupt merchant ! and the insolvent herd
We feasted and made merry cry in scorn,
" How pride has fallen ! — Lo, the bankrupt mer-
        chant ! "   *
My daughter, thou hast saved us.
10   Pauline.   And am lost !
    M. Deschap. Come, let me hope that Beauseant's
        love —
    Pauline.   His love !
Talk not of love. Love has no thought of self !
15 Love buys not with the ruthless usurer's gold
The loathsome prostitution of a hand
Without a heart ! Love sacrifices all things
To bless the thing it loves ! *He* knows not love.
Father, his love is hate — his hope revenge !
20 My tears, my anguish, my remorse for falsehood —
These are the joys that he wrings from our despair !
    M. Deschap. If thou deem'st thus, reject him ! Shame
        and ruin
Were better than thy misery. Think no more on 't.
25 My sand is well-nigh run — what boots it when
The glass is broken ? We 'll annul the contract, —
And if to-morrow in the prisoner's cell
These aged limbs are laid, why still, my child,
I 'll think thou art spared ; and wait the Liberal Hour
30 That lays the beggar by the side•of kings !

PAULINE. No, no, forgive me! You, my honor'd
father, —
You, who so loved, so cherished me, whose lips
Never knew one harsh word ! I 'm not ungrateful ;
I am but human ! — hush ! *Now*, call the bridegroom. 5
You see I am prepared — no tears — all calm ;
But, father, *talk no more of love !*
M. DESCHAP. My child,
'T is but one struggle ; he is young, rich, noble ;
Thy state will rank first 'mid the dames of Lyons ; 10
And when this heart can shelter thee no more,
Thy youth will not be guardianless.
PAULINE. I have set
My foot upon the ploughshare —' [M. DESCHAPPELLES
retires] — I will pass 15
The fiery ordeal. [*aside*] Merciful Heaven, support me !
And on the absent wanderer shed the light
Of happier stars — lost evermore to me !

[*Enter*, C. I.., MADAME DESCHAPPELLES, BEAUSEANT, GLAVIS, *and*
NOTARY, *who confers with* M. DESCHAPPELLES, *and then sits at* 20
table, R.]

MME. DESCHAP. Why, Pauline, you are quite in *déshabillé* — you ought to be more alive to the importance of
this joyful occasion. We had once looked higher, it is
true ; but you see, after all, Monsieur Beauseant's father 25
was a marquis, and that's a great comfort. Pedigree
and jointure ; — you have them both in Monsieur Beauseant. A young lady decorously brought up should only
have two considerations in her choice of a husband : First,
is his birth honorable ? Secondly, will his death be ad- 30

vantageous? All other trifling details should be left to parental anxiety.

BEAU. [L. C., *approaching and waving aside* MADAME] Ah, Pauline ! let me hope that you are reconciled to an event
5 which confers such rapture upon me.

PAULINE. . I am reconciled to my doom.

BEAU. Doom is a harsh word, sweet lady.

PAULINE. [*aside*] This man must have some mercy — his heart cannot be marble. [*aloud*] Oh, sir, be just, be
10 generous ! Seize a noble triumph, a great revenge ! Save the father, and spare the child.

BEAU. [*aside*] Joy — joy alike to my hatred and my passion ! The haughty Pauline is at last my suppliant. [*aloud*] You ask from me what I have not the sublime
15 virtue to grant — a virtue reserved only for the gardener's son ! I cannot forego my hopes in the moment of their ' fulfilment ! I adhere to the contract — your father's ruin or your hand.

PAULINE. Then all is over.· Sir, I have decided.

20 [*The clock strikes one;* BEAUSEANT *retires to* L. *of table and sits examining the papers.*]

[*Enter* DAMAS *and* MELNOTTE, C. L.]

. DAMAS. Your servant, cousin Deschappelles. Let me introduce Colonel Morier.

25 MME. DESCHAP. [*curtseying very low*] What, the celebrated hero? This is, indeed, an honor !

[*She crosses ; seems to converse with* MELNOTTE, *who bows as she returns to the table,* R. ; MELNOTTE *throws himself into a chair,* L. U. F.]

DAMAS. [*to* PAULINE] My little cousin, I congratulate you. What, no smile, no blush? You are going to be divorced from poor Melnotte, and marry this rich gentleman. You ought to be excessively happy!

PAULINE. Happy!   5

DAMAS. Why, how pale you are, child! Poor Pauline! Hist — confide in me! Do they force you to this?

PAULINE. No!

DAMAS. You act with your own free consent?

PAULINE. My own consent — yes.   10

DAMAS. Then you are the most — I will not say what you are.

PAULINE. You think ill of me — be it so — yet if you knew all —

DAMAS. There is some mystery — speak out, Pauline.   15

PAULINE. [*suddenly*] Oh, perhaps you can save me! you are our relation — our friend. My father is on the verge of bankruptcy; this day he requires a large sum to meet demands that cannot be denied; that sum Beauseant will advance, this hand the condition of the barter. Save me 20 if you have the means, save me! You will be repaid above.

DAMAS. [*aside*] I recant; women are not so bad after all! [*aloud*] Humph, child! I cannot help you, I am too poor.   25

PAULINE. The last plank to which I clung is shivered.

DAMAS. Hold! you see my friend, Morier. Melnotte is his most intimate friend; fought in the same fields, slept in the same tent. Have you any message to send to Melnotte? any word to soften this blow?   30

[*She bows;* DAMAS *goes to* MELNOTTE, *who rises and comes forward,* L. C.]

PAULINE. He knows Melnotte, he will see him, he will
bear to him my last farewell.   [*approaches* MELNOTTE; *he*
5 *bows to her, and, overcome by his emotion, turns towards* L.]   He
has a stern air — he turns away from me, he despises me !
Sir, one word, I beseech you.

MEL. Her voice again ! How the old time comes o'er
me !

10   DAMAS. [*to* MADAME] Don't interrupt them.   He is
going to tell her what a rascal young Melnotte is ; he
knows him well, I promise you.

MME. DESCHAP. So considerate in you, cousin Damas !

[DAMAS *approaches* DESCHAPPELLES ; *converses apart with him in*
15 *the dumb show.* DESCHAPPELLES *shows him a paper, which he*
inspects and takes.]

PAULINE. Thrice have I sought to speak ; my courage
    fails me.

Sir, is it true that you have known — nay, are
20 The friend of Melnotte ?

MEL.   Lady, yes ! — Myself
And misery know the man !

PAULINE.   And you will see him,
And you will bear to him — ay — word for word,
25 All that this heart, which breaks in parting from him,
Would send, ere still for ever?

MEL.   Lady, speak on !

PAULINE. Tell him, for years I never nursed a
    thought

30 That was not his ; — that on his wandering way,

Daily and nightly, pour'd a mourner's prayers;
Tell him ev'n now that I would rather share
His lowliest lot, — walk by his side, an outcast, —
Work for him, beg with him, — live upon the light
Of one kind smile from him, — than wear the crown   5
The Bourbon lost !

    MEL. [*aside*]   Am I already mad?
                    [*aloud*] You love him thus,
And yet desert him?

    PAULINE.   Say, that if his eye   10
Could read this heart, — its struggles, its temptations, —
His love itself would pardon that desertion !
Look on that poor old man, — he is my father;
He stands upon the verge of an abyss !
He calls his child to save him !   Shall I shrink   15
From him who gave me birth? — withhold my hand,
And see a parent perish?   Tell him this,
And say that we shall meet again in Heaven !

    MEL. Night is past — joy cometh with the morrow ! —
[*goes to* DAMAS, *who is* L.] What is this riddle? — what   20
The nature of this sacrifice?

    BEAU. [*at the table*] The papers are prepared — we only
    need
Your hand and seal.

    MEL.   Stay, lady — one word more.   25
Were but your duty with your faith united,
Would you still share the low-born peasant's lot?

    PAULINE. Would I?   Ah, better death with him I love
Than all the pomp — which is but as the flowers
That crown the victim !   [*turning away*]   I am ready.   30

[MELNOTTE *goes to* DAMAS, *who has got the paper from the table*]

DAMAS. [*showing paper*]   There—
This is the schedule — this the total.

BEAU. [*to* DESCHAPPELLES, *showing notes*] These

5 Are yours the instant she has signed ; you are
Still the great House of Lyons !

[*The* NOTARY *is about to hand the contract to* PAULINE, *when*
MELNOTTE *seizes it and tears it.*]

BEAU. [*going* L.]   Are you mad ?

10 M. DESCHAP. [L. C.] How, sir? What means this
insult ?

MEL. [C.] Peace, old man !
I have a prior claim. Before the face
Of man and Heaven I urge it ; I outbid

15 Yon sordid huckster for your priceless jewel.

[*giving a pocket-book*]

There is the sum twice told ! Blush not to take it —
There is not a coin that is not bought and hallow'd
In the cause of nations with a soldier's blood !

20 BEAU. Torments and death !

PAULINE.   That voice ! Thou art —

MEL.   Thy husband !

[PAULINE *rushes into his arms*]

Look up ! look up, Pauline ! — for I can bear

25 Thine eyes. The stain is blotted from my name.
I have redeem'd mine honor. I can call
On France to sanction thy divine forgiveness !
Oh, joy ! — oh, ˉapture ! By the midnight watchfires
Thus have I seen thee ! thus foretold this hour !

And 'midst the roar of battle thus have heard
The beating of thy heart against my own !

[*places* PAULINE *in a chair; the* NOTARY *goes off,* C. L.]

BEAU. Fool'd, duped, and triumph'd over in the hour
Of mine own victory !   Curses on ye both !   5
May thorns be planted in the marriage-bed !
And love grow sour'd and blacken'd into hate —
Such as the hate that gnaws me !
DAMAS.   Curse away !
And let me tell thee, Beauseant, a wise proverb   10
The Arabs have : " Curses are like young chickens,
[*solemnly*] And still come home to roost ! "
BEAU.   Their happiness
Maddens my soul ! I am powerless and revengeless !

[*to* MADAME]   15
I wish you joy !   Ha, ha ! the gardener's son !

[*Exit,* L.C.]
[PAULINE *rises and comes forward,* R. C. MELNOTTE *grasps* DAMAS'
    hand]
PAULINE.   Oh !   20
My father, you are saved — and by my husband !
Ah ! blessed hour !   [*she embraces* MELNOTTE]
MEL.   Yet you weep still, Pauline.
PAULINE. But on thy breast ! — *these* tears are sweet
    and holy !   25
M. DESCHAP. You have won love and honor nobly,
    sir,
Take her ; be happy both !
MME. DESCHAP.   I 'm all astonish'd !
Who, then, is Colonel Morier ?   30

DAMAS.   You behold him !

MEL. Morier no more after this happy day !

[*crosses*, R.C.]

I would not bear again my father's name

5 'Till I could deem it spotless !   The hour 's come !

Heaven smiled on conscience !   As the soldier rose

From rank to rank, how sacred was the fame

That cancell'd crime, and raised him nearer thee !

MME. DESCHAP. A colonel and a hero !   Well that 's

10   something !

He 's wondrously improved !   [*crosses to him*] I wish you

joy, sir !

MEL. Ah ! the same love that tempts us into sin,

If it be true love, works out its redemption !

15 And he who seeks repentance for the Past

Should woo the Angel Virtue in the future.

MME. DESCHAPPELLES.	MELNOTTE,	PAULINE.
R.C.	C.	L.C.

M. DESCHAPPELLES,		DAMAS.
20 R.		L.

[*CURTAIN.*]

XI.

I. *Bismarck to Motley.*

BERLIN, May 23, 1864.

JACK MY DEAR, — Where the devil are you, and what
do you do that you never write a line to me? I am
working from morn to night like a nigger, and you have 5
nothing to do at all, — you might as well tip me a line as
well as looking on your feet tilted against the wall of
God knows what a dreary color. I cannot entertain a
regular correspondence; it happens to me that during
five days I do not find a quarter of an hour for a walk; 10
but you, lazy old chap, what keeps you from thinking of
your old friends? When just going to bed in this moment my eye met with yours on your portrait, and I
curtailed the sweet restorer, sleep, in order to remind
you of Auld Lang Syne. Why do you never come to 15
Berlin? It is not a quarter of an American's holiday journey from Vienna, and my wife and me should be so happy
to see you once more in this sullen life. When can you
come, and when will you? I swear that I will make out
the time to look with you on old Logier's quarters, and 20

drink a bottle with you at Gerolt's, where they once would not allow you to put your slender legs upon a chair. Let politics be hanged and come and see me. I promise that the Union Jack shall wave over our house,
5 and conversation and the best old hock shall pour damnation upon the rebels. Do not forget old friends, neither their wives, as mine wishes nearly as ardently as myself to see you, or at least to see as quickly as possible a word of your handwriting.

10 *Sei gut und komm oder schreibe.*

> *Dein,*
>
> V. BISMARCK.

Haunted by the song, " In good old Colony Times."

II. *Motley to his mother.*

15 VIENNA, August 3, 1864.

MY DEAREST MOTHER, — The prominent topic of the last week has been the peace negotiations between the two great German powers (Prussia and Austria) and Denmark. The preliminaries were signed yesterday, and the
20 armistice prolonged for six weeks. In short, the peace is made.

This is all the commentary I shall make to-day on the Schleswig-Holstein history. To me the most interesting part of these Vienna Conferences was that they brought
25 my old friend Bismarck to this place. He thinks it about as possible to transplant what is called parliamentary government into Prussia, as Abraham Lincoln be-

lieves in the feasibility of establishing an aristocracy in
the United States. I venerate Abraham Lincoln exactly
because he is the true honest type of American Democracy. There is nothing of the shabby genteel, the
would-be-but-could n't-be fine gentleman; he is the 5
great American Demos, honest, shrewd, homely, wise,
humorous, cheerful, brave, blundering occasionally, but
through blunders struggling onward towards what he believes the right. I have a great faith in Grant; I think
he is the man we have been wanting for these three years, 10
but I don't feel absolutely certain. But this I will say,
that if he takes Richmond before Christmas, his Vicksburg and Virginia campaigns will prove him the greatest
general now living. But this is a great *if*, I confess.
Still, I think he will do it. Good-bye, my dearest mother. 15
I am delighted to hear of you as improving in health
and spirits. Try to write me half-a-dozen lines when
you can. It is such a pleasure to see your handwriting.

Ever your affectionate son,

J. L. M. 20

III. *Motley to his daughter.*

VIENNA, August 16, 1864.

MY DEAREST LILY, — We have a telegram this morning,
date August 6, telling us that Grant has been repulsed at
Petersburg. . . . This time I really believe we have had 25
a defeat, notwithstanding that the telegraph says so, because I have been feeling these three days, ever since the
attack was in progress, that it could not result otherwise.

Since the days of Fort Donelson, few attacks made in front upon entrenchments by either belligerent have succeeded. It seems to me that they cannot succeed ; and if anything could stagger my profound faith in Grant, it would be many repetitions of such assaults. If he can't make Lee attack him — which I always thought would be his game — I shall be disappointed.

The only ripple we have had on our surface is when the bold Bismarck made his appearance. Your mother has told you about him, and it was the greatest delight to me to see him again. He and Werther dined with us one day *en famille*, and we drank three bottles of claret (not apiece) ; but we sat until half-past nine at table, much to the amazement of the servants ; for what well-conducted domestic in Vienna can tolerate any remaining at table after the finger-bowls? Of course, the " Fremdenblatt " and all the other journals announced next morning that " Sir Motley," the American Envoy, had given a " gala dinner " to Minister Bismarck, Count Rechbarg, the Danish Plenipotentiary, and a string of other guests, most of whom I have not the pleasure of knowing by sight. *En revanche*, three days afterwards, as I believe your mother has informed you, we did give a dinner of a dozen, and the journals conscientiously stated next morning that Baron Werther had given a " gala dinner " to M. de Bismarck, adding a list of *convives*, not one of whom was of the party.

Ever your affectionate

P.

IV. *Bismarck to Motley.*

VARZIN, August 7, 1869.

DEAR MOTLEY, — Your writing to me was one of the best ideas that you have had for a long time, and you are certain to have many good ones. Your accusation against 5 me that I had not answered you, sounds to me, however, quite incredible. You say so, therefore it must be true ; but the consciousness of my virtue is so strong in me, that I prefer to doubt the regularity of the North German Postal Service, which is confided to my care, rather than believe 10 in my personal negligence. No post in these days is worth anything ; the world generally keeps growing worse. — Doubt that the stars are fire, etc., but never doubt my virtue. For three weeks my paper has been lying ready to write to you in London to ask you if you have not a 15 week or two to spare for me ; to make up for your secret flight across the ocean, you should do us the favor to banish all ink, house-hunting, and Englishmen for a time from your mind, and transport your wigwam to the Pomeranian woods. The affair is as easy in these days for an 20 ocean traveller as it used to be to go from Göttingen to Berlin. You give your arm to your wife, enter a cab with her, in twenty minutes you are at the station, in thirty hours in Berlin, and from there, in half a day, here ; leaving Berlin at nine o'clock you are here for dinner. It 25 would be delightful. My wife, daughter, myself, and my sons, whom I expect in two days, would be as pleased as children, and we would be as merry again as in old days. Personally, I cannot travel at this moment without upset-

ting all the reasons for which my leave is granted, otherwise I would come and find you and bring you to the
backwoods here;⌉but please come, throw all cares and
worries behind the stove, where you will be sure to find
5 them unconsumed on your return, and arrange to stay a
short or a long time, — the longer the better; but give us
the pleasure of your coming.   I have absorbed myself so
in the thought that I shall be ill if you say no, and that
would have the worst effect on politics.   My respectful
10 remembrances to your wife,

Your true friend,

V. Bismarck.

V. Bismarck to Motley.

Varzin, July 6, 1872.

15   My dear Motley, — I was the more agreeably surprised in seeing your handwriting, as I guessed before
opening the letter that it would contain the promise of a
visit here.   You are thousand times welcome, and doubly
if accompanied by your ladies, who, I am sure, never
20 have seen a Pomeranian on his native soil.   We live here
somewhat behind the woods, but Berlin once reached
the journey is not a difficult one.   The best train leaves
Berlin in the morning between eight and nine o'clock, —
I believe 8.45, Stettiner Bahhof; fifteen or twenty minutes
25 to drive from any hotel about the Linden.   You go by
railway as far as Schlawe, where you arrive at about four
o'clock afternoon, and from where a trumpet-sounding
postilion brings you to Varzin just in time for the dinner-

bell, before six o'clock.   If you will have the goodness to
send me a telegram on your departure from Berlin, or the
evening before, I shall make everything ready for you at
Schlawe, so that you only have to step from the waggon
to the wagen. | The Pomeranian gods will be gracious 5
enough for me to give you a sunny day, and in that case
I should order an open carriage, and one for luggage.
Only let me know by the telegram your will about this,
and about the number of in- or outside places wanted.

My wife is still at Loden.   I expect her to be back on 10
the 9th inst., but *la donna è mobile!*   At all events, she
will not be detained by female frailty beyond the end of
the week.   She will be equally glad to see you again ;
your name is familiar to her lips, and never came forth
without a friendly smile.   The first day that you can dis- 15
pose of, at all events, is the best one to come to see us,
though we think to remain here until the end of summer.
You do not mention that Mrs. Motley will accompany
you, and by this silence I take it for granted that she
will, as *Mann und Weib sind ein Leib.*   We will be 20
happy to see her with you, and *en attendant* give my
most sincere regards to her and to Mrs. Ives.

Most faithfully your old friend,

V. BISMARCK.

VI. *Motley to his wife.* 25

VARZIN, July 25, 1872.

MY DEAREST MARY, — I had better write a line to
tell you that we have arrived in safety, although I fear

that I shall hardly be able to say much just now, as I
wish to go downstairs to the breakfast room. Lily told
you all there was to say of Berlin. We had a pleasant
half-hour with the Bancrofts, who were very cordial, and
5 we promised to go and see them on our return. We
left Berlin at a quarter to nine yesterday morning ; reached
Schlawe station at half-past four.

We had an hour and a half's drive from the station to
Varzin. As the postilion sounded his trumpet, and we
10 drove up to the door, Bismarck, his wife, M——, and
H——, all came out to the carriage and welcomed us in
the most affectionate manner. I found him very little
changed in appearance since '64, which surprises me.
He is somewhat stouter, and his face more weather-
15 beaten, but as expressive and powerful as ever. Madame
de Bismarck is but little altered in the fourteen years that
have passed since I saw her. They are both most kind
and agreeable to Lily, and she feels already as if she had
known them all her life. M—— is a pretty girl, with
20 beautiful dark hair and gray eyes, — simple, unaffected,
and, like both father and mother, full of fun. The manner of living is most unsophisticated, as you will think
when I tell you that we marched straight from the carriage into the dining-room (after a dusty, hot journey by
25 rail and carriage of ten hours), and made to sit down and
go on with the dinner which was about half through, as,
owing to a *contretemps*, we did not arrive until an hour
after we were expected. After dinner Bismarck and I had
a long walk in the woods, he talking all the time in the
30 simplest and funniest and most interesting manner about

all sorts of things that had happened in these tremendous
years, but talking of them exactly as every-day people
talk of every-day matters, — without any affectation. The
truth is, he is so entirely simple, so full of *laissez-aller*,
that one is obliged to be saying to one's self all the time, 5
"This is the great Bismarck, — the greatest living man,
and one of the greatest historical characters that ever
lived." When one lives familiarly with Brobdignags it
seems for the moment that everybody was a Brobdignag
too, that it is the regular thing to be ; one forgets for 10
the moment one's own comparatively diminutive stature.
There are a great many men in certain villages that we
have known who cast a far more chilling shade over those
about them than Bismarck does.

In the evening we sat about most promiscuously, — 15
some drinking tea, some beer, some seltzer water ; Bismarck smoking a pipe. He smokes very little now, and
only light tobacco in a pipe. When I last knew him, he
never stopped smoking the strongest cigars. Now, he
tells me, he could n't to save his life smoke a single cigar ; 20
he has a disgust for them. A gentleman named Von
Thadden and his wife are the only guests, and they go
this afternoon, — a Pomeranian friend. He made the
campaign of Königgrätz ; and Bismarck was telling innumerable anecdotes about that great battle, and subse- 25
quently gave some most curious and interesting details
about the negotiations of Nikolsburg. I wish that you
could have heard him. You know his way. He is the
least of a *poseur* of any man I ever saw, little or big.
Everything comes out so offhand and carelessly ; but I 30

wish there could be an invisible, self-registering Boswell
always attached to his button-hole, so that his talk could
be perpetuated. There were a good many things said by
him about the Nikolsburg Conference confirming what I
5 had always understood.

The military opinion was bent on going to Vienna after
Sadowa. Bismarck strongly opposed this idea. He said
it was absolutely necessary not to humiliate Austria, to do
nothing that would make friendly relations with her in
10 the future impossible. He said many people refused to
speak to him. The events have entirely justified Bismarck's course, as all now agree. It would have been
easy enough to go to Vienna or to Hungary, but to return would have been full of danger. I asked him if he
15 was good friends with the Emperor of Austria now. He
said Yes, that the Emperor was exceedingly civil to him
last year at Salzburg, and crossed the room to speak to
him as soon as he appeared at the door. He said he
used when younger to think himself a clever fellow
20 enough, but now he was convinced that nobody had any
control over events, — that nobody was really powerful or
great ; and it made him laugh when he heard himself
complimented as wise, foreseeing, and exercising great
influence over the world. A man in the situation in
25 which he had been placed was obliged, while outsiders,
for example, were speculating whether to-morrow it would
be rain or sunshine, to decide promptly it will rain,
or it will be fine, and to act accordingly with all the
forces at his command. If he guessed right, all the
30 world said, "What sagacity; what prophetic power!"

if wrong, " all the old women would have beaten me with broomsticks."

If he had learned nothing else, he said, he had learned modesty. Certainly a more unaffected mortal never breathed, nor a more genial one. He looks like a Co- 5 lossus, but his health is somewhat shattered. He can never sleep until four or five in the morning. Of course work follows him here, but as far as I have yet seen it seems to trouble him but little. He looks like a country gentleman entirely at leisure. 10

The woods and park about the house are fine, but un- kempt and rough, unlike an English country place. We have had, since I began to write, long walks and talks in the woods, an agreeable family dinner, and then a long drive through the vast woods of beeches and oaks 15 of which the domain is mostly composed. I don't in- tend to Boswellise Bismarck any more. It makes me feel as if I were a New York Herald interviewing re- porter. He talks away right and left about anything and everything, — says among other things that nothing could 20 be a greater *bêtise* than for Germany to attack any foreign country ; that if Russia were to offer the Baltic provinces as a gift, he would not accept them. As to Holland, it would be mere insanity to pretend to occupy or invade its independence. It had never occurred to him or to 25 anybody. As to Belgium, France would have made any terms at any time with Germany if allowed to take Bel- gium. I wish I could record the description he gave of his interviews with Jules Favre and afterwards with Thiers and Favre, when the peace was made. 30

One trait I must n't forget, however. Favre cried a little, or affected to cry, and was very pathetic and heroic. Bismarck said that he must not harangue him as if he were an Assembly; they were two together for
5 business purposes, and he was perfectly hardened against eloquence of any kind. Favre begged him not to mention that he had been so weak as to weep, and Bismarck was much diverted at finding in the printed account afterwards published by Favre that he had made a great
10 parade of the tears he had shed.

I must break off in order to commit this letter to the bag. Of course I don't yet know how long we shall stay here; I suppose a day or two longer. I will send you a telegram about a change of address, so don't be fright-
15 ened at getting one.

Ever yours,

J. L. M.

XII.

FROM THE LIFE AND LETTERS OF
BAYARD TAYLOR.

I. *To Jervis McEntee.*

GOTHA, GERMANY, July 3, 1872.

HERE we are, at last ! I can scarcely believe that nearly
a month has gone by since you left us on the steamer's
deck at Hoboken.   The intervening time has been so 5
pleasant that one day has only repeated the impression
left by the previous one.   We went out on the smoothest
of oceans that day, and carried calm weather with us.   I
was not the least sea-sick, for the first time in my life, and
M. only for half a day.   The passengers were agreeable, 10
the fare and attendance remarkably good, and so the time
went by so rapidly that the Scilly Islands seemed only a
short distance from the light-house off Sandy Hook.   We
touched at Plymouth on the evening of the tenth day,
found the Channel a sheet of glass, Normandy and 15
Cherbourg flooded with sunshine, the Strait of Dover in a
most benevolent and Christian mood, and the dreaded
North Sea an imitation of the Mediterranean.   At
Hamburg my brother and sister-in-law were waiting for
us on the quay.   We landed at their door, and sat down 20

to their table with much the same feeling as if we had
gone from New York to dine in Brooklyn.

Two more weeks have gone since then, and now I am
quietly settled here in my father-in-law's house, with my
5 books, papers, and amateur sketching-traps in his old
library at the foot of the astronomical tower. I breathe an
atmosphere of old vellum binding, queer instruments, dust,
and astrological mysteries, very much like Faust in the
opening scene. Under me is a garden of gooseberries,
10 then the trees of the park, a bit of the old ducal castle,
and a good, broad stretch of sky. Here I mean to write,
dabble in colors, smoke, and "invite my soul" to whatever sort of banquet she may prefer. I tell you, old
fellow, it does one great good to get away, now and then,
15 from the grooves in which one's life must run. Distance
has the effect of time, in a measure. You walk farther
away from your canvas in this great studio of the world,
and see the truer relations of the work in hand. I have a
smouldering instinct that I must give this summer to
20 physical interests mainly; therefore, we still hold to the
plan of a watering-place. But we shall not go until some
time in August, and thus hope to hear from you before
we leave. My brother-in-law from Russia is here with his
family, — wife and five children, — and the stately old
25 house is full of noises. I am "uncled" from morning till
night. . . .

M. joins me in best love to G. and you, and Vauxes,
and all our friends. Both of us feel more clearly than
ever before how much we have left behind, — how much
30 that we cannot expect to find anywhere else in the world.

Our ties, now, have the light and sparkle and strength and smoothness of ripe old wine, and this is the best gift the years bring. Do let me hear from you soon, and tell me all your plans and interests and labors.

II. *To A. R. MacDonough.* 5

GOTHA, GERMANY, July 16, 1872.

. . . I have done nothing since leaving home, except to read a few books which I shall need to consult for Goethe's biography. But last week I went with my wife on a three days' trip to Ilmenau, Rudolstadt, and the 10 region thereabouts, — classic localities ! At Ilmenau a curious thing happened. The *Oberkellner* said : " The hotel is full ; I must put you in Goethe's room." It was the room where Goethe celebrated his last (eighty-second) birthday, in 1831 ; and there I discovered a new 15 fact in his biography. It is interesting, rather than im-portant ; and proves, among other things, that Lewes took more from Viehoff's " Life of Goethe " than he acknowledges. The next day we stopped at Volkstedt, and saw the room where Schiller lived in 1788, then 20 crossed the Saale and walked to Rudolstadt by the path he followed when he visited the Lengefelds. We saw also the *Grenzhammer*, a forge where he studied the *staffage* for his ballad of " Fridolin." Unfortunately, the lodge on the `Kickelhahn, where Goethe wrote " Ueber allen 25 Gipfeln " with a pencil on the wall, was burned down about eighteen months ago. . . .

III. *To T. B. Aldrich.*

GOTHA,   October 28, 1872.

. . . A week ago the Grand Duke of Saxe-Weimar invited me to visit him at the Wartburg; this on account
5 of " Faust." We dined in the Hall of the Minstrels, where Tannhäuser sang, — actually the same old Byzantine hall, — and sat on mediaeval chairs. All their five Roilighnesses (as Yellowplush says) were very amiable, and the two princesses were charming. This invitation is
10 a good thing for my plans; for the Grand Duke invited me to Weimar, and all the Goethean records and archives will now be open to me. At present I am only collecting materials, which will be a work of some months.

Here we are living very quietly. I work half the day
15 compiling for Scribners, and thus earn the right to use the other half for myself. Moreover, I paint in oil, and of such is not the Kingdom of Heaven! How I should like to have an autumn evening at Cambridge with you, and Longfellow, and Howells!
20   Tell Longfellow from me that the Weimar Princesses have read all his works, and the Hoffräulein, Baroness ——, a very charming person, begged me to say that her enthusiasm for him is so great that it led her to cut his name out of a traveller's register at Bruges. This
25 was at the beginning of dinner, and all the ceremonious Highnesses showed so much interest in Longfellow that I forgot ceremony and felt quite at home all the evening. So that I owe to him!

IV. *To E. C. Stedman.*

GOTHA, GERMANY, Jan. 16, 1874.

. . . So much was crowded into my two months' sojourn in Weimar, that I hardly know where to begin
to tell you about it. I had not been there many 5
days before I discovered that my translation was generally and favorably known; so I began to call, without
ceremony, upon the people I wanted to know, and was
received with open arms. During the last three weeks I
was invited out to supper every evening, and thus drew 10
deep draughts of the social atmosphere. I made no
secret of my plan, and every one seemed desirous to
be of some service. With Baron Gleichen, Schiller's
grandson, I established a hearty friendship. I am to
go with him to his father's castle of Bonnland in the 15
spring, and examine all the MSS. and relics of Schiller
which the family possesses. Wolfgang von Goethe, who
is both eccentric and misanthropic, thawed toward me,
and I assure you it was a great satisfaction to visit him
in Goethe's house, and to see the same luminous large 20
brown eyes beaming on me as he talked. I was startled
at his personal resemblance to the poet. Herder's grandson invited me to supper before I ever saw him, and
Wieland's granddaughter, a sculptress, invited me to give
my German lecture on American Literature in Weimar. 25
One evening, at the hotel, an interesting looking man of
forty, with a brown beard, took his seat opposite to me,
and we fell into conversation. Presently Mr. Hamilton
(of the noble Scotch clan, who lives in Weimar) came in,

and introduced him to me as Baron von Stein, grandson
of Frau von Stein! Fraulein Frommann, foster-sister
of one of Goethe's loves (Minna Herzlieb), though a
woman of seventy-five, knows and remembers everything,
5 and she told me many interesting anecdotes. She was
for many years companion to the present Empress
Augusta, and enjoys much consideration; so when she
said to me, "I feel *safe* with you; I can tell you all,
knowing that you will use it only as I could wish," and
10 repeated the same thing to others, I was at once placed
in the very relation to all which I wished to have established. I called on the famous old painter, Preller, whose
illustrations of the Odyssey are finer (because simpler
and severer) than anything of Kaulbach's. I remarked
15 that he had a copy of Trippel's glorious bust of Goethe,
and said : "I have this bust at home, and opposite to it
the Venus of Milo, as the woman form corresponding to
this male form." His eyes shone ; he rose up without
a word, grasped my arm, and turned me around. There
20 was the Venus of Milo, opposite Goethe ! "I never pass
her," said Preller, "without pausing an instant, and saying to myself, 'My God, how beautiful she is!'" Well,
after that Preller and I became fast friends. He was a
protégé, a half-pupil of Goethe, whose son died in his
25 arms. Afterwards, when Goethe lay dead, Preller stole
into the room and made a wonderful drawing of the head.
Now, after forty years, he voluntarily made the first copy
of it, with his own hands, as a present for me ! You may
guess how I value it.
30   Schiller's grandson is an excellent artist. His pictures

are astonishingly like McEntee's. I spent many hours in
his studio. Schoell, one of the best Goethe scholars in
Germany (now chief librarian at Weimar), is enthusiastically in favor of my biographical plan. He is utterly dissatisfied with Lewes. He told Lewes many particulars 5
which Lewes distorted in the most ridiculous manner.
Several persons told me that Lewes pumped lackeys and
old servants while in Weimar, and took no pains to get
acquainted with the intelligent intimate friends of Goethe.
I can't say how much truth there is in this; *I* am most 10
happy to find that I have nothing of my own conception
of Goethe to *unlearn*, after knowing Weimar. My plan,
at last, stands round and complete before my mind, and
I only need life and health to give it a permanent form.
I wish I had space to tell you more of what I learned, 15
and how immensely I have been encouraged.

My lecture was a 'great triumph. It was given in the
hall of the Arquebusiers, a society dating from the Middle Ages. The whole court came, Grand-Duke and
Duchess, Hereditary Grand-Duke and Duchess, the two 20
charming Princesses, and Prince Hermann, with adjutants and ladies of honor. The Grand-Duke came up
to me with a mock reproach, and said: " There's one
serious fault in the lecture: you have not mentioned
yourself! But come and dine with me to-morrow, and 25
we'll talk more about it." Which I did. The dinner
was superb; two Weimar friends of mine were invited,
otherwise only the family. I assure you it gave me a
thrill of pride to stand in Weimar, with the grandchildren
of Carl August, Goethe, Schiller, Herder, and Wieland 30

among my auditors, and vindicate the literary achievement of America.   I lashed properly the German idea
of the omnipotency of money among us ; recited passages
from Halleck, Poe, Emerson, Bryant, and Whittier, and
5 said a good word for E. C. S., R. H. S., T. B. A., and
W. D. H.   The lecture seems to have made considerable
impression, as an account of it has since gone the rounds
of most of the German papers.

I must return to Weimar for another month in the
10 spring, and finish my studies there.   Then Dr. Hirzel of
Leipzig, who has the best Goethe library in the world,
allows me to make use of certain materials, which will
give me in a fortnight what would otherwise require a
year's drudgery.   I want to come home next summer,
15 ready to begin to write.   The whole work, then, can be
done in three years more, even allowing occasional inter-
ludes of poetry, as they come to me.

V. *To his mother.*

AMERICAN LEGATION, BERLIN, May 18, 1878.

20   I write to you again, intending this letter to be read
by all.   We are very busy just now getting settled and
paying the round of formal visits which is required of us.
I have already used a hundred and fifty cards, and or-
dered three hundred more to be printed.   The Crown
25 Prince received me last Friday (yesterday week, I mean)
with the greatest friendliness.   He came up to me with
outstretched hand, saying, in English, " Oh, I know you

already ! My wife was talking about your ' Faust ' only a few weeks ago." My hearty reception by the imperial family is known, of course, to the diplomatic corps, and hence all the other ambassadors are very polite and obliging. . . .   5

M. and L. nearly saw the attempt to assassinate the Emperor. He passed them hardly two minutes before the man fired. I went to the palace at once, and was one of the first to offer my congratulations. Yesterday I received, officially, the Emperor's thanks. Last night 10 there was a magnificent torchlight procession of students.

We are busy looking out for a residence. We can get a superb one for about fifteen hundred dollars a year (adding the office rent, which the government pays), with a grand ballroom and no end of bedrooms. I think 15 we shall take it. Furnished apartments can scarcely be had, but furniture is now very cheap, and we think we can save enough from the salary by Oct. 1st to buy all that is necessary. So far as I can judge, the expenses will be just about what I calculated. M. and L. are out 20 this afternoon, leaving cards, with Harris (our mulatto man), gorgeous in his gold-banded stove-pipe hat. No one else has a colored footman except Prince Karl, and Harris adds immensely to our respectability. I find that our experience in St. Petersburg is of great value now. 25 We know what to do, and people are rather surprised to find that we know it. All this tells in such an artificial society as we move in. The business of the legation is less than I supposed ; the two secretaries take all the bother off my hands, and I am in capital spirits about my liter- 30

ary work.   The weather is wonderful; it is full summer;
all windows open, even at night, and cloudless skies, day
after day.

VI. *To Mr. and Mrs. R. H. Stoddard.*

5   ˉ AMERICAN LEGATION, BERLIN, June 10, 1878.

. . . I reached here May 4th, and have had my hands
full ever since.   Besides the business of the legation and
the presentations to the high personages, I have already
distributed more than four hundred cards in necessary
10 formal calls.   Now I am nearly through, — only two
princes more.   On Saturday I had an hour's talk with
Bismarck in the garden behind his palace; he being
accompanied by a huge black dog, and I by a huge
brown bitch.   I tell you he is a *great* man !   We talked
15 only of books, birds, and trees, but the man's deepest
nature opened now and then, and I saw his very self.
The attempts on the Emperor's life have produced an
effect only a little less profound than the murder of
Lincoln.   The excitement is all the stronger because it is
20 silent, but now it is subsiding, and to-day (the second
Pentecost holiday) the people begin to look cheerful
again. . . .

VII. *To W. M. Evarts.*

LEGATION OF THE UNITED STATES,
BERLIN, July 1, 1878.

. . . It had been announced in various journals that
General Grant would proceed directly from Amsterdam to 5
Copenhagen without visiting Berlin, and my first intimation of his coming was through a letter from my colleague,
Mr. Birney, United States Minister resident at the Hague,
received on the 22d ultimo. I communicated immediately with him and with Mr. A. M. Simon, the United 10
States Vice-Consul at Hanover, and ascertained the day
and hour of General and Mrs. Grant's arrival here. It
was then impossible — since the stay of the distinguished
visitors would be brief — to arrange in advance for such
interviews and honors as might be procured for them at 15
a time when both assumed an exceptional importance.
The Emperor is unable to receive any one, and I was
informed by the proper officials that the Empress, for
this reason, would probably feel bound to maintain her
privacy in the palace. Prince Frederick Charles is ab- 20
sent on a visit to England, and Count Moltke is residing
on his estate in Silesia, at some distance from Berlin.
Furthermore, the presence of the European Congress, and
the number of prearranged dinners and social assemblages
arising therefrom, seemed to limit the amount of atten- 25
tion which at any other time would have been so freely
accorded to the ex-President.

On Wednesday, the 26th ultimo, after having arranged
for a reception by his Imperial Highness the Crown

Prince and by Prince von Bismarck, I travelled as far as
Stendal (about sixty-five miles), there met General and
Mrs. Grant, and accompanied them to Berlin. The
secretaries of this legation, the consular officials, and a
5 number of the American residents were at the station to
welcome the distinguished guests; the hour was too late
for any other testimony of respect.

The following afternoon I accompanied General Grant
to the palace of the Crown Prince, where he was first
10 received by all the adjutants and court officials of the
latter, and conducted to the audience room. The Crown
Prince then entered in his uniform of field marshal,
greeted General Grant most cordially, and conversed with
him for three quarters of an hour. At the close of the
15 interview he invited him and Mrs. Grant, together with
myself, to dine at the new palace in Potsdam the next
evening.

On returning home I was surprised to find a letter from
Count Nesselrode, court marshal of the Empress, in-
20 forming me that her majesty would receive me on Friday
afternoon. From the absence of certain customary
formalities on reaching the palace and the quiet manner
of my reception, I suspect that it was meant to be private
quite as much as official. The Empress took occasion to
25 express to me the Emperor's interest in General Grant's
history, his desire to meet him personally, and his deep
regret that this was now impossible. Her words and
manner implied an authorization that I should repeat
these expressions to General Grant. She then spoke
30 very freely and feelingly of the disturbances occasioned

by the distress of the laboring class, declared her belief that a period of peace would be the best remedy, and finally said, "The Emperor knew that I should see you to-day. He has the peace of the world at heart, and he desires nothing so much as the establishment of friend- ship between nations. I ask you to make it your task to promote the existing friendship between your country and ours. You cannot do a better work, and we shall most heartily unite with you in doing it. This is the Emperor's message to you, and he asked me to give it to you in his name as well as my own." She bowed and left me. The deep, earnest, pathetic tones of her voice impressed me profoundly. I kept her words carefully in my memory, and have repeated them with only such changes as the translation makes necessary.

The same afternoon I accompanied General and Mrs. Grant to Potsdam. The fact that the dinner was given specially in their honor was evident on reaching the station. They were ushered into the imperial waiting-room, from which a carpet was spread to the state car. On reaching Potsdam, the first court equipage conveyed them, together with Mr. von Schlözer, German minister at Washington, and myself, to the palace, the other guests following us. Before the dinner General Grant and Mrs. Grant and myself were received by the Crown Princess in private audience. The company numbered about fifty, including the Prince of Hohenzollern, Prince Augustus of Würtemberg, the members of the imperial ministry, and all the chief officials of the court. Mrs. Grant was seated beside the Crown Prince, and General

Grant opposite, beside Mr. von Bülow, both being the
places of honor. I˙ did not consider it consistent with
the dignity of the government I represent to make any ˜
stipulation concerning etiquette in advance, or even to
5 ask any question, and I am consequently all the more
gratified to ˙find that it would have been unnecessary.
During the return to another station, by a longer drive
through the park, General Grant received every mark of
respect from the people, who crowded the streets to see
10 him pass.

VOCABULARY.

VOCABULARY.

A.

ability, Begabung, f.

able, to be a., können, wissen.

abolish, vernichten.

about, worüber, umher, an, hinsichtlich.

above, über.

abreast, neben einander, in einer Reihe.

absence, Abwesenheit, f., Unterlassung, f.

absent, abwesend, fern.

absolute, unbedingt.

absorb, vertiefen in (acc.), vertieft sein in (dat.).

absurd, albern, Unsinn, m., -s.

abyss, Abgrund, m., -es, -ünde.

accept, annehmen.

accompany, begleiten, mitkommen.

accord, zeigen, erweisen.

accordingly, demgemäss, darnach.

account, Bericht, m., -es, -e ; Beschreibung, f.

accusation, Klage, f., Beschuldigung, f.

accustomed, gewohnt.

achievement, Leistung, f.

acknowledge, anerkennen für (acc.), zugeben, gestehen.

acquaintance, Bekanntschaft, f., Bekannter, m., -s., —.

acquainted, to become a., kennen zu lernen.

acquire, erlangen, gewinnen, erwerben.

across, über.

act, That, f., —, -en ; Aufzug, m., -s, -üge.

act, handeln.

action, Handlung, f. ; Wirkung, f.

actually, wirklich.

add, hinzufügen, miteinschliessen; added to, und auch.

address, Benehmen, n., -s, Anrede, f. ; Adresse, f.

address, richten an (acc).

adhere, bestehen auf (dat.), bleiben dabei.

adherent, Anhänger, m., -s, —.

adieu, adieu, auf wiedersehen.

adjutant, Adjutant, m., -en, -en.

admirable, vortrefflich, ausgezeichnet.

admiration, Bewunderung, f.

admire, bewundern.

admonitory, mahnend.

advance, in a., zum voraus ; in a. of, vor (dat.) . . . voraus.

advance, Fortschritt, m., -s, -e.

advance, befördern, weiter bringen; (lend) vorschiessen, leihen.

advantageous, vorteilhaft.
adventure, Geschichte, f., Erfahrung, f., Zufall, m , -s, -älle.
advise, Ermahnung, f.
Aegean, das Ägéische Meer.
aeon, an æon ago, vor Jahrhunderten.
affable, freundlich, leutselig.
affair, Verhältnis, n., -isses, -isse, Geschichte, f., Sache, f.
affect, scheinen, sich stellen.
affectation, Ziererei, f., Verstellung, f.
affection, Liebe, f.
affectionate, liebend, liebevoll, herzlich.
after-effect, Nachwirkung, f.
afternoon, Nachmittag, m., -s, -e ; in the a., nachmittags.
afterward, später, nachher.
again, wieder.
against, gegen ; a. it, dagegen, dawider.
age, Alter, n., -s, —.
aged, greis, alt.
agitated, aufgeregt.
agitation, Bewegung, f.
ago, seit, vor (dat.).
agonized, ängstlich, grässlich.
agony, Angst, f., Ängste.
agree, zugeben.
agreeable, angenehm (gegen), freundlich (gegen).
aim, Ziel, n., -s, -e.
air, Luft, f., -üfte.
Alhambra, f.
alike, auch, gleich ; a. . . . and, sowohl . . . als.
alive, empfindlich (dat.), be a. to, lebhaft empfinden.
all, ganz, all.
alley, Gasse, f. ; Pass, m., -es, -ässe.

alliance, Verbindung, f.
allow, lassen, erlauben.
almost, beinahe, fast.
aloft, in der Höhe.
alone, nur, allein.
along, hin, an (dat.) . . . entlang.
aloud, laut.
already, schon.
also, auch.
altered, verändert.
alternately, abwechselnd, wechselsweise.
always, immer.
amazement, Erstaunen, n., -s, Verwunderung, f.
ambassador, Botschafter, m., -s, —.
America, n., -s.
American, amerikanisch ; Amerikaner, m., -s, —.
amateur, Liebhaber, m., -s, — Dilettanten —.
amiable, liebenswürdig.
amid, unter (dat.).
amidst, in mitten (gen.), mitten in (dat.).
amount, Anzahl, f.
Amsterdam, Amsterdam, n., -s.
amuse, amüsieren.
ancestor, Ahn, m., -en, -en.
ancient, alt, altertümlich.
and, und.
anecdote, Geschichte, f.
anew, von neuem, wieder.
angel, Engel, m., -s, —.
anguish, Qual, f., -en. Angst, f., Ängste.
anniversary, Jahrstag, m., -es, -e.
animal, Tier, n., -s, -e.
announce, melden.
annually, jährlich, alljährlich.
annul, annullieren, für nichtig erklären, ungültig machen.

answer, versöhnen, abbüssen ; antworten (dat.).

antagonist, Gegner, m., -s, —.

antique, altertümlich.

anxiety, Sorgfalt, f. ; to have a. about, sich um (acc.) kümmern.

any, jed-er, all.

anything, etwas, alles, jedes.

apart, entfernt, beiseite.

apartment, Wohnung, f.

apiece, jeder.

Apollo, Apóll (-o), m, -s.

apologetic, Apologie, f., Verteidigung, f.

apostle, Apostel, m., -s, —, Bekenner, m., -s, —.

appear, erscheinen, veröffentlicht werden ; aussehen, scheinen.

appearance, to make an a., sich zeigen, zum Vorschein kommen.

appetite, Appetit, m., -s.

approach, Anzug, m., -s, -üge.

approach, (sich) nahen (dat.), sich nähern (dat.).

apron-strings, Gängelbänder, n. plu., Schürzenbänder, n. plu.

arch, Pforte, f., a. of triumph, Siegesbogen, m., -s, -ögen, or — ; Gewölbe, n., -s, —.

architecture, Baukunst, f. ; Bauwerke, n. plu.

archives, Archiv, n., -s, -e.

archway, Thorweg, m , -s, -e ; Bogengang, m., -s, -änge ; Thorgewölbe, n., -s, —.

ardent, heiss.

ardently, sehnlich, eifrig.

arquebusiers, Armbrust-Schützengesellschaft, f.

argumentation, Disputieren, n. ; Beweisführung, f.

Ariadne, Ariadne, f.

aright, recht.

arise, erstehen, aufkommen, entspringen (daraus).

aristocracy, Aristokratie, f. ; Adelstand, m., -s.

Arkansaw, Arkansaw (-Fluss), m., -s.

arm, Waffe, f. ; Arm, m., -s, -e.

arm, stählen (gegen), sich gefasst machen auf (acc.).

arm-chair, Lehnstuhl, m., -s, -ühle.

armistice, Waffenstillstand, m., -s.

army, Armée, f. ; Heer, n., -s, -e.

around, um (acc.)

arouse, wecken, rufen.

arrange, abmachen, einrichten, Vorkehrungen treffen.

arrival, Ankunft, f.

arrive, ankommen.

arrogant, arrogánt, anmassend, hochmütig.

arrow, Pfeil, m., -s, -e.

arróyo, arroyo, m., -s.

art, Kunst, f., -ünste.

artificial, förmlich, gekünstelt.

artist, Künstler, m., -s, —.

as, wie, so, als.

ascertain, erfahren, ermitteln.

ashes, Asche, f.

aside, beiseite, auf der Seite.

ask, bitten (acc. of person and *um* with acc. of thing), fragen ; a. a question, eine Frage zu thun (or, stellen).

aspire, aufstreben, emporstreben, streben (nach).

assassinate, morden, meuchlings überfállen.

assault, Sturmanlauf, m., -s, -äufe ; Angriff, m., -s, -e.

assemblage, Versammlung, f.

assembly, Versammlung, f.
assert, behaupten.
assiduous, sorgsam, emsig, fleissig.
assume, annehmen, voraussetzen.
assure, versichern ; assured, sicher.
astonished, erstaunt.
astonishingly, merkwürdig.
astrological, astrologisch.
astronomical tower, Sternwarte, f.
astrologer, astrolog, m., -en, -en ; Sterndeuter, m., -s, —.
astute, scharfsinnig.
at home, zu Haus, bei uns ; at (the University), an or auf; at hand, in der Nähe.
Athenaeum, Athenaeum, m., -s.
athlete, Athlét, m., -en (-s), -en.
Atlas, Atlas, m., -es.
atmosphere, Luft, f., Atmosphäre, f.
attach, anhängen, befestigen (an).
attachment, Neigung, f., Liebe, f.
attack, Angriff, m., -s, -e.
attack, angreifen.
attain, erzielen.
attempt, Versuch, m., -s, -e ; Attentát, n., -s, -e.
attend, begleiten.
attendance, Bedienung, f.
attendant, en a., unterdessen, im Erwarten.
attention, Aufmerksamkeit, f.
attest, bezeugen, beweisen.
audible, hörbar ; become a., laut werden
audience-room, Audienzsaal, m., -s, -säle.
auditor, Zuhörer, m., -s, —.
August (month), Augúst, m., -s ; (proper name), Aúgust, m., -s.

Augusta, f.
Augustus, Augustus, m.
Auld Lang Syne, the same, or : die gute alte Zeit (f.).
Austria, Österreich, n.
author, Schriftsteller, m., -s — ; Veranlasser, m., -s, —.
authority, Ansehen, n., -s, Einfluss, m., -es.
authorization, Ermächtigung, f.
authorize, bestätigen, billigen.
autobiography, Selbstbiographie, f., eigne Lebensbeschreibung, f.
autumn, Herbst —, m., -es, -e.
avenger, Rächer, m., -s.
away, fort, los.
awe, Schauder, m., -s, Grauen, n., -s ; of death, Todesschauer, m., -s.
awkward, unbehilflich, linkisch. ungeschickt.
axe, Axt, f., Äxte.
azote, Stickstoff, m., -s.

B.

baby, Kindlein, n., -s.
Bacchus, Bacchus, m.
bachelor, Junggesell, m., -en, -en.
back, zurück, wieder ; b. hair, Nackenhaar, n., -s, -e.
back, Rücken, m., -s, —.
background, Hintergrund, m., -s.
backward, rückwärts.
backwoods, same word, or : Hinterwälder, Urwälder, m. plu.
bad, schlimm, schlecht.
baffle, verhindern, verderben ; (of plans) vereiteln.
bag, Postbeutel, m. -s.
Baiae, Bajä, n., -s.

balance, balancieren, wagehalten, im Gleichgewicht halten.
balcony, Balkón, m., -s.
ball, Ball, m., -s, -älle.
ballad, Ballade, f.
ballroom, Ballsaal, m., -s, -säle.
Baltic, baltisch, Ostsee —.
Bancroft, Bancroft, -s, -s.
band, Kapelle, f.
banish, verbannen.
bankrupt, bankbrüchig, bankerott (adj. and noun).
bankruptcy, Verderben, n., -s ; on the verge of b., auf dem Punkte stehen Bankerott zu machen.
banquet, Fest, n., -es, -e.
banquette, Banquette, f., or Bankett, n., -s.
barb, Spitze, f.
bare, bloss (-gestellt).
barefooted, barfüssig; b. Friar, Barfüssermönch, m., -es, -önche.
Baron, Barón, m., -s, -e, Freiherr, m., -n, -n.
barricade, Barrikade, f. Verschanzung, f.
barter, Tausch, m., -es, Handel, m., -s.
base, Grund, m., -es, Fuss, m., -es, Unterbau, m., -s, Basis, f.
basket, Korb, m., -s, -örbe.
batter, einschlagen, eindrücken.
battery, Batterie, f.
battle, Kampf, m., -s, -ämpfe Schlacht, f.
battlement, Zinne, f.
beam, strahlen (auf, acc.), anleuchten.
bear, haben, tragen, mitteilen, sagen, ertragen.
beard, Bart, m., -s.
beat, Schlag, m., -s, -äge ; b. of time, Pulsschlag.

beat, schlagen, klopfen, zertreten, prügeln.
beating, klopfen, n., -s.
Beauseant, Beauseant, m., -s.
beautiful, schön.
beauty, Schönheit, f.
beckon, winken.
become, werden.
bed, Beet, n., -s, -e ; Bett, n., -s, -en ; Lager, n,, -s, —.
bedroom, Schlafzimmer, n., -s, —.
beech, Buche, f.
beer, Bier, n., -s, -e.
beer-barrel, Bierfass, n., -es, -ässer.
beer-drinking, Biertrinken, n., -s.
before, vor, vorher, vormals, ehe, bevor.
beg, bitten.
begin, beginnen, anfangen.
beggar, Bettler, m., -s, —.
behind, hinter.
behold, beschauen.
Belgium, Belgien, n., -s.
belief, Überzeugung, f.; Glaube (an, acc.), m., -ens.
believe, glauben (von), erwarten (von).
belligerent, kriegführende Partei (f., -en) or Macht, f., -ächte.
belong, gehören (dat. alone or zu with dat.).
beloved, geliebt, teuer.
below, unten, unter.
Ben, Ben.
bench, Bank, f., -änke, Schulbank.
beneath, unter.
Benevento, Benevént, n., -s.
beneficent, wohlthätig.
benevolent, wohlwollend, gütig.
benignant, wohlwollend, gütig, heiter.

bent, gebückt; b. upon, darauf
bestehen, dahin gehen.
Bergstrasse, Bergstrasse, f.
Berlin, Berlín, n., -s.
beseech, bitten (um, acc.)
Besen, Besen, m., -s, —.
besides, ausser (dat.).
best, best.
bêtise, Bêtíse, f., dummer Streich,
m., -s., -e, Dummheit, f.
better, besser.
between, zwischen, dazwischen,
unter.
beyond, hinter, dahinter.
Bible, Bibel, f., -n.
bid, wünschen, heissen.
big, gross, dick.
bill, Rechnung, f.
binding, Einband, m., -s.
bind, festbinden, sich verpflichten.
biographical, biographisch.
biography, Biographíe, f., Lebensbeschreibung, f.
bird, Vogel, m., -s, -ögel.
birth, Geburt, f., Rang, m , -es,
Stand, m., -es, Leben, n., -s.
birthday, Geburtstag, m., -s.
birthplace, Geburtsort, m., -s.
birthright, Geburtsrecht, n., -es.
Bismarck, Bismarck.
bitch, Hündin, f.
bit, Stück, n., -es, -e ; some b. of
satire, irgend eine Spottrede, f.
Byzantine, byzantinisch.
black, schwarz, dunkel, düster ;
b. (horse), Rappe, m., -n, -n.
blackened, schwarz werden.
black-robed, schwarzgekleidet.
blame, tadeln.
bland, sanft, mild.
blanket, (Lager-) Decke, f., wol-
lene Decke.
blaze, schimmern.

bless, segnen.
blessing, Segen, m., -s.
blind, blind.
bliss, Glückseligkeit, f.
blood, Blut, f.
bloodshot, mit Blut unterláufen,
aufgeschwollen.
bloom, Duft, m., -s.
blot, austilgen, auslöschen.
blow, wehen, flattern.
blow, Schlag, m., -s, -äge.
blue, blau.
blunder, Irrtum, m., -s, -ümer.
blundering, im Irrtum.
blush, erröten.
blush, Erröten, n., -s.
bobbing, herumhüpfend.
body, Körper, m., -s, —.
bold, kühn.
Boniface, Bonifacius, Bonifáz, m.
Bonnland, Bonnland, n., s.
book, Buch, n., -s, -ücher ; Liste,
f., Verzeichnis, n., -nisses, -nisse ;
Register, n., -s, —.
boon, Segen, m., -s, Lohn, m., -s,
Gut, n., -es, -üter.
boot, daran liegen.
booted, gestiefelt.
booty, Beute, f.
born, geboren.
Boswell, Boswell, m.
Boswellize, boswellisieren, den
B. spielen.
both, beide, b. and, sowohl . . .
(als) auch, nicht nur . . . sondern auch.
bother, Plage, f., Quälerei, f.
bottle, Flasche, f.
boulder, Stein, m., -s, -e, Block,
m., -s, -öcke, Steinmasse, f.
Bourbon, Bourbone, m., -n, -n.
bow, sich verbeugen, sich neigen,
grüssen.

BOX 99 CAMPAIGN

box, Loge, f., Stuhl, m., -s, -ühle.
boy, Knabe, m., -n, -n.
braced, erfrischt; b. back, zurück-
gebogen, zurückgeworfen.
branch, Zweig, m , -s, -e.
branded, gebrandmarkt.
brander, Brandfuchs, m., -es,
-üchse.
brave, tapfer, mutig, tüchtig.
brawl, rauschen.
break, brechen, zerbrechen; (of
the day) anbrechen; b. away,
losbrechen (von), lossagen.
breakfast, Frühstück, n., -s.
breakneck, halsbrecherisch.
breast, Brust, f., -üste.
breath, Atemzug, m., -s, -üge.
breathe, atmen, einatmen.
breed, erwecken, erzeugen, erziehen.
breeze, Lüftchen, n., -s, Lufthauch,
m., -s, Luftzug, m., -s.
bridal, Ehe, f., Vermählung, f.
bride, Braut, f., -äute, Gemahlin, f.
bridegroom, Bräutigam, m., -s.
bridge, Brücke, f.
bridle, Zügel, m., -s.
brief, kurz.
bright, hell, glänzend.
broom-stick, Besenstiel, m., -s, -e.
brilliant, leuchtend, glänzend.
brim, Rand, m., -s, -änder.
bring, b. out, herausbringen; b.
up, erziehen.
broad, breit, weit, einfach, deutlich.
Broad-Stone, der breite Stein,
m., -s.
broadsword, Rapier, n., -s.
Brobdignag, the same, or: Riese,
m., -n, -n.
bronzed, verbräunt.
Brooklyn, Brooklyn, n., -s.

brother, Bruder, m., -s. Brüder.
brother-in-law, Schwager, m.,
-s, -äger.
brown, braun.
Brüges, Brügge, n., s.
buckskin, ledern (aus Bocksfell
gemacht).
build, bauen, erbauen.
building, Gebäude, n., -s, —.
bull-dog, Bull-Dogge, f.
burn, brennen, anbrennen.
burst, Ausbruch, m., -s.
burst, einschlagen (in, acc.); geraten (in, acc.); zerspringen; losbrechen; steigen (über, acc.).
bushel, Scheffel, m., -s, —.
bush, Busch, m., -es. -üsche, Ge-
büsch, n., -es, -e.
business, Geschäft, n., -s, -e.
business (adj.), geschäftlich.
bust, Büste, f.
busy, sich beschäftigen (mit).
but, aber, ausser.
butcher, schlachten.
button-hole, Knopfloch, n., -s,
-öcher.
buy, kaufen.
by, mit, bei, von.

C.

cab, cab, n., -s, Droschke, f.,
Wagen, m., -s, —.
cadence, Takt, m., -s, -e.
calculate, berechnen.
call, nennen, heissen; wecken;
rufen (in, acc.); visit, besuchen.
California, Califórnien, n., -s;
(adj.) Californisch.
calm, ruhig, heiter.
Cambridge, Cambridge, n., -s.
campaign, Feldzug, m., -s, -üge.

can, können, wissen, vermögen.

cancel, ausstreichen, verlöschen.

candle, Licht, n., -s, -er.

cane, Stock, m., -s, -öcke, Stöckchen.

cañon, Schlucht, f., Pass, m., -es, -ässe.

cant, c. names, Spitznamen, m. plu.

canvas, Leinwand, f.

cap, Mütze, f. Couleurmütze, f., Cereviskäppchen, n., -s.

capital, Kapital, n, -s, -e and -ien, Vermögen, n, -s.

captain, Hauptmann, m., -s, plu. Hauptleute; Käpitän, m., -s, -e.

car, state-c., Staatswagen, m., -s, —.

caravan, Karawane, f.

carcass, Leichnam, m., -s, -e, Leiche, f.

card, Karte, f.

care, Leitung, f., Aufsicht, f.

careful, sorgsam, vorsichtig, sorgfältig.

careless, rücksichtslos, unbekümmert, unbefangen, sorglos.

Carl, Karl, m., -s.

Carmagnole, Carmagnole, f.

carpet, Teppich, m., -s, -e.

carriage, Haltung, f., Wagen, m., -s, —.

carry, tragen, gewinnen.

carving, Bildwerk, n., -s, -e, Schnitzwerk, n., -s, Bildhauerei, f.

case, Fall, m., -s, -älle.

cast, Abguss, m., -es, üsse.

castellated, betürmt, bezinnt, mit Zinnen versehen.

castle, Schloss, n., -es, -össer.

catch, einholen, fangen; stölpern, fehltreten; packen, ergreifen.

Catholic, Kathólik, m., -en, -en; (adj.) kathólisch.

caudal, Schwanz-.

cause, Sache, f., -n.

cause, verursachen.

celebrate, feiern.

celebrate, berühmt.

cell, Zelle, f. Kerkerloch, n, -s, -öcher.

centre, Mittelpunkt, m., -s, -ünkte; in the c. of, mitten in or auf.

century, Jahrhundert, n., -s, -e.

ceremonious, feierlich, anständig.

ceremony, Feierlichkeit, f. Ceremonîe, f. Etikétte, f.

certain, bestimmt, gewiss, sicher.

certainly, sicherlich, gewiss, freilich.

chafe, reizen

chain, ketten, (an, acc)

chair, Stuhl, m., -s, -ühle.

challenge, fordern, herausfordern, gebieten.

chameleon, Chamäleon, n, -s, -s.

champion, Kämpe, m., -n, -n.

chance, by c., or c. to, zufällig, zufälligerweise.

change, Wechsel, m, -s, Änderung, f.

change, (ver-)tauschen (für, gegen, mit, um), wechseln, úm schlagen, verändern.

channel, Bett, n, -s, -en, Kanál, m., -s, -äle.

chap, Kerl, m., -s -e, (-s) Patrón, m., -s, -e.

chapel, Kapélle, f., Kirche, f.

character, Charákter, m, -s, —, guter Ruf, m., -s.

charge, anschreiben, nehmen (für), fordern von . . . für; hin donnern, hinstürmen.

Charles, Karl, m, -s.
charm, Zauber, m., -s, —.
charming, reizend, allerliebst.
chase, jagen, Jagd machen.
chase, Jagd, f., -en.
chasm, Grund, m., -es, -ünde, Tiefe, f., Schlucht, f., -en.
check, without c., ohne Bedenken, ohne Zaudern.
check, bändigen.
cheek, Wange, f., Gesicht, n., -s, -er.
cheer, erheitern, ermuntern, sich trösten, Mut fassen.
cheerful, munter, froh, beruhigt, fröhlich.
Cherbourg, Cherbourg, n., -s.
cherish, sorgen (für), pflegen.
chest, Brust, f.
chicken, Hündchen, n.
chief, grösst, Haupt-, Ober-.
chief, Haupt, n, -es, -äupter, Führer, m., -s, —.
child, Kind, n., -s, -er.
childhood, Kindheit, f.
childlike, kindlich.
chilling, frostig.
chimney, Kamín, m., -s, -e.
chin, Kinn, n., -s, -e.
chirp, zirpen.
choose, wählen.
chorus, Chor, m., -s, -öre.
Christian, christlich.
Christmas, Weihnachten, pl.; Ch. jollities, Weihnachtsfestlichkeiten, fröhliche Christfeste.
church, Kirche, f.
cicerone, Führer, m., -s, —.
cigar, Cigarre, f.
circle, Kreis, m., -es, -e, Umfriedung, f.
city, Stadt, f., ädte.
civil, höflich (gegen, acc.).

civilization, Bildung, f., Gesittung, f., Kultur, f., Civilisatión, f.
civilize, civilisieren, bilden.
claim, Recht, n., -s, -e, Anspruch, m., -s, -üche.
clamber, ansteigen.
clan, Clan, m., -s, -s, Geschlecht, n., -s, -er, Stamm, m., -s, -ämme.
claret, Rotwein, m., -s, -e.
class, Klasse, f.
classic, klassisch.
classic, Klassiker, m., -s, —.
classmate, Klassenkamerad, m., -en and -s, -en, Universitätsfreund, m., -s, -e.
Claudian, Claudian, m., -s.
clay, Thon, m., -s, -e; of c., thönern.
clear, klar, hell, deutlich.
cleave, bleiben; sich in (acc.) spalten.
clever, klug.
cliff, Felsklippe, f., Fels, m, -en, -en.
climate, Klima, n., -s, -ta and -te.
cling, sich nisten (an, acc. and dat.), fest halten, fassen, sich klammern (an, acc.).
clipping, Scheren, n., -s.
clique, Clique, f., Gesellschaft, f., Genossenschaft, f.
cloak, Mantel, m., -s, -äntel.
clock, Uhr, f, -en.
cloister, Kloster, n, -s.
close, dicht, nah.
close, schliessen.
clothes, Kleider, n. plu.
cloudless, wolkenlos, hell, klar.
clutch, greifen (nach).
coal, Kohle, f.
coat, Rock, m., -s, -öcke.

cock, Hahn, m., -s, -ähne.
cock, spannen (den Hahn).
coin, Geldstück, n., -s, ücke, Goldstück.
cold, Kälte, f.
cold, kalt.
collar, Kragen, m., -s, —.
colleague, Kollége, m., -en, -en.
collect, sammeln, versammeln.
college, Universitäts-, Studenten-; on the c. benches, im Hörsaal, im Kollegium, auf den Bänken.
colonel, Oberst, m., -en, -en.
colony, Kolonie, f., Kolonial-.
color, Farbe, f.
colored, farbig, bunt, schwarz.
colossus, Kolóss, m., -es, -s.
colt, Füllen, n., -s, —.
column, Säule, f.
column-like, säulengleich.
combing, Kämmen, n., -s.
combatant, Streiter, m., -s, —, Kämpfender, m., -n, -n.
come, kommen; c. up, aufgehen, heraufsteigen; c. off with, davontragen; c. in, eintreten; c. back, wieder zurückkehren; come upon, treffen.
comfort, Trost, m., -es.
command, befehlen.
command, Führung, f., Befehl, m., -s, -e, Verfügung, f.
commander-in-chief, Oberbefehlshaber, m., -s,—, Feldherr, m., -n, -n.
commanding, überwiégend, überrágend.
commend, empfehlen.
commentary, Bemerkung, f., Beobachtung, f.
commit, überliéfern, (dat.), werfen (in, acc.).

communicate, mitteilen, sich brieflich in Verbindung setzen.
companion, Reisegefährte, m., -n, -n; Gesellschafterin, f.
companionship, Kameradschaft, f.
compare, vergleichen.
comparatively, verhältnismässig.
compile, an Sammelwerken arbeiten, sammeln.
complete, ganz, vollkommen, fertig, zu Ende, vorüber.
compliment, Komplimente machen, schmeicheln (dat.).
compose, is c., bestehen aus.
composure, Ruhe, f., Gleichgültigkeit, f.
comprehend, begreifen, verstehen.
comprehensible, begreiflich.
comprehensive, umfássend.
comrade, Gefährte, m., -n, -n.
conception, Meinung, f., Auffassung, f.
concerning, inbetreff (gen.), hinsichtlich (gen.).
condemn, verdammen.
condescension, Herablassung, f.
condition, Zustand, m., -s, -ände, Bedingung, f.
conduct, fähren, begleiten.
conductor, Kondukteur, m., -s, -e, Führer, m., -s, —, Schirrmeister, m., -s, —.
confer, sprechen (mit); c. rapture, glücklich machen.
conference, Unterhandlung, f., Beratschlagung, f.
confess, gestehen.
confide, sich verlassen auf (acc.), Vertrauen haben in (dat.).
confirm, bestätigen.

congratulate, gratulieren (dat.), Glück wünschen (dat.).
congratulation, Glückwunsch, m., -es, -ünsche.
Congress, Kongréss, m., -es, -e.
conscience, Gewissen, -n., -s.
conscientiously, gewissenhaft.
consciousness, Gefühl, n., -s, -e, Bewusstsein, n., -s.
consecrate, weihen.
consent, free c., freiwillig, freier Wille, m., -ens.
consent, einwilligen (darin).
consequence, no c., es thut nichts.
consequently, daher.
consider, halten (für), überlégen, bedenken.
considerable, gross, viel, bedeutend.
considerate, rücksichtsvoll.
consideration, Rücksicht, f., -en, Ansehen, n., -s.
consist, bestehen (aus or in, dat.) darin.
consistent, vereinbar (mit), im Einklang (mit).
constant, fortwährend, stet; beständig, treu.
consular, Konsular-.
consult, nachschlagen, zu Rate ziehen.
contain, enthalten.
content, Zufriedenheit, f.
contentious, streitlustig.
contents, Inhalt, m., -s.
contest, Kampf, m., -s, -ämpfe; Opposition, f.
continent, Festland, n., -s, Erdteil, m., ·s, ·e, Kontinént, m., -s, -e.
contract, Kontrákt, m., -s, -e, Vertrag, m., -s, -äge.

contretemps, Zufall, m., -s, -älle.
control, Macht, f.
convenience, Bequemlichkeit, f.
conversation, Unterhaltung, f., Unterredung, f., Gespräch, n., -s, -e.
converse, sprechen, sich unterhalten (mit).
convince, überzeúgen.
convives, Gäste, m., plu.
cool, kühl.
cool, kühlen, abkühlen.
coolness, Ruhe, f.
Copenhagen, Kopenhagen, n., -s.
cordial, freundlich, herzlich.
cork, Kork, m., -s, -e and -örke, Korkstöpsel, m., -s, —.
corn, Mais, m., -es.
corner, Ecke, f., Eck-.
corps, n., —, —.
correspond, passen (zu), entsprechen (dat.).
correspondence, Briefwechsel, m., -s, —.
corridor, Gang, m., -s, -änge.
cost, to the c. of, zum Kosten, zum Besten (gen.).
cost, kosten (dat. or acc. of person); schwerfallen (dat.).
cosy, gemütlich, traulich.
cough, Husten, m., -s.
couldn't be, the same, or : der es nicht vermag.
Count, Graf, m., -en, -en.
count, messen (nach), rechnen, zurücklegen.
country, Land, n., -es, -e and -änder, Gegend, f. Land- ; c. place, Landsitz, m., -es, -e.
coupé, n., -s, -s.
couple, Paar, n., -es, -e.
courage, Mut, m., -s.
courageous, herzhaft, mutig.

course, Kurs, m., -es, -e, Richtung, f.; Verfahren, n., -s.
course, schweifen über (acc.)
court, Hof, m., -s, -öfe.
court-marshal, Hofmarschall, m., -s, -s and -älle.
courtesy, Höflichkeit, f.
cousin, Cousine, f.; Vetter, m., -s, —.
cover, bedecken, bekränzen; bewachsen.
coward, Memme, f.
crag, Fels, m., -en, -en.
cranium, Schädel, m., -s, —.
cranny, Spalte, f.
cravat, Halstuch, n., -s, -ücher.
crawl, kriechen, away, weg.
cream-colored, geltweiss.
creature, Geschöpf, n., -es, -e.
credit, Credit, m., -s, Zahlungsfähigkeit, f.
crevice, Riss, m., -es, -e.
cricket, Grille, f., Heinchen, n.
crime, Verbrechen, n., -s, —.
crimson, rot.
cripple, verkrüppeln, verwunden.
criticism, Kritik, f.
cross, sich kreuzen; kreuzweise legen; hinübergehen, auf die andre Seite gehen, gehen (durch or über, acc.).
cross, Kreuz, n., -es, -e.
crosswise, kreuzweis.
croupe, carry en c., hinter sich aufsitzen lassen.
crowd, Gedränge, n., -s, Menge, f.
crowd, füllen, sich drängen (in, dat.), c. into, sich zusammendrängen (bei), einschliessen (in, acc. or dat.).
crown, Krone, f.; Kron-.
crown, bekränzen, bedecken.

cruel, schwer, schrecklich, unbarmherzig.
crumble, zertrümmern, zerstören.
crush, c. of a, wimmelnd.
crush, zertreten, zermalmen.
cry, Ruf, m., -s, -e, (nach).
cry, rufen; c. out, ausrufen, ausschreien.
cultivate, bilden.
curiosity, Neugierde, f.
curious, merkwürdig, seltsam, eigentümlich.
curl, Locke, f., Löckchen, n, -s.
curl, kräuseln.
curly-pated, krauslockig, krausköpfig.
currency, c. of talk, Redefluss, m., -es.
current, Strömung, f.
curse, Fluch, m., -es, -üche.
curse, verfluchen.
curtail, verkürzen.
curtain, Vorhang, m., -s, -änge.
curtsey, sich beugen or verbeugen.
curve, Krümmung, f.
cushion, Kissen, n., -s, —, Polster, n., -s, —.
customary, üblich, gewöhnlich.
cut, schneiden, ausschneiden, zerschneiden; c. to resemble, nachmeisseln (dat.); c. off, abschneiden.

D.

dabble, pfuschen, künsteln, klecksen.
daily, täglich, bei Tag.
dame, Dame, f.
damnation, Verderben, n., -s, Verdammnis, f.

dance, tanzen.
danger, Gefahr, f.
Danish, dänisch.
dare, wagen.
daring, kühn, verwegen.
dark, dunkel, schwarz.
dark-haired, mit dunkelm (or, schwarzem) Haar.
Darmstadt, Darmstadt, n., -s.
dash, giessen in (acc.); sausen (durch), stürmen, jagen.
date, Datum, n., -s, -ta and -ten.
dated, datiert, Dato.
daughter, Tochter, f., -öchter.
day, Tag, m., -s, -e; all his d., sein Lebenlang.
daylight, Tag, m., -s, Morgen, m., -s, —.
dead, tot.
deal, great d., viel, sehr viel, höchst.
dear, lieb, teuer.
death, Tod, m., -s, Todes —; to be in at the d., beim Halali dabei sein.
debris, Trümmer, plu., Überreste, plu.
decay, Verfall, m., -s; bring d., in Verfall bringen, schwächen.
deceive, betrügen.
deck, Deck, Verdeck, n., -s, -e.
decide, (sich) entscheiden (für, über, acc.), sich entschliessen (zu).
decorous, anständig.
deed, That, f., Handlung, f.
deem, denken, meinen, glauben.
deep, geräumig, tief, voll, inner, gross, innig.
defeat, Niederlage, f.
defile, Pass, m., -es, -ässe.
define, d itself, sich auszeichnen, hervortreten in (dat.).

definite, bestimmt.
dejection, Traurigkeit, f., in d., betrübt.
delicious, köstlich; d. place, kühler Ort.
delight, Behagen, n., -s, Freude, f.
delight, to be d., sich freuen, erfreut sein.
delightful, reizend.
dell, Thal, n., -s, -äler.
Delphic, delphisch.
demand, Forderung, f., Nachfrage, f., Wunsch, m., -es, -ünsche.
democracy, Demokratie, f., Volksherrschaft, f.
Demos, Demos, m., Volk, n., -s, -ölker.
dense, dick.
deny, leugnen; ablehnen, abschlagen.
depart, abfahren; entfliehen, scheiden.
departure, Abreise, f., Abfahrt, f.
depth, Tiefe, f.
deride, verspotten, verhöhnen.
descend, aussteigen, absteigen.
description, Beschreibung, f.
desert, verlassen.
desert, wüst, öde.
desert, Wüste, f., Einöde, f.
desertion, Verrat, m., -s.
deserve, verdienen.
déshabillé, in Morgenkleidung.
desire, Wunsch, m., -es, -ünsche.
desire, wünschen, wollen.
desirable, wünschenswert.
desk, Pult, n., -s, -e.
desolation, Einöde, f.
despair, Verzweiflung, f.
despise, verachten.
desponding, verzagend, niedergeschlagen.

destroy, zerstören, vernichten.
destruction, Verderben, n., -s.
detail, Einzelnkeit, f., Kleinigkeit, f.
detain, abhalten.
development, Entwichlung, f.
device, Spiel, n., -s, -e, Sache, f.
devil, Teufel, m., -s, —.
devilish, verteufelt.
devoted, treu, ergeben.
dexterous, geschickt.
dialect, college d., Studentensprache, f., burschikos.
die, sterben.
differ, abweichen (von).
difference, Unterschied, m., -s, -e.
different, verschieden (von), nicht ähnlich (dat.); anders.
difficult, beschwerlich, schwer, ermüdend.
diffuse, verbreiten.
dignity, Würde, f.; d. of carriage, würdige Haltung, f.
diligence, Diligence, f., Eilwagen, m., -s, —.
dim, trübe, düster.
diminutive, klein.
dine, speisen.
dingy, dunkel, verblasst.
dining-room, Speisesaal, m , -s, -säle.
dinner, Mittagsessen, n., -s, Essen, n., -s, Diner or Diné, n., -s, -s.
dinner-bell, Tischklingel, fem., Tischzeit, f., Mittagsessen, n., -s.
dinner-table, Speisetisch, m., -es, -e.
dip, sich senken.
diplomatic, diplomatisch.
direct, unmittelbar.
directly, stracks, gerade.

dirty, schmutzig.
disappoint, enttäuschen.
discharge, (sich) münden (in, acc.), sich ergiessen.
discobolus, Diskuswerfer, m., -s, —.
discord, Zwietracht, f.
discourse, Rede, f.
discover, entdecken, erfahren.
discuss, erörtern.
disentangle, (sich) zurückziehen (aus).
disgust, to have a d., Ekel empfinden (vor, dat.).
dislodge, vertreiben.
dismount, absteigen.
dispose, verfügen (über, acc.).
dissatisfied, unzufrieden (mit).
distance, Ferne, f., Strecke, f., Distanz, f., Entfernung, f.; at wide d., weit entfernt.
distant, fern, weit.
distinct, deutlich.
distinction, Auszeichnung, f.
distinguish, (sich) unterscheiden, (sich) auszeichnen.
distort, verstellen, verdrehen.
distress, Not, f.
distribute, abgeben, verteilen.
disturb, stören.
disturbance, Unruhe, f.; Störung, f.
divert, amüsieren.
divine, göttlich.
divine, erraten.
division, d. room, Kollegenzimmer, Klassenzimmer, n., -s, —. Hörsaal, m., -s, -säle.
divorce, Scheidung, f.
do, thun, machen, schaffen.
doctor, Doktor, m., -s, -en.
dog, Hund, m., -es, -e, Kerl, m., -s, -e.

domain, Bereich, m. and n., -s, -e ; Gut, n., -s, -üter.

domestic, Diener, m., -s, — ; plu.: Dienerschaft, f.

Domino, Domino, m., (-s), -s.

doom, Schicksal, n., -s, -e, Los, n., -es, -e.

door, Thür, f., -en.

d'or, d'Or.

doubly, doppelt.

doubt, Zweifel, m., -s, —.

doubt, zweifeln (an, dat.).

Dover, Dover, n., -s.

down, nieder, unten, abwärts, herunter.

downstairs, hinunter, hinab.

downward, nach unten.

dozen, Dutzend, n., -s, -e.

drag, hinabziehen, hinabzerren.

drain, leeren.

draught, Zug, m., -s, -üge.

draw, ziehen ; holen ; d. breath, (Atem, m., -s.), einatmen ; stossen (in, acc.) ; d. nearer, näher hinrücken.

drawing, Zeichnung, f.

drawn, blank.

dread, fürchten.

dreaded, befürchtet.

dream, träumen, hinbrüten (über, acc.).

dreamily, träumerisch, sinnend, nachdenklich.

dreary, traurig.

dress, Kleid, n., -s, -er ; Uniform, f.

dress, to be dressed, tragen, gekleidet sein (in, dat.).

drink, trinken.

drive, Fahrt, f.

drive, verscheuchen, jagen, treiben ; fahren, anfahren (vor, dat.).

drizzle, rieseln.

drop, fallen (lassen), entgleiten (dat.), entfallen (dat.), sinken, herabfallen ; d. into, besuchen.

drudgery, mühevolle Arbeit, f.

drunk, betrunken.

dry, trocken, ausgetrocknet.

Dryad, Dryáde, f.

ducal, herzoglich.

Duchess, Herzogin, f., -innen.

duel, Duell, n., -s, -e, Zweikampf, m., -s, -ämpfe.

duelist, Duellánt, m., -en, -en, Zweikämpfer, m., -s, —, Schläger, m., -s, —.

dull, starr, dumm.

dumb, stumm.

dupe, betrügen.

dust, Staub, m., -s.

dusty, staubig.

Dutch, holländisch.

duty, Pflicht, f.

dynasty, Herrschergeschlecht, n., -es, -er, Dynastíe, f.

E.

each, jeder.

eager, eifrig, bereit.

eagerness, Ungestüm, n., -s.

ear, Ohr, n., -s, -en.

earn, verdienen.

ease, to be at e., sich behaglich fühlen, sich zwanglos bewegen.

easy, leicht.

eccentric, wunderlich.

echo, Echo, n., -s, -s, Wiederhall, m., -s, -e.

echo, wiederhallen.

economical, genau, sparsam.

edge, Spitze, f., Kante, f., Ecke, f.

edge, e. on, weiter hinfahren, vorwärtsrücken.

edition, Ausgabe, f., Auflage, f.

educate, erziehen.

education, Ausbildung, f., Erziehung, f.

educator, Erzieher, m., -s, —.

effect, Wirkung, f., Einfluss, m., -es, -üsse.

effort, Anstrengung, f.

eight, acht.

eighteen, achtzehn.

eighty, achtzig.

eighty-second, zweiundachtzigst.

elastic, Gummiband, n., -s, -änder.

electric, electrisch.

elegant, zierlich, vornehm.

eleven, elf.

Elizabeth, Elisabeth, f.

eloquence, Beredsamkeit, f.

elsewhere, anderswo.

embarrassed, unbehülflich, verlegen, linkisch.

embrace, umármen.

embroider, sticken, verbrämen.

emotion, Bewegung, f.

emperor, Kaiser, m., -s, —.

employment, Beschäftigung, f.

empress, Kaiserin, f.

emulate, wetteifern (mit).

enchant, bezaubern.

encompass, umfássen.

encourage, aufmuntern, ermutigen.

end, Ende, n., -s, -n ; no end of, zahllos, ohne Ende.

endow, ausstatten, versehen.

energy, Eifer, m , -s.

England, England, n., -s.

English, englisch.

Englishman, Engländer, m., -s, —.

enjoy, geniessen, besitzen, einnehmen, sich erfreuen (gen.).

enormous, ungeheuer, gross.

enough, genug.

ensue, entstehen.

enter, eintraten, beginnen, auftreten, besteigen.

entertain, unterhálten, führen.

enthusiasm, Bewunderung, f., Begeisterung, f.

enthusiastically, e. in favor, ganz entzückt (von), günstig gelegen (für).

entirely, ganz, gänzlich, durchweg, ganz und gar, völlig.

entrenchment, Schanze, f.

envoy, Gesandte (r), m., -en, -en.

envy, beneiden.

equal, thy e., deinesgleichen.

equally, gleich, ebenso.

equipage, Equipage, f.

equip, ausrüsten.

erect, hoch aufgerichtet, aufrecht.

errand, Gang, m., -s, -änge, Ritt, m., -s, -e.

error, Irrtum, m , -s, -ümer.

escape, verschwinden, vorüber sein.

estate, Gut, n., -s, -üter.

establish, stiften, (be)gründen, schliessen, anknüpfen.

establishment, Stiftung, f , Gründung, f.

eternity, Ewigkeit, f.

etiquette, Etikette, f.

Euclid, Euclídes, m., -s.

Europe, Európa, n., -s.

European, europäisch.

evangelical, evangelisch.

even, auch, einmal.

evening, Abend, m., -s, -e.

event, Ereignis, n., -isses, -isse ; at all events, jedenfalls.

ever, immer, sonst.

evermore, auf ewig, auf immer.

ever-running, immerfliessend.

every, jeder, all.

every-day, alltäglich, gemein.

everything, alles.

everywhere, überall.

exactly, gerade.

exalted, hochgestiegen, erhaben.

examination, Prüfung, f., Examen, n., -s, -imina.

examine, untersúchen, besichtigen.

example, Beispiel, n., -s, -e ; for e., zum B.

exceedingly, äusserst.

excellent, vortrefflich, vorzuglich, ausgezeichnet.

except, ausser, nur nicht, ausgenommen.

exceptional, ausserordentlich.

excessively, übermässig.

excite, aufregen.

excitement, Aufregung, f., Erregung, f.

exclaim, rufen, ausrufen.

excuse, Entschuldigung, f.

execute, ausführen, handeln.

executioner, Henker, m., -s, —, Scharfrichter, m., -s, —.

exercise, üben, ausüben.

exertion, Anstrengung, f.

exeunt, gehen ab.

exist, bestehen.

existence, Leben, n., -s.

expect, erwarten.

expenses, Ausgaben, f. plu.

experience, Erfahrung, f.

explain, erklären.

explode, explodieren, zerplatzen, zerspringen.

explosive, knallend.

ex-President, Ex-Präsidént, m., -en, -en.

express, äussern, erzählen, ausdrücken, sprechen (von).

expression, Ausdruck, m., -s, -ücke, Miene, f.

expressive, ausdrucksvoll.

extend, ausstrecken, hinwegreichen.

extensive, ausgedehnt, gross.

exultant, frohlockend.

eye, Auge, n., -s, -n.

eyelid, Augenlid, n., -s, -er.

F.

façade, Vorderseite, f., Fassade, f.

face, Gesicht, n., -s, -er.

facetious, spasshaft, witzig, lustig.

fact, Thatsache, f.

fail, fehlen.

faint, matt.

fair, schön.

fairly, ganz.

faith, Glaube(n), m., -ens, Treue, f., Vertrauen, n., -s (zu).

faithful, treu, ergebenst.

faithless, untreu, treulos.

fall, fallen, stürzen, anfangen ; f. out, herauslaufen ; f. into, geraten in (acc.).

fall back, zurückfallen.

falsehood, Falschheit, f., Treulosigkeit, f.

familiar, bekannt, vertraut.

familiarly, auf intimem Fusse.

family, Famílie, f., Familien-.

famous, berühmt.

fancy, Phantasíe, f.

fantastic, phantastisch.

far, fern, weit.
far-away, fern.
fare, Beköstigung, f., Speise, f., Küche, f., Tisch, m., -es.
fare, gehen (mit), stehen (mit).
farewell, Lebewohl, n., -s, -(s) and -e.
farther, weiter; f. on, weiter hin.
fashion, Weise, f., Mode, f., Art, f.; in the old f., wie domals.
fat, fett, dick.
fate, Schicksal, n., -s, -e.
father, Vater, m., -s, -äter.
father-in-law, Schwiegervater, m., -s.
fault, Fehler, m., -s, —.
favor, begünstigen.
favor, Gefallen, m., -s, Freude, f., Gunst, f.; plu., Gunstbezeigungen; in favor of, günstig (dat., or zu, or für).
favorite, Lieblings-.
fear, fürchten.
fearful, furchtsam.
feasibility, Möglichkeit, f.
feast, bewirten.
feather, Feder, f., -n.
feeble, schwach.
feed, leben (von).
feel, fühlen, ahnen, spüren; to make felt, sich geltend machen.
feeling, Gefühl, n., -s, -e.
feelingly, mit Gefühl, lebhaft.
fellow, Kerl, m., -s, -e, Kamerad, m., -en and -s, -en.
female, weiblich.
feminine, weiblich.
ferocious, grausam, grimmig.
fervid, brünstig.
fevered, fieberisch.
few, wenig, ein paar.
field, Feld, n., -s, -er, Schlacht, f.; Feld-.

fifteen, fünfzehn.
fifty, fünfzig.
fight, fechten, kämpfen, ausfechten, sich schlagen; f. duels, sich duellieren.
figure, Gestalt, f.
fill, füllen, erfüllen, einnehmen.
filthy, garstig, schlecht.
finally, endlich.
find, finden, einem vorkommen.
fine, schön, fein, klar.
finger-bowl, Fingerbecken, n., -s, —.
finish, enden, vervollständigen, fertig machen, vollenden; to be finished, fertig sein, zu Ende sein.
fin, Flosse, f.
fire, feuern, abfeuern, losdrücken; to set on f., anzünden.
firm, fest.
firmness, Festigkeit, f.
first, erst, erstens, vorher; the f. to, zuerst.
fissure, Spalt, m., -es, -e.
five, fünf.
fix, weilen (auf, dat.), heften (auf, acc.).
flank, Flanke, f., Weiche, f.
flank, flankieren.
flathead, Flachkopf-.
fleck, (be-)flecken.
fleeting, flüchtig, vorüberfliegend.
Flemish, flämisch, niederländisch.
flesh, Fleisch, n., -es.
flicker, zittern.
flight, Flug, m., -s, Flucht, f.
flinch, ermatten, nachlassen, matt werden.
fling, ausschlagen, brausen, sich werfen, sich öffnen, weichen.

flood, überströmen, umfliessen.
flood, Flut, f.
flourish, blühen, hervortreten.
flow, fliessen, strömen.
flower, Blume, f.
Fluxions, Fluxionen, f. plu.
fly, fliegen.
foam, Schweiss, m., -es.
foam, schäumen.
foe, Feind, m., -s, -e.
foliage, Laubwerk, n., -s, Laub, n., -s.
follow, folgen (dat.), verfolgen (acc.).
follower, Anhänger, m., -s, —.
fool, Narr, m., -en, -en.
fool, bethören, täuschen, betrügen.
foolish, dumm.
foot, Fuss, m., -es, -üsse, Huf, m., -s, -ufe.
footing, Fussraum, m., -s.
footman, Lakai', m., -en and -s, -en, Diener, m., -s —.
footprint, Fußstapfe, f., Spur, f.
for, denn, da.
force, zwingen (zu), aufzwingen.
force, Kraft, f., -äfte; by f. of, Kraft or vermöge (gen.).
fore, Vorder-.
forego, aufgeben.
forehead, Stirn, f., -en.
foreleg, Vorderbein, n., -s, -e.
foremost, die Ersten.
foresee, voraussehen.
forest, Wald, m., -s, -älder.
foretell, ahnen, vorstellen, einbilden.
forge, Schmiede, f., Schmelzofen, m., -s, -öfen, Hüttenwerk, n., -s, -e.
forget, vergessen.
forgive, vergeben (dat.).

forgiveness, Vergebung, f.
fork, Gabel, f., -n.
form, Gestalt, f., Form, f.
form, bilden.
formal, förmlich, ceremoniös, formell.
formality, Formalität, f., Förmlichkeit, f.
formally, förmlich.
Fort Donelson, die Festung Donelson, Fort (n.) Donelson.
fortnight, vierzehn Tage.
fortunately, glücklicherweise, zum Glück.
fortune, Glück, n., -s, Schicksal, n., -s, -e ; Vermögen, n., -s.
forty, vierzig.
forward, heran-, näher.
foster-sister, Pflegeschwester, f., -n.
found, gründen, stiften.
founder, Gründer, m., -s, —.
four, vier.
fourteen, vierzehn.
Fox-Commerce, Fuchs - Kommers, m., -es, -e.
Fox-Song, Fuchslied, n., -s, -er.
foyer, Foyer, m. and n., -s, -s, Vorhalle, f.
frailty, Gebrechlichkeit, f.
frame, umrähmen, umränken.
franchise, Freiheit, f.
Frankfort, Frankfurt, n., -s.
Franklin, Franklin.
Frederick, Friedrich, m., -s.
free, frei, ungehindert, offen.
freely, tüchtig, in vollem Masse.
Fremdenblatt, n., -s, -ätter.
French, französich.
Frenchman, Franzose, m., -n, -n.
frenzy, Wahnsinn, m., -s, Tollheit, f., in a f., wütend, tobend.
frequent, besuchen.

freshen, erfrischen.
friar, Mönch, m., -es, -önche.
friend, Freund, m , -es, -e.
friendliness, Freundlichkeit, f.
friendship, Freundschaft, f.
frighten, erschrecken.
from, aus, von.
front, Stirn(e), f. ; in f., vorne, von vorne, voraus.
frosty, frostig, Schnee-.
frowning, düster.
frozen, hard f., festgefroren, eingefroren.
fruit, Frucht, f., üchte.
fruit-tree, Obstbaum, m., -s, -äume.
fulfil, erfüllen, vollziéhen, vollbringen, halten.
fulfilment, Erfüllung, f.
full, voll, ganz; f. of danger, gefahrvoll.
full-length, in Lebensgrösse, f.
fumble, zupfen an (dat.).
fume, f. of beer, Bierdunst, m., -s.
fun, full of f., voll heiterer Laune, immer lustig.
funny, possierlich, lächerlich, komisch, drollig.
furnish, versehen, versorgen.
furnished, möbliert.
furniture, Möbel, n., -s, —.
further, no f., kein . . . mehr.
furthermore, ausserdem.
future, Zukunft, f. ; in the f., zukünftig, nachher.

G.

gain, g. strength, erstarken ; g. booty, Beute machen.
gala, g. dinner, Gala-Diner, n., -s, -s.

gale, Wind, m., -s, -e.
gallant, brav.
gallery, Gallerie, f.
gallop, sprengen, galloppieren.
game, Spiel, n., -s, -e, Plan, m., -s, -e and -äne.
gap, Öffnung, f., Einschnitt, m., -s, -e.
garden, Garten, m., -s, -ärten.
gardener, Gärtner, m., -s, —.
garnish, ausschmücken.
gash, Hieb, m., -s, -e.
gate, Thor, n., -s, -e.
gather, lasten (auf, dat.).
gaunt, mager.
gauntlet, Handschuh, m., -s, -e.
gauzy, durchsichtig.
gayety, Fröhlichkeit, f.
gaze, g. at, schauen, beschauen.
General, Generál, m., -s, -e (and -äle).
general, allgemein, Gesamt-.
generally, überhaupt, im Allgemeinen, allgemein.
generous, gütig, wohlwollend, edelmütig, grossmütig.
genial, warm, herzlich, leutselig.
genius, Genie, n., -s, -s.
genteel, vornehm, fein, nett.
gentleman, Herr, m., -n, -en.
German, deutsch.
Germany, Deutschland, n., -s.
Gerolt, Gerolt, m., -s.
gesture, Gebärde, f.
get, steigen (in, acc.), haben, bekommen, werden ; get away, entwischen, wegkommen ; g. over, überwinden.
ghost, Schatten, m., -s, —.
ghost-like, wie ein Gespenst.
giant, Riese, m., -n, -n.
giant, riesenhaft, riesig.
gift, Geschenk, n., -s, -e, Gabe, f.

gild, vergolden.

girl, Mädchen, n., -s.

girth, Gurt, m., -s, -e.

give, geben, gewähren, bestimmen, anbieten, g. life to, beleben.

glad, to be g., sich freuen, erfreut sein.

glade, Lichtung, f.

gladly, gern.

glass, Glas, n., -es, -äser, Spiegel, m., -s, —.

gleam, Schimmer, m., -s, —.

gleam, schimmern.

glide, gleiten.

glimmer, dämmern, schimmern.

glitter, funkeln.

glorify, verherrlichen.

glorious, herrlich, prachtvoll.

glove, Handschuh, m., -s, -e.

glow, Schein, m., -s, -e; Inbrunst, f.

glow, glühen.

gnaw, nagen (acc., or an with dat.).

go, gehen; g. down, untergehen; g. the rounds, die Runde machen; g. off, fortjagen.

goal, Ziel, n., -s, -e.

goblet, Krug, m., -s, -üge, Passglas, n., -es, -äser.

God, Gott, m., -es.

Goethean, Goethe-.

gold, Gold, n., -s.

gold - banded, goldumrändert, goldbetresst.

golden, golden.

good, gut.

good-bye, Lebewohl.

good-natured, gutmütig, gefällig, gemütlich.

goodness, Güte, f.

good-woman, gutes Weibchen.

gooseberry, Stachelbeere, f.

gorge, Schlucht, f., -en.

gorgeous, prachtvoll, prangend.

gospel, Evangelium, n, -(s), -lien.

gossip, Geschwätz, n., -es, -e.

govern, regieren, herrschen.

government, Regierung, f.

gracious, gnädig, lieblich.

gradually, allmählig.

grain, Korn, n., -s, örner.

grand, gross, grössartig, erhaben, Grande —.

grandchild, Enkel, m., -s, —.

granddaughter, Enkelin, f.

Grand-Duke, Grossherzog, m.; -s, -öge.

grandeur, Herrlichkeit, f., Grösse, f.

grandfather, Grossvater, m., -s, -äter.

grandson, Enkel, m., -s, —.

grant, zugeben, bewilligen.

grapple, nachgreifen, nachstreben, anfassen.

grasp, umklämmern, umfässen, greifen, nehmen, anfassen, fassen.

grass, Gras, n., -es, -äser, Wiese, f.

gratify, befriedigen.

grave, Grab, n., -s, -äber.

gray, grau.

graze, grasen.

great, gross.

Greek, Grieche, m., n, -n.

green, grün, ungefahren.

Grenzhammer, m., -s.

grief, Schmerz, m., -es, -en.

grisette, Grisette, f.

grisly, greulich, grausig.

groan, stöhnen.

groove, Geleise, n., -s, —.

grotto, Grotte, f.

ground, Erde, f., Boden, m., -s, —,
Grund, m., -s; grounds, Anla-
gen, f. plu.
grow, wachsen, werden.
grudge, with a g., unwillig.
guardianless, schutzlos, unver-
sorgt.
guard-room, Wachtstube, f.
guess, erraten, vermuten, treffen,
denken or einbilden (with dat.
of reflexive pronoun).
guest, Gast, m., -s, -äste.
guide, leiten.
gully, Kluft, f., -üfte.
gush, rauschen, hervorquellen,
strömen.
gutter, Gosse, f.

H.

ha, ha.
habit, Lebensweise, f., Gewohn-
heit, f.
Hague, der Haag, -s.
hail, preien (acc.), anrufen; within hailing distance, um einander zurufen zu können, im Bereich der Stimme.
hair, Haar, n., -s, -e.
hale, gesund, wohl, frisch.
half, halb.
half-a-dozen, ein halb(es) Dutzend, ein paar.
half-hour, eine halbe Stunde.
half-open, halb geöffnet.
half-past five, halb sechs, um h.
s. Uhr.
half-past four, halb fünf.
half-pupil, halb (und halb) ein
Schüler.
half-yearly, halbjährig.
hall, Saal, m., -s, Säle.

hallow, heiligen, weihen.
Hamburg, Hamburg, n., -s.
hand, Hand, f., -ände; in h.,
unter der Hand; unter Händen;
on one's hands, auf Händen,
auf dem Halse, or unterhanden
haben.
hand, einhändigen, überreichen.
handsome, hübsch, schön.
handsomely, reichlich.
hand-writing, Handschrift, f.,
Hand, f.
hang, hangen; to h. about, bleiben (an, dat.); h. him, zum
Teufel (Henker) mit ihm.
Hanover, Hannover, n., -s.
happen, geschehen, begegnen,
passieren; happened to, zufälligerweise.
happiness, Glück, n., -s.
happy, glücklich.
harangue, haranguieren, anre-
den.
hard, fest, hart, schwer.
harden, abhärten.
hard - faced, mit harten (Ge-
sichts)-Zügen.
hardly, kaum, schwerlich.
hard-won, schwererrungen.
harsh, herb, hart.
haste, Hast, f.
hasty, rasch.
hat, Hut, m., -s, üte.
hate, Hass, m., -es.
hatred, Hass, m, -es.
haughty, stolz.
haunt, bannen, bezaubern, verfolgt.
have, haben, brauchen, müssen.
hazy, leicht, neblig.
he, er.
head, Kopf, m., -s, öpfe, Haupt,
n., -s, -äupter.

headlong, ungestüm, tollkühn, unbesonnen.
health, Gesundheit, f.
hear, hören (von).
heart, Herz, n., -ens, -en; at h., im Herzen.
heart-beat, Herzschlag, m., -s, -äge.
heartily, herzlich, von ganzem Herzen.
heartrending, herzzerreissend.
hearty, munter, gesund, herzlich.
heat, Hitze, f., heiss.
heathen, Heide, m., -n, -n.
heaven, Himmel, m., -s, —; by Heavens, beim Himmel.
heavy, gewaltig, tief; schwer.
heed, sich bekümmern (um), hören.
Heidelberg, n., -s.
Heiligenberg, m., -s.
heir, Erbe, m., -n, -n.
heiress, Erbin, f.
help, helfen.
help, Hilfe, f.
hell, Hölle, f.
hemisphere, Halbkugel, f., n.
hence, deshalb.
hen, Huhn, n., -s, -ühner.
Herald (N. Y.), Herald, m., —.
herd, Bande, f., Rotte, f.
here, hier.
hereditary, Erb-.
hero, Held, m., -en, -en.
heroic, heroisch, ritterlich.
hesitate, zögern.
hew, hauen (auf, acc.).
hide, verbergen, verstecken.
high, hoch, gross, wichtig.
Highness, Hoheit, f.
hill, Berg, m., -s, -e, Hügel m., -s, —.
hillside, Bergeshang, m., -s, Abhang des Berges.

hind, Hinter
hinderance, Hindernis, n., -isses, -isse.
hip, Hüfte, f.
hist, still, höre mal.
historical, historisch, geschichtlich.
history, Geschichte, Lebensgang, m., -s.
hit, 's sitzt, getroffen.
hoard, anhäufen.
hoarse, heiser; in a h. whisper, heiser flüsternd.
hoary, greis, grau.
hock, Rheinwein, m., -s.
Hoffräulein, n., -s.
hold, halten, tragen; (es) aushalten, (es) aufnehmen (mit); hold out, aushalten.
hold, Halt, m., -s, -e.
Holland, n., -s.
holiday, Feiertag, m., -s, -age, plu. also die Ferien.
hollow, hohl.
holy, heilig, Heiligen —; the h. tablets, i. e. das Heiligtum.
home, zu Haus, nach Haus; at h. (bei uns) zu Haus.
homely, einfach, gemütlich.
homeward, nach Hause, way h., Rückweg, m., -s.
honest, ehrlich, tüchtig, echt, redlich.
honeymoon, die Flitterwochen, f. plu.
honor, Ehre, f.; ladies of h., Hofdamen, f. plu.
honorable, ehrenvoll, ehrenhaft, gut; ehren-.
hoof, Huf, m., -s, ufe.
hoof-mark, Hufspur, f., -en.
hope, Hoffnung, f.; in hopes, in der Hoffnung.

hope, hoffen ; **I h.,** hoffentlich.
horizon, Horizónt, m., -es, -e.
horribly, fürchterlich.
horse, Pferd, n., -s, -e.
horseman, Reiter, m., -s, —.
hot, heiss.
hotel, Hotel, n., -s, -s, (Gast-)
Hof, m., -s, -öfe.
hour, Stunde, f.
house, Haus, n., -es, -äuser.
house - hunting, Häusermieten,
n., -s.
however, jedoch, aber.
huckster, Käufer, m., -s, —,
Händler, m., -s, —.
hue, Farbe, f.
huge, riesig, kolossal.
human, menschlich, sterblich, ein
Mensch.
humbug, "Humbug," m., Wind-
beutel, m., -s.
humiliate, demütigen.
humorous, spasshaft, lustig.
hundred, Hundert, n., -s, -e, hundert —.
hurry, eilen.
husband, Gemahl, m., -s, -e.
hush, still.
hymn, Hymne, f., Kirchenlied, n.,
-s, -er.

I.

I, ich.
icy, Eis-.
idea, Vorstellung, f., Meinung, f.,
Ansicht, f.
if, wenn.
illegal, ungesetzlich.
ill, schlecht.
ills, Schmerzen, m. plu.
illustration, Darstellung (aus), f.,
Abbildung, f.

image, Bild, n., -s, -er.
imaginable, denkbar, was man
sich denken kann.
imitate, nachahmen (dat.).
imitation, Nachahmung, f.
immediately, sofort, sogleich.
immensely, sehr viel, ungeheuer,
unendlich, unermesslich, bedeutend.
imminent, dringend, nah.
impatiently, ungeduldig.
imperial, kaiserlich, Kaiser-.
impertinent, unverschämt.
impetuous, heftig, ungestüm.
importance, Wichtigkeit, f., Bedeutung, f.
important, wichtig, bedeutend.
impose, i. upon, täuschen, betrügen, zum Besten haben.
imposing, überwältigend, bedeut-
sam ; imposánt.
impossible, unmöglich.
impostor, Betrüger, m., -s, —
impression, Eindruck, m., -s,
-ücke.
impressive, wirkungsvoll, impo-
nierend.
imprisonment, Einschränkung,
f., Gefangenschaft, f.
improve, verbessern, verschö-
nern.
improvise, improvisieren, aus
dem Stegreif dichten.
impulse, Trieb, m., -s, -e, Drang,
m., -s.
in, in, hin, hinein, bei, dabei.
incarnate, lebendig, leibhaftig.
incline, neigen (zu).
include, mit einschliessen ; in-
cluded, darunter.
incredible, unglaublich.
indeed, wahrhaftig, wirklich, freilich, in der That.

independence, Unabhängigkeit, f.
independent, unabhängig.
Indian, Indianer, m., -s, —; I. corn, Mais, m., -es.
India-rubber, Gummi elasticum, n.
indignation, Unwillen, m., -s; in i., entrüstet (über, acc.).
individual, Individuum, n., -s, -uen, Persönlichkeit, f.
indwelling, inwohnend.
inexpressibles, i. e. Hosen, f. plu.
infinite, unendlich, unverwüstlich.
influence, Einfluss, m., -s, -üsse, Wirkung, f.
infold, umfássen, einschliessen.
inform, mitteilen, benachrichtigen, melden.
information, Kenntnisse, f. plu.
inherit, ererben.
initiate, einführen; to be initiated, aufkommen.
ink, Tinte, f.
inn, Wirtshaus, n., -es, -äuser.
innumerable, zahlreich, unzählig.
inquire, erfragen (acc.).
inquisitive, neugierig.
insanity, Wahnsinn, m., -s.
inside, inwendig; the i., das Innere.
insipid, geschmacklos.
insist, (darauf) bestehen.
insolent, frech, unverschämt.
insolvent, zahlungsunfähig.
inspect, betrachten, besehen.
instance, for i., zum Beispiel, n., -s, -e.
instant, Augenblick, m., -s, -e; the i., sobald.
instantly, sogleich.

instinct, Ahnung, f.
instruction, Anweisung, f., Befehl, m., -s, -e, Vorschrift, f.
instrument, Instrumént, n., -s, -e.
insult, Beleidigung, f.
insulate, isolieren, absondern.
intellectual, geistig, Geister-.
intelligent, gebildet, wohl unterrichtet.
intend, wollen, meinen, beabsichtigen, sollen.
interest, Teilnahme, f., Interesse, n., -s, -n, Rücksicht, f.
interest, interessieren.
interesting, interessánt, anziehend, reizend.
interlude, Zwischenpause, f., Zwischenspiel, n., -s, -e, Intermezzo, n., -s, -s.
intermediate, dazwischenliegend, dazwischenbefindlich.
internal, inner, innerlich.
interrupt, stören.
intervening, i. time, Zwischenzeit, f.
interview, interviewen.
interview, Unterredung, f., Besuch, m., -s, -e, Zusammenkunft, f., -ünfte.
intimate, vertraut, teuer, intím.
intimation, Anzeige, f., Andeutung, f.
into, in (acc.), hinein.
intolerance, Intoleranz, f., Unduldsamkeit, f.
intoxicated, betrunken.
introduce, vorstellen (acc. and dat.), einführen.
invade, gefährden, angreifen.
inverted, umgekehrt, umgestürzt.
invisible, unsichtbar.
invite, einladen, auffordern.
invitingly, einladend.

iron-gray, Eisenschimmel, m.,
-s, —.
irregular, unregelmässig.
is, ist, heisst.
island, Insel, f., -n.
isle, Insel, f., -n.
isolate, trennen, absondern.
issue, herauskommen.
Italian, italienisch.
Italy, Italien, n., -s.
ivy, Epheu, m., -s.

J.

Jack, Hans, m.
jackass, Esel, m., -s, —.
jacket, Wams, m. and n., -es,
-ämser, Jacke, f.
January, Január, m., -s, -e.
jealousy, Eifersucht, f.
jewel, Kleinod, n., -s, -e and -ien.
join, sich anschliessen (dat.), sich
ergiessen (in, acc.), einfallen (in,
acc.); nehmen, fassen, drücken,
festhalten; eintreten (in, acc.).
joint, Gelenk, n., -s, -e.
jointure, Leibgedinge, n., -s.
joke, Witz, m., -es, -e.
jollity, Festlichkeit, f.
journal, Zeitung, f., Blatt, n., -s,
-ätter.
journey, Reise, f.
joy, Wonne, f., Freude, f.
joyful, freudig, freudvoll.
judge, beurteilen, taxieren (nach),
urteilen.
judgment, Urteil, n., -s, -e.
July, Júli, m., —, -(s).
jump, hüpfen, springen.
June, Júni, m., —, -(s).
Jupiter, Jupiter, m., -s.
just, gerade, so; gerecht, recht.
justify, réchtfertigen.

K.

keep, halten, hindern; k. on, festhalten; k. near the fashions,
mit der Zeit zu gehen, sich der
Mode anschliessen; k. separate, unterscheiden; k. growing, immer werden.
kick, einen Fusstritt geben.
Kickelhahn, m., -s.
kind, Art, f.
kind, freundlich, gütig.
king, König, m., -s, -e.
kingdom, Reich, n., -s, -e.
knee, Knie, n., -s, -(e).
kneel, knien.
kneipe, Kneipe, f.
knife, Messer, n., -s, —.
knightly, ritterlich.
knit, verknüpfen (zu).
knock, klopfen.
know, kennen, wissen, sehen.
knowledge, Wissen, n., -s, Gedächtnis, n., -isses, -isse, Wissenschaft, f., Erkenntnis, f.,
-isses, -isse.
known, bekannt.

L.

labor, Arbeit, f.
labor, arbeiten, streben (nach).
lack, fehlen (dat.).
lackey, Lakai', m., -en and -s, -en,
Diener, m., -s, —.
lady, Dame, f.
laissez-aller, sichgehenlassen.
land, Land, n., -s, -ande and -änder.
land, landen, absteigen, aussteigen.
Landsmannschaft, f.
lane, Gasse, f.

large, gross.
lariat, Tüder, m., -s.
lash, geisseln.
last, weitest, letzt.
later, höher.
laughter, Gelächter, n., -s.
laurel, Lorber —.
lava, Lava —.
law, Gesetz, n., -es, -e.
lawyer-work, juristische Lauf-
bahn, f.
lay, legen.
lazy, faul, träge.
lead, führen, leiten; l. off, voraus-
kommen, voransprengen.
lead, Blei, n., -s.
league, Stunde, f.; many a l.,
stundenlang, meilenweit.
lean, (sich) lehnen.
lean, mager.
leap, springen, hinwegsetzen (über,
acc.).
leap, Bewegung, f., Munterkeit,
f.; Sprung, m., -s, -ünge.
learn, lernen.
learning, Gelehrsamkeit, f.,
Kenntnisse, f. plu., Wissenschaft, f.
least, kleinst.
leather, ledern.
leave, lassen, verlassen, hinter-
lássen.
leave, Urlaub, m., -s.
leave, Blatt, n., -s, -ätter.
lecture, Vorlesung, f., Vortrag,
m., -s, -äge.
lecture-room, Hörsaal, m., -s,
-säle, Vorlesungszimmer, n., -s,
—.
left, übrig.
leg, Bein, n., -s, -e.
legation, Legatión, f., Gesandt-
schaft, f.

legend, Legende, f.
legion, Legión, f., Schar, f., -en.
legitimate, gesetzmässig, recht.
Leipzig, n., -s.
leisure, Musse, f.; at l., M. haben.
Lengefelds, Lengefelds, die Familie Lengefeld.
length, at l., endlich.
less, weniger, minder.
Lessing, m., -s.
let, lassen.
letter, Brief, m., -s, -e.
level, Ebene, f.
level, flach.
level, fällen, niederfällen.
Leviathan, Leviáthan, m., -s, -e;
huge l., Riesenschiff, n., -s, -e.
liberal, gütig, freundlich.
Liberalism, Liberalismus, m., —.
Freisinnigkeit, f.
liberty, Freiheit, f.
librarian, Bibliothekár, m., -s, -e.
library, Bibliothék, f.
lie, liegen.
lie, Lüge, f.
lieutenant, Lieutenant (Leut-
nant), m., -s, -s.
life, Leben, n., -s, —.
lift, erheben, sich höher zeigen,
ermuntern, erwecken, stärken,
treiben (zu).
light, Licht, n., -s, -e and -er,
Glanz, m., -es.
light, leicht.
lighted, beleuchtet. .
light-house, Leuchtturm, m., -s,
-ürme.
like, ähnlich (dat.), gleich (dat.),
wie.
likely, wahrscheinlich.
likewise, auch, ebenso.
limb, Zweig, m., -s, -e, Glied, n.,
-s, -er.

limit, verhindern (dass).
linden, Linde, f. ; "die Linden,"
(street).
line, Spur, f.; Zeile, f.; Umriss,
m., -es, -e.
line, begrenzen.
lion, Löwe, m., -n, -n.
lip, Lippe, f.
list, wollen.
listen, zuhören (dat.).
literature, Litteratur, f.
literary, litterarisch.
little, klein.
live, glühend.
lively, lebhaft.
living, lebend, lebendig.
Livy, Livius, m.
load, Ladung, f., Fuder, n., -s, —.
loafer, Bummler, m., -s, —, Müs-
siggänger, m., -s, —.
loan, Anleihe, f.
loan, verleihen.
loathsome, ekelhaft, ekel.
local, kleinstädtisch, örtlich, an
den Ort gebannt.
locality, Ort, m., -s, -Örter (Orte),
Örtlichkeit, f., Boden, m., -s.
lock, Locke, f., -n.
lodge, Hütte, f.
Lodi, n., -s.
Logier, m., -s.
loiter, zögern.
London, n., -s.
loneliness, Einsamkeit, f.
long, lang, ·gross; as l. as, so
lang (als) ; l. odds of a start,
ein grosser Vorsprung voraus.
long-faced, mit dem langen Gesicht.
longitude, Länge, f., die Länge-
grade, m. plu.
look, sehen; zusehen; aussehen;
ausblicken, l. out for, suchen,

aussuchen; l. forward, vor sich
hinblicken; l. higher, höher
hinaufwollen; l. off towards,
nach . . . zusehen.
loose, schlaff, frei, los.
lope, Schritt, m., -s, Gangart, f.
lose, verlieren, einbüssen.
lot, Geschick, n., -s, -e, Los, n., -es,
-e.
loud, laut.
love, Liebe, f.
lover, Liebhaber, m., -s, —.
lovely, lieblich, schön.
low, niedrig.
low-born, von niedriger Geburt.
lowly, niedrig, bescheiden.
lucky, glücklich.
luggage, Gepäck, n., -s.
lull, sich legen.
luminous, leuchtend, strahlend,
hell.
lurid, leuchtend, düster, trüb.
lustre, Glanz, m., -es.
lusty, fröhlich, lustig, tüchtig,
weidlich, gehörig.
Luther, m., -s.
Lyons, Lyon, n., -s.

M.

macheer, (Machete?) Schwert,
n., -s, ·er, Messer, n., -s, —.
machine, Maschine, f.
mad, toll.
madame, Madame, f., gnädige
Frau, f.
madden, rasend (wütend) machen, von Sinnen bringen.
madness, Wahnsinn, m., -s.
magnificent, herrlich, prächtig,
prachtvoll.
magnitude, Grösse, f.

Main, Main, m., -s.
mainly, hauptsächlich.
maintain, behaupten, halten ; m.
  privacy, zurückgezogen bleiben.
majestic, majestätisch, herrlich,
  gross.
major, Majór, m., -s, -e.
majority, Mehrheit, f., die Meisten.
make, machen, lassen, werden,
  schliessen ; to m. good, geschmeidig machen, temperieren ; to m. merry, aufmuntern,
  erheitern ; to m. out, ausfinden,
  herausschlagen.
male, männlich.
malicious, boshaft.
man, Mann, m., -s, -änner, Mensch,
  m., -en, -en.
manage, führen, leiten, treiben,
  einrichten.
Manfredi, Manfred, m., -s.
manhood, Mannesalter, n., -s.
mankind, Menschheit, f.
Mannheim, n., -s.
manly, männlich.
manner, Weise, f., Miene, f.
manuscript, Handschrift, f., -en.
many, manch, viel.
marble, Marmorbildwerk, n., -s,
  -e.
march, marschieren, schreiten.
mark, bezeichnen, auszeichnen,
  stempeln, ausprägen.
mark, Beweis, m., -es, -e, Zeichen,
  n., -s, —.
marquis, Marquis, m., —, —.
marriage, Ehe, f., Heirat, f., Vermählung, f.
marriage-bed, Ehebett, n., -es,
  -en.
marry, (ver)heiraten.

Mars, Mars, m., —.
marshal, Marschall, m., -s, -s and
  -älle.
martial, kriegerisch.
martyr, Märtyrer, m., -s, —, Dul-
  der, m., -s, —.
marvel, m. at, bewundern.
marvellous, merkwürdig, erstaunlich.
Marylander, Maryländer, m., -s,
  —.
mask, Maske, f. ; masked —,
  Masken-.
masonry, of m., gemauert.
mass, m. of ruins, Ruinenmasse,
  f.
massacred, verstümmelt.
master, Meister, m., -s, —, Herr,
  m., -n, -en.
master, bewältigen.
material, Material, n., -s, -alien,
  das Stoffliche, Stoff, m., -s, -e.
mathematical, mathematisch.
matter, Ding, n., -s, -e, Sache, f.,
  Gegenstand, m., -s, -ände.
maxim, Maxíme, f., Grundsatz,
  m., -es, -ätze, Regel, f., -n.
may, Mai, m., -s, -e(n).
may, mögen, können.
mayor, Bürgermeister, m., -s, —,
  Schultheiss, m., -en, -en.
mean, heissen, bedeuten.
means, Mittel, n., -s, —, Vermögen, n., -s, —.
means, by no m., keineswegs.
meanwhile, inzwischen, indessen.
measure, messen.
measure, Versmass, n., -es, -e,
  Massstab, m., -s, -äbe ; in some
  m., in gewissem Masse.
Mediterranean, Mittelmeer, n.,
  -s.
mediæval, mittelalterlich.

medley, Gemisch, n., -es, Gedränge, n., -s.

meet, begegnen (dat.), treffen (acc.) zusammentreffen (mit), sich nahen ; well met, einem willkommen sein.

melancholy, Schwermut, f. Melanchthon, m., -s.

mêlée, Gemetzel, n., -s.

melt, verschmelzen, verschwimmen.

member, Mitglied, n., -s, -er.

memory, Gedächtnis, n., -isses, -isse, Andenken, n., -s, Erinnerung, f.

mention, erwähnen, melden, erzählen.

Menzel, m., -s.

merchant, Kaufmann, m., -s.

merciful, barmherzig, gütig.

merciless, unbarmherzig, erbarmungslos.

mere, lauter, bloss.

merit, verdienen.

merry, froh, munter ; make m., erheitern, aufmuntern.

message, Botschaft, f., Auftrag, m., -s, -äge, Wort, n., -s.

method, Art (f.) and Weise (f.).

metropolis, Hauptstadt, f., -ädte.

Mexico, n., -s.

middle, mittelst.

middle ages, das Mittelalter, -s.

midnight, (mitter)nächtlich, Mitternacht, f., -ächte.

midway, mitten (in, dat.).

might, Macht, f., -ächte.

mighty, gewaltig.

mile, Meile, f.

military, militärisch, des Militärs, n.

mind, Gedächtnis, n., -isses, -isse, Geist, m, -es, -er, Verstand, m , -s.

mine, Grube, f., Bergwerk, n., -s, -e.

mingle, vermischen, hineinziehen (in, acc.).

ministry, Ministerium, n., (-s), -rien.

minor, kleiner, jünger.

minister, Minister, m., -s, —.

minster, Münster, n., -s, —.

minstrel, Sänger, m., -s, — ; Sänger —.

miracle, Wunder, n., -s, —.

misanthropic, menschenfeindlich, Menschenhasser, m., -s, —.

misery, Elend, n., -s, Jammer, m , -s, Unglück, n., -s.

miss, vermissen, nicht sehen.

missionary, Missionär, m., -s, -e.

mistaken, misverstanden, falsch.

mistress, Herrin, f.

moan, without a m., ohne zu ächzen, stumm.

moat, Stadtgraben, m., -s, -äben.

mock, scheinbar, scherzhaft, Schein-.

modern, modern, neuer.

modesty, Bescheidenheit, f.

moment, Augenblick, m., -s, -e ; at the same m., zu gleicher Zeit.

money, Geld, n., -s, -er.

monk, Mönch, m., -s, -e.

monkey, Möncherei, f.

month, Monat, m., -s, -e.

mood, Stimmung, f.

moon, Mond, m., -s, -e.

moony, m. face, Mondgesicht, n., -s. ; also, Vollmondgesicht.

more, mehr, länger.

moreover, dabei, sodann.

morning, Morgen, m., -s, —.

morning-gown, Schlafrock, m., -s, -öcke.

morrow, good m., guten Morgen.
mortal, Mensch, m., -en, -en, ein
  Sterblicher.
Mossy-Head, bemoostes Haupt,
  n., -s, -äupter.
most, meist.
mostly, hauptsächlich.
motley, bunt.
motionless, regungslos.
motto, Motto, n., -(s), -s.
mould, Staub, m., -s.
mountain, Berg, m., -s, -e or das
  Gebirge.
mountain-flank, Bergflanke, f.,
  Bergwand, f., -ände.
mountain-town, Gebirgstädt-
  chen, n., -s.
mount, aufsteigen, besteigen.
mounted, beritten.
mourner, der Trauernde; m.'s
  prayer, trauernd beten.
mouth, Mund, m., -s, -e and -ünder,
  Maul, n., -s, -äuler.
Mr., Herr, m., -n, -en.
Mrs., Frau, f.
Mss., Handschriften, f. plu.
mulatto, Mulatte, m., -n, -n.
mule, Maultier, n., -s, -e.
multitude, Menge, f., das grosse
  Publikum.
murderer, Mörder, m.; -s, —.
murky, dicht.
muscle, Muskel, m., -s, -n.
Musen-Almanach, m., -s, -e,
music, Musik, f.
must, müssen.
mustache, Schnurbart, m., -s,
  -ärte.
mysterious, geheimnisvoll, heimlich.
mystery, Geheimnis, n., -isses,
  -isse.
mythology, Mythologie, f.

N.

naked, nackt, bloss, entblösst.
name, nennen.
name, Name(n), m., -ens, -en.
namely, nämlich.
nankeen, Nanking —.
narrow, eng.
nasty, schmutzig, ekelhaft.
Nasty-Fox, krasser Fuchs, m.,
  -es, -üchse.
nation, Nation, f., Volk, n., -s,
  -ölker.
national, national.
native, eigen, heimisch, Vater-.
nativity, place of n., Geburts-
  stätte, f.
natural, natürlich.
nay, nein, ja.
near, nah (dat.), neben.
nearing, sich näher zeigen.
nearly, beinah, fast.
neatly, hübsch, nett.
necessary, nötig, notwendig.
necessity, Not, f.; matters of n.,
  notwendige Dinge, n. plu.
neck, Hals, m., -es, -älse, Nacken,
  m., -s, —; by a n., um eine
  Halslänge; neck and neck,
  Nacken an Nacken.
Neckar, m., -s.
need, Not, f., -öte.
need, brauchen, bedürfen, nötig
  sein, müssen.
neglect, vernachlässigen.
negligence, Nachlässigkeit, f.
negotiation, Unterhandlung, f.,
  Verhandlung, f.
neighborhood, Nachbarschaft, f.
neither, weder, keins von Beiden.
nerve, Nerv, m., -s and -en,
  -en.
nerve, erstärken, antreiben.

nervous, nervös, aufgeregt, reizbar; nervig, kräftig.
nether, Unter-; n. limbs, Beine.
never, niemals, nimmer.
new, neu.
new-comer, Neuling, m., -s, -e.
New England, Neu-England, n., -s.
newspaper, Zeitung, f.
New York, New-York —, Neu-York, n., -s.
niche, Nische, f.
nigger, "Nigger," Neger, m., -s, —.
night, Nacht, f., -ächte, Abend, m., -s, -e; last n., gestern A.
nightingale, Nachtigall, f., -en.
nightly, bei Nacht.
nine, neun; half past n., halb zehn.
nineteenth, neunzehnt.
ninety, neunzig.
no, kein, nein.
nobility, Adel, m., -s.
noble, herrlich, edel, ehrlich.
nook, Plätzchen, n., -s, Winkel, m., -s, —.
noon, Mittag, m., -s, -e.
nor, noch, weder.
Normandy, Normandie, f.
north, Nord-.
northern, nordisch.
North Sea, Nordsee, f.
northward, to the n., nach Norden, nordwärts.
northwest, Nordwest-.
nose, Nase, f.
nostril, Nüster, f., -n.
not, nicht.
notable, merkwürdig.
notary, m., Notár(ius), -s, e.
notch, Einschnitt, m., -s, -e, Thor, n., -s, -e.

note, Wechsel, m., -s, —, (Bank-) Note, f.
noteworthy, merkwürdig.
notwithstanding, trotz (dat.); trotzdem, ungeachtet dass, obgleich.
nourish, bewahren, halten.
now, jetzt; n. and then, dann und wann; the Now, die Gegenwart.
nowise, keineswegs.
number, Anzahl, f., Zahl, f.
nurse, hegen.

O.

oak, Eiche, f.; Eichen —.
Oberkellner, m., -s, —.
object, Gegenstand, m., -s, -ände, etwas.
oblige, to be obliged, müssen.
obliging, verbindlich, gefällig.
observation, Bemerkung, f.
obstacle, Hindernis, n., -isses, -isse.
obtain, bekommen, haben.
occasion, Gelegenheit, f., Ereignis, n., -isses, -isse.
occasion, verursachen, veranlassen.
occasional, gelegentlich.
occasionally, zuweilen.
occupy, besetzen.
occur, einfallen (dat.), vorkommen (dat.).
ocean, Ocean, m., -s, -e.
ocean-stream, Meeresstrom, m., -s, -öme, Weltstrom.
o'clock, Uhr, f.
octagon, achteckig.
October, Oktober, m., -s, —.
odds, see long.

odor, Duft, m., -es, üfte.
Odyssey, Odyssee, f.
off, ab, zurück, fort.
offend, empören, ärgern.
offensive, beleidigend.
offer, darbringen, erbieten, anbieten.
offhand, aus dem Stegreif, leicht, unbefangen, frei.
office, Bureau, n., -s, -s and -x; B—.
official, Beamte, m., -n, -n.
official, offiziell.
Oh, Ach so.
oilcloth-covered, mit Wachstuch überzogen.
old, alt.
Old Ones, Alte, alte Häuser.
omen, Zeichen, n., -s, —, Omen, n., -(s), Omina.
omnibus, Omnibus, m., — and -usses, — and -usse.
omnipotency, Allmacht, f.
on, an, auf, über; fest.
once, einmal; at o., sogleich.
one, einer, man; eins.
only, einzig; nur, allein, bloss.
open, offen, frei.
open, öffnen, sich öffnen [nach, in (acc.)].
opening, Gelegenheit, f.; Anfangs-.
opera, Oper, f.
opinion, Meinung, f.
opponent, Gegner, m., s, —
opportunity, Gelegenheit, f.
oppose, bekämpfen.
opposite, gegenüber.
opposition, Gegenpartei, f.
ordeal, Probe, f.
order, Stand, m., -es, -ände.
order, bestellen, lassen (with verb).

ornament, (aus)schmücken.
orthodox, the o., die Orthodoxen, die Rechtgläubigen.
other, ander; on the other hand, im Gegenteil.
otherwise, anders, sonst, ausserdem.
ought, sollen.
out, aus.
outbid, überbieten (für).
outcast, ein Verbannter.
outrun, überflügeln, übertréffen.
outside, ausserhalb; äusser (adj.).
outsider, ein Fernstehender, Uneingeweihter.
outstretch, ausstrecken.
over, über, vorbei.
overcome, überwínden, überwältigen.
overgrown, überwáchsen.
overhead, droben.
overlook, hinausblicken (über, acc.); overlooking, mit dem Blick auf (acc.).
overshadowed, überschattet.
overthrow, úmwerfen.
owe, verdanken (acc. and dat. of person).
own, eigen.
oxygen, Sauerstoff, m., -s, -e.

P.

pace, Schritt, m., -s, -e.
packing, as adj., drückend.
pack-mule, Saumtier, n., -s, -e, Maultier, n.
paganism, Heidentum, n., -s.
pain, Schmerz, m., -es, -en.
paint, malen, zeichnen, darstellen.
painter, Maler, m., -s, —.
pair, Paar, n., -s, -e, zwei.

palace, Palais, n., —, —
pale, blass, bleich.
pallid, bleich.
paper, Papier, n., -s, -e.
parade, to make a ·p., prunken (mit), sich viel darauf zu Gute thun (dass).
parch, dörren.
pardon, verzeihen (dat.).
parental, elterlich, väterlich.
parents, Eltern, Ahnen ; a p.. der Vater.
Paris, n.
park, Park, m., -s, -e·
parliamentary, parlamentarisch.
parsonage, Pfarrhaus, n., -es, -äuser.
part, Teil, m., -s, -e ; Gegend, f.
part, scheiden (von einander), trennen.
particular, Einzelnheit, f.
party, Gesellschaft, f.
pass, passieren or reisen (durch); verfliessen, vergehen ; vorbeireiten ; hinziehen ; bestehen, ertragen ; p: out, heraustreten (auf).
pass, Pass, m., -es, -ässe.
passage, Stelle, f.; Durchgang, m., -s, -änge.
passenger, Passagier, m., -s, -e, der Mitreisende.
passion, Leidenschaft, f., Liebe, f.
past, Vergangenheit, f.
past, nach.
pastor, Pfarrer, m., -s, —, Pastor, m., -s, -en.
path, Pfad, m., -es, -e, Weg, m., -s, -e, Bahn, f.
pathetic, pathetisch, rührend.
pathway, see path.
Pauline, f.
pause, (still) stehen.

Pausilippo, m., -s.
pavement, Pflaster, n., -s, — Fussboden, m., -s. See path.
pay, bezahlen, machen, abstatten.
pea, Erbse, f. .
peace, Friede(n), m., -ens ; Friedens-; peace! ruhig.
peaceful, friedlich. .
peak, Spitze, f.
peasant, Bauer, m , s and -n, n ; Bauern-.
peasantry, Bauer(n)schaft, f.
pectoral, Brust-.
pedantic, gelehrt, lehrhaft.
pedestal, Fussgestell, n., -s.
pedigree, Stammbaum, m., -s, Herkunft, f.
peep, (hinein) gucken.
pen, Feder, f.
pencil, Bleistift, m., -s, -e.
Pentecost, Pfingst-.
people, Leute, plu.; Volk, n., -s, ·ölker, Bevölkerung, f.
perch, anbringen, befestigen, einpferchen.
perfect, vollkommen.
perfectly, völlig.
performance, Unternehmen, n., -s.
period, Periode, f.
perish, sterben.
permanent, dauerhaft.
permit, to be permitted, dürfen.
perpetuate, aufbewahren.
person, Mensch, m., -en, -en, Person, f., Persönlichkeit, f.
personage, see person ; high p., Hoheit, f.
personal, persönlich, eigen.
personally, persönlich.
Peter, Peter, Petrus, m.
Petersburg, n., -s.
pew, p. bench, Kirchenstuhl, m., -s, -ühle.

phalanx, Schar, f., -en
philosopher's walk, Philosóphen-
weg, m , -s.
philosophic, philosophisch.
physical, körperlich.
physics, Physik, f.; in p., physi-
kalisch.
pick, zählen; p. up, aufheben.
picture, Bild, n., -s, -er, Gemälde,
n , -s, —.
piece, Stück, n., -s, -e.
piercing, durchdringend.
pinch, kneipen, n., -s, Angriff, m.,
-s, (auf, acc.).
pinched, gekniffen.
pine, Fichte, f.
pinion, Fittich, m., s, -e
pink, ausschneiden.
pinnacle, Gipfel, m., -s, —.
pipe, Brunnenrohr, n., -s, -e, or
Brunnenröhre, f.; Pfeife, f.
Pipers - Doomsday, Pfeifenge-
richt, n., -s.
pistol, Pistole, f.
place, Platz, m., -es, -ätze, Plätzchen, n., -s, Ort, m., -s, -en and
-örter, Stätte, f.; Stelle, f.; to
this p., hierher.
place, stellen, legen, setzen, sein,
bringen, drücken.
plain, einfach.
plain, Ebene, f., Prairie —.
plan, Plan, m., -s, -e and -äne,
Entwurf, m., -s, -ürfe.
planet, Planét, m., -en, -en.
planetary, planetarisch, weltbür-
gerlich.
plank, Brett, n., -s, -er.
plant, stecken, pflanzen.
plaster of Paris, Gips, m , -es, -e.
play, spielen.
plaything, Spielzeug, n., -s, -e,
Spielzeit, f.

plead, flehen, Ansprüche machen
(auf, acc.).
pleasant, angenehm, lieblich.
please, gefallen; be pleased, sich
freuen; please! bitte.
pleasure, Vergnügen. n , -s, Freude, f.
plenipotentiary, (adj.), ausserordentlich.
plough-share, Pflugschar, f., -en.
plunge, fallen, stürzen, straucheln.
Plymouth, n., -s.
pocket, Tasche, f.
pocket-book, Beutel, m., -s, —.
poem, Gedicht, n., -s, -e.
poet, Dichter, m., -s, —.
poetic, poetisch.
poetry, Poesie, f.
point, Punkt, m., -s, -e, Hinsicht,
f.
point, sichten, zeigen, hinweisen
(nach).
pointed, zugespitzt.
poke, stecken.
polemic, Polémik, f.
polemic, polemisch, streitbar,
streitartig.
polish, Vollendung, f., Verfei-
nerung, f.
polished, fein.
polite, höflich.
politician, Politiker, m., -s, —.
politics, Politík, f.
Pomatum-Stallions, Pomadenhengst, m., -es, -e.
Pomeranian, pommersch; (noun)
Pommer, m., -n, -n.
pomp, Pracht, f.
poodle, Pudel, m., -s, —.
poor, arm.
Pope, Papst, m., -es, -äpste.
popular, volkstümlich.
portcullis, Fallgatter, n., -s, —.

porter, Hausknecht, m., -s, -e.
portion, Teil, m., -s, -e.
portmanteau, Reisetasche, f.
portrait, Bild, n., -s, -er.
poseur, m., as adj., prahlerisch.
position, Stellung, f.
possess, besitzen.
possession, Besitz, m., -es.
possibility, Möglichkeit, f.
possible, möglich.
possibly, möglicherweise.
post, Post, f., -en.
postal service, Postwesen, n., -s.
postilion, Reitknecht, m., -s, -e.
post-road, Poststrasse, f.
posture, Stellung, f., Haltung, f.
potent, wirksam.
Potsdam, n., -s.
pounce, p. upon, bestürmen.
pour, giessen, aushauchen.
Poussades, Poussaden, f. plu.
power, Kraft, f., -äfte, Macht, f.,
 -ächte, Gabe, f.
powerful, kräftig, mächtig.
powerless, kraftlos.
practical, praktisch.
praise, rühmen, preisen.
pray, beten ; pray! bitte.
prayer, Gebet, n., -s, -e.
preach, predigen.
pre-arrange, vorausbestimmen.
precious, kostbar.
precisely, gerade, Punkt.
prefer, vorziehen.
preliminaries, Präliminarien, Vor-
 bereitungen.
prepare, bereiten.
prepared, bereit, fertig.
preponderating, überwiegend,
 überrägend.
presence, Gegenwart, f.
present, Gegenwart, f.; Geschenk,
 n., -s, -e.

present, p. oneself, sich vorstellen ; p. itself, sich darstellen.
present, jetzig; anwesend ; at p.,
 gegenwärtig.
presentation, Vorstellung, f.
presently, bald.
preside, Präsident sein.
President, Präsident, m., -en, -en.
press, Gedränge, n., -s.
press, p. on, vorwärts dringen;
 p. after, nachfolgen, nacheilen.
pretend, sich stellen, daran denken.
pretty, niedlich, hübsch, schön.
previous, vorig.
priceless, unschätzbar.
prick, stacheln, treiben, (zu).
pride, Stolz, m., -es.
priest, Priester, m., -s, —.
prim, steif.
prince, Prinz, m., -en, -en.
princess, Prinzessin, f.
principal, bedeutendst, Haupt-.
principle, Grundsatz, m., -es, -ätze.
print, drucken.
prior, älter.
prisoner's cell, Kerkerloch, n., -s,
 Gefängnis, n., -isses.
privacy, Zurückgezogenheit, f.
private, einzeln, eigen, Privat-.
probably, wahrscheinlich, vermut-
 lich.
problem, Aufgabe, f.
proceed, hervorgehen (von), reisen.
proceeding, Schritt, m., -s, -e,
 Unterhandlung, f.
procession, Zug, m., -s, -üge.
produce, hervorbringen.
profession, Beruf, m., -s, -e, Beschäftigung, f.
professional, professionell, be-
 rufsmässig, von Beruf.
professor, Professor, m., -s, -en.

profound, tief.
profusely, reichlich.
progress, Fortschritt, m., -s, -e, Beförderung, f.; in p., im Gange, angefangen, unterwegs.
prolix, weitläufig.
prominent, Haupt-.
promiscuously, unbefangen, zwanglos.
promise, versprechen (dat.), versichern (acc. or dat.).
promise, Versprechen, n., -s.
promontory, Vorgebirge, n., -s, Klippe, f.
promote, befördern.
promotion, Beförderung, f., Aufrücken, n., -s, Avancement, n., -s.
promptly, rasch.
pronounce, halten.
proper, gehörig, richtig, beteiligt.
properly, gehörig.
prophecy, Weissagung, f., Prophezeiung, f.
prophetic, Propheten-.
prospect, Aussicht, f., -en.
prosperity, Wohlfahrt, f.
prostitution, Feilbieten, n., -s, Entehrung, f., Unzucht, f.
protégé, Zögling, m., ·s, Schützling, m., -s.
Protestant, Protestant, m., -en, -en.
proud, stolz.
prove, zeigen, beweisen.
proverb, Sprichwort, n., -s, -örter.
provide, versorgen.
province, Provinz, f., -en.
Prussia, Preussen, n., -s.
public, öffentlich, Volks-.
public, Publikum, n., -s.
publish, veröffentlichen.
puff, (Wind-) Stoss, m., -es, -össe.

pulpit, Kanzel, f., -n., Katheder, n., -s.
pump, ausfragen.
purple, bläulich.
purpling, dunkelnd.
purpose, Vorhaben, n., -s, Entschluss, m., -es, -üsse, Zweck, m., -s, -e.
pursue, verfolgen.
pursuit, Verfolgung, f.
push, verfolgen; p. behind, zurückdrängen; p. on, weiter eilen, vorwärts dringen.
put, p. in, bringen (in, acc.), geben (in, acc.); p. on, aufsetzen; p. out of, befreien (von).

Q.

quadrangle, Viereck, n., -s, -e, Hof, Schlosshof, m., -s, -öfe.
qualify, befähigen, berechtigen.
quarter, Weltteil, m., -s, -e, Gegend, f., -en, Viertel, n., -s, —, Quartier, n., -s, -e, Wohnung, f.
quarter to nine, drei Viertel neun.
quay, Kai, m., -s, -e.
queer, wunderlich, seltsam, eigentümlich.
question, Frage, f.
question, fragen, zweifeln.
quick, rasch, schnell.
quicken, beschleunigen.
quiet, still, ruhig.
quiet-looking, ruhig aussehen.
quite, ganz.

R.

race, Volk, n., -s, -ölker, Geschlecht, n., -s, -er. Rasse, f.; Wettrennen, n., -s, —.

9

rail, schelten, spötteln.
rail, Geländer, n., -s, Wandleiste, f., Balustrade, f. ; by r., auf der Eisenbahn.
railway, Eisenbahn, f., Bahn, f., by r., mit der E., or, zu E.
rain, Regen, m., -s.
rainy, regnerisch.
raise, heben, in die Höhe ziehen.
range, Gebirge, n., -s, Bergkette, f.
range, reihen ; r. up, sich an einander reihen, ereilen, einholen.
rank, sich reihen (zu).
rank, Rang, m., -es, -änge, Stellung, f.
rapid, schnell, rasch.
rapture, Wonne, f., Glück, n., -s.
rascal, Taugenichts, m., Schurke, m., -n, -n.
rather, lieber, ziemlich.
ravine, Schlucht, f., -en.
reach, erreichen.
reach, ankommen, (in, dat.), erlangen.
read, lesen, vorlesen.
readings, Stúdien, f. plu.
ready, fertig, bereit, im Begriff.
really, wirklich.
rear, emporheben.
reason, for the very r. that, gerade deshalb, weil.
reason, Grund, m., -s, -ünde.
rebel, Rebéll, m., -en, -en.
recall, sich besinnen (gen.), sich erinnern (gen., or an with acc.).
recant, widerrúfen.
receive, erhalten, empfangen, begrüssen.
reception, Empfang, m., -s
recite, hersagen, ergründen, vortragen, anführen.

recognize, erkennen (als).
recollect, sich erinnern (gen., or an with acc.).
recommendation, Empfehlung, f.
record, Verzeichnis, n., -isses, -isse.
record, aufzeichnen.
reconcile, versöhnen (mit).
recover, retten, erhaschen.
rector, Rektor, m., -s, -en.
red, rot.
redeem, retten, erlösen.
redemption, Erlösung, f.
reduce, umwandeln (in, acc.), zurückführen (auf, acc.).
reflect, zurückstrahlen.
reform, reformatorisch.
refresh, erholen.
refuse, versagen (dat.), nicht wollen.
regain, wieder gewinnen, zurück erhalten, wieder einnehmen.
regards, Grüsse (an, acc.), m. plu.
regardless, nicht achtend, rücksichtslos, ohne sich zu bekümmern (um).
regiment, Regiment, n., -s, -er.
regimentals, Uniformen, f. plu.
region, Gegend, f., Landschaft, f.
register, traveller's r., Fremdenbuch, n., -s, -ücher.
regret, Bedauern, n., -s.
regular, regelmässig; the r. thing, ganz in der Ordnung.
regularity, Regelmässigkeit, f.
reign, Herrschaft, f.
rein, Zügel, m., -s, —.
reiterate, wiederhólen.
reject, zurückweisen.
rejoice, sich freuen.
relation, Verwandte, m., -n, -n ; Beziehung, f., Verhältnis, n., -isses, -isse.

relics, Reliquien, f. plu.
relieve, abhelfen, erleichtern (einem etwas).
religion, Religion, f.
religious, religiös.
remain, bleiben, verweilen.
remaining, übrig.
remark, Bemerkung, f.
remarkably, ausserordentlich.
remedy, Heilmittel, n., -s, —.
remember, sich erinnern (gen., or an with acc.), ins Gedächtnis zurückrufen, nicht vergessen, denken (an, acc.).
remembrance, Erinnerung, f.; Empfehlung, f.
remorse, Vorwurf, m., -s, -ürfe, Reue, f.
renounce, verleugnen, versagen.
renown, renommieren.
renowner, Renommist, m., -en, -en.
rent, gesprengt.
rent, Miete, f.
repay, wieder bezahlen, belohnen.
repeat, wiederhólen.
repentance, Busse, f.
repetition, Wiederholung, f.
reply, erwiedern.
reporter, Berichterstatter, m., -s, —.
repose, Ruhe, f.
represent, vertreten.
reproach, Vorwurf, m., -s, -ürfe, Tadel, m., -s.
repulse, zurückschlagen, zurückwerfen.
require, bedürfen, kosten (dat.), erfordern, nötig sein.
rescue, retten.
resemblance, Ähnlichkeit, f.
resemble, gleichen (dat.), ähnlich (dat.) sein; see cut.

reserve, Rückhalt, m., -s, -e.
reserve, vorbehalten.
reside, wohnen.
residence, Wohnung, f.
resident, Einwohner, m., -s, — ;
minister resident, Ministerresident, m., -en, -en.
resonant, stampfend, klingend.
resort, benutzen.
resounding, hallend.
respect, Beziehung, f., Hinsicht, f.; Achtung, f.
respectability, Vornehmheit, f., Ansehen, n., -s, Würde, f., Achtbarkeit, f.
respectful, achtungsvoll.
respective, gegenseitig.
rest, Rast, f.
rest, übrig, ander.
rest, bleiben, ruhen, weilen.
" Restauration," f.
restore, wiedersetzen (in, acc.).
restorer, Erneuerer, m., -s, —.
result, Wirkung, f.
result, enden.
retire, zurückziehen.
retort, Kolben, m., -s, —.
retreat, Schlupfwinkel, m., -s, —, Ruheplätzchen, n., -s.
return, Rückkehr, f., Rückreise, f.
return, zurückkehren.
revanche, en r., the same, or, zur Vergeltung.
revenge, Rache, f.
revengeless, ohne Rache, f.
Reverie, f., Träumerei, f.
reverse, Unglück, n., -s.
reward, belohnen.
Rhine, Rhein, m., -s.
Rhone, R. valley, Rhonethal, n., -s.
rhymed, gereimt.
rhythmical, taktmässig, abgemessen, eintönig.

ribbon, Band, n., -s, -änder.
rib, Rippe, f.
rich, fruchtbar, gesegnet, reich, an (dat.), schön.
Richmond, n., -s,
riddle, Rätsel, n., -s, —.
ride, reiten, fahren.
rider, Reiter, m., -s, —.
riding, Reit-.
ridge, Bergrücken, m., -s, —.
ridiculous, lächerlich.
rift, sich aufthun, sich öffnen.
rift, Riss, m., -es, -e.
right, recht; rechts; to set r, gut machen, wieder in Ordnung bringen.
right, Recht, n., -s, -e.
right and left, rechts und links, hin und her.
ring, klirren, klingen; r. through, durchfáhren.
ring, Klingen, n., -s, Schlag, m., -s, -äge.
ripe, reif, gut.
ripen, zur Reife bringen.
ripeness, Reife, f.
ripple, Bewegung, f., Erregung, f.
rise, sich erheben.
rise, Beförderung, f.
rival, Nebenbuhler, m., -s, —.
rivalry, Kampf, m., -s, -ämpfe, Streit, m., -s, -e.
river, Fluss, m., -es, -üsse; Strom, m., -s, -öme.
road, (Land-)Strasse, f., Fahrweg, m., -s, -e.
road-maker, wegebauend.
roar, Gebrüll, n., -s, r. of laughter, schallendes Gelächter.
rock, Fels, m., -en, -en; Stein, m., -s, -e.
Roilighnesses, the same, or, (königliche) Hoheiten.

roll, r. of blankets, aufgerollte Decken, f. plu.
roll, drehen; r. together, zusammenrollen.
rolling, wellenförmig.
Roman, römisch.
romantic, romantisch.
Rome, Rom, n., -s.
roof, Dach, n., -s, -ächer.
room, Zimmer, n., -s, —, Stube, f.
roost, to r., zum Schlafen.
rose-bush, Rosengebüsch, n., -es, -e.
rosy, rosig.
rough, hart, rauh, verwildert.
round, rund, roll; herum.
round, Runde, f., Reihe, f.
royal, königlich.
rouse, ermannen, auf !
ruin, Ruine, f., Verderben, n., -s.
ruined, zerstört, verfallen.
run, fortfliessen, weiterziehen, laufen, hinziehen, ablaufen, hinfahren; r. over, durchblättern.
runner, Laufbursch, m., -en, -en.
rush, stürzen, eilen, sich werfen.
rush, Sprung, m., -s, -ünge.
Russia, Russland, n., -s.
Russie, de R., russisch.
rusty, rostig, alt.
ruthless, unbarmherzig.

S.

Saale, f.
sacred, heilig.
sacrifice, Opfer, n., -s, —.
sacrifice, aufopfern, preisgeben.
saddle, Sattel, m., -s, -ättel.
Sadowa, n., -s.
safe, sicher, gerettet.
safety, in s., sicher, wohlbehalten.

sagacity, Klugheit, f., Scharfsinn, m., -s.
sage, Salbei, f.
saint, Sankt-.
salary, Gehalt, n. and m., -s, -e.
salutation, Gruss, m., -es, -üsse.
Salzburg, n., -s.
same, selb, gleich.
sanction, genehmigen, bestätigen.
sand, i. e. Uhr, f., Stundenglas, n., -es.
Sandwich, Sandwich-.
Sandy-Hook.
satellite, Satellit, m., -en, -en.
satire, Spottrede, f., Witz, m., -es, e.
satisfaction, Vergnügen, n., -s.
saunterings, Streifereien, f. plu.
save, bewahren (vor, dat.), retten (von); aufsparen.
saw-teeth, i. e., Zackenkante, f.
Saxe-Weimar, Sachsen-Weimar, n., -s.
say, sagen.
saying, Sprichwort, n., -s, -örter.
Scandinavian, Skandinavisch.
scar, Narbe, f.
scarred, narbig.
scarcely, kaum.
scatter, zerstreuen.
scene, Scene, f., Ort, m., -s, -e.
schedule, Verzeichnis, n., -isses, -isse, Liste, f.
scheme, Plan, m., -s, -e und -äne.
Schläger, m., -s, —.
Schleswig-Holstein, schleswig-holsteinisch.
scholar, Schüler, m., -s, —, Gelehrte, m., -n, -n.
school, Schule, f.
school-mate, Schulkamerad, m., -en and -s, -en.

science, Wissenschaft, f.
Scilly Islands, Scilly-Inseln, f. plu.
scorching, brennend.
scorn, Verachtung, f.; in s., spöttisch, höhnisch.
Scotch, schottisch.
scream, Schrei, m., -s, -e.
scream, schreien.
sculptor, Bildhauer, m., -s, —.
sculptress, Bildhauerin, f.
sculpture-gallery, Skulpturensammlung, f.
sea, Meer, n., -s, -e.
seal, Siegel, n., -s, —.
seam, durchlaufen, durchädern.
seasick, seekrank.
season, Jahreszeit, f.
seat, Platz, m., -es, -ätze, Sitz, m., -es, -e, Bank, f., -änke; to be firm in one's seat, festsitzen.
seat, sich setzen.
second, Sekundant, m., -en, -en; Sekúnde, f.
second, zweit.
secondly, zweitens.
secret, Geheimnis, n., -isses, -isse.
secret, heimlich, geheimnisvoll.
secretary, Sekretär, m., -s, -e, Schriftwart, m., -s, -e.
secure, bestellen, belegen.
security, Sicherheit, f.
see, sehen, einsehen.
seek, suchen, versuchen; s. repentance, Busse thun wollen.
seem, scheinen.
seize, ergreifen.
seldom, selten.
select, gewählt, ausgewählt.
self, Selbst, n.
self-possessed, besonnen.
self-registering, selbstregistrierend.

seltzer water, Selterwasser, n., s.

senior, Senior, m., -s, -en.

sense, Gefühl, n., -s, -e.

sensible, verständig.

separate, von einander gehen, scheiden, trennen.

sere, dürr, öde.

serene, heiter.

serious, ernsthaft, bedenklich.

seriously, ernstlich.

sermon, Predigt, f.

servant, Diener, m., -s, —.

serve, dienen (dat.); s. as, dienen als.

service, Dienst, m., -es, -e.

set, setzen; s. forth, ausgehen, s. down as, halten für; s. in, beginnen; s. up, erfrischen; s. upon, hängen or setzen (an, acc.); s. to, setzen an (acc.).

set, aufgesetzt.

settle, abmachen, einrichten; s. down, sich niederlassen.

seventeenth, siebzent.

seventy, sieb(en)zig.

seventy-five, fünfundsiebzig.

several, mehrere.

severe, ernst.

shabby, schäbig, abgeschabt.

shade, Schatten, m., -s, —; in the s., im Dunkeln, im Hintergrund.

shady, schattig.

shaggy, zottig.

shake, schweben, wallen, zittern, zusammenzucken.

shaky, stolpernd, unsicher.

shame, Schande, f.

shape, Gestalt, f.

share, teilen.

sharp, scharf, tief.

shatter, zerbrechen, erschüttern.

shaved, geschoren.

shed, breiten (über, acc.), s. the light on, leuchten lassen (über, dat., auf, acc.).

sheeny, glänzend.

sheet, Platte, f., Stück, n., -s, -e; a s. of glass, spiegelglatt.

shelter, schützen.

shelter, for s., zum Schutz, m., -es.

shift, ändern.

shine, schimmern, leuchten.

ship, Schiff, n., -s, -e.

shirt, Hemd(e), n., -es, -en.

shiver, zerscheitern.

shoot, schiessen.

shooting-jacket, Jagdrock, m., -s, -öcke.

short, kurz.

shortcomings, Fehler, m., -s, —.

shot, Schuss, m , -es, -üsse, Kugel, f, -n.

shoulder, Schulter, f., -n.

show, Spiel, n., -s, -e.

show, zeigen, verraten, anweisen (acc. and dat.), beweisen. .

show-room, Ausstellungszimmer, n., -s, —; show-rooms, Zimmer die gezeigt werden.

shrewd, klug, verschlagen.

shriek, schreien.

shrink, weichen, verzagen, zurück schaudern (vor, dat.); s. back, zurückfahren.

shut, (zu)schliessen.

side, Seite, f. ; Seiten- ; take sides for, Partei nehmen für.

Sierra, f.

sigh, Seufzer, m., -s, —.

sight, Sehenswürdigkeit, f., Blick, m., -s, -e, Anblick ; by s., von Ansehen.

sight-seeing, Sehenswürdigkeiten besuchen.

sign, Spur, f

sign, unterzeichnen, unterschreiben.

signal, Zeichen, n., -s, —.

silent, stumm, schweigsam; to be s., schweigen.

Silentium, n., -s.

Silesia, Schlesien, n., -s.

silk, Seide, f.

silver-haired, silberhaarig.

simple, einfach.

simplicity, Einfachheit, f.

Simplon, m.

sin, Sünde, f.

since, seit, seitdem.

sincere, aufrichtig.

sing, singen.

single, einzig.

single, s. out, herauslesen (aus), auserwählen, ausersehen (zu).

sink, (hin)sinken, herabsinken, sich neigen.

sinner, Sünder, m., s, —.

Sion, or Sitten, n.

sir, Sir, Herr, m., -n, -en.

sister-in-law, Schwägerin, f.

sit, sitzen, sich setzen; s. in, besitzen; s. for it accordingly, demgemäss sitzen.

situation, Lage, f.

six, sechs.

six-shooter, Revolver, m., -s, —, sechsläufige Pistole, f.

sixty-five, fünfundsechzig.

sketching-traps, plu. of Zeichenapparát, m., -s, -e, or Malgerät, n., -s, -e.

skulk, schlendern, schweifen.

skull, (Hirn)schädel, m., -s, —.

skull-cap, Tellermütze, f.

sky, Himmel, m., -s.

slave, Sklave, m., -n, -n.

slay, schlagen, töten.

sleep, schlafen.

slender, dünn.

slight, schlank.

slip, s. out of, abgleiten (an, dat.); entschwinden (dat).

slippery, glatt, schlüpfrig.

slow, langsam.

small, klein.

smart, schön, sauber.

smile, Lächeln, n., -s.

smile, lächeln, günstig sein (dat.).

smiling, lachend, sonnig.

smite, schlagen (auf, acc.); s. off, herunterschlagen.

smoke, Qualm, m., -s.

smoke, rauchen.

smoky, rauchig, raucherfüllt.

smooth, zart, glatt, ruhig, still.

smoothness, Sanftheit, f., Milde, f.

smouldering, dunkel, dumpf.

snaffle, Trense, f.

snatch, ergreifen.

snuff, take s., eine Prise nehmen.

soap, Seife, f.

social, gesellschaftlich.

society, Gesellschaft, f., Verein, m., -s, -e.

soft, zart, sanft.

soften, lindern, mildern.

soil, Grund (m., -s,) und Boden (m., -s), Bodenart, f., -en.

sojourn, Aufenthalt, m., -s.

solemn, feierlich, ernst.

solidarity, Solidarität, f., Einheit, f.

solidity, Solidität, f., Dauerhaftigkeit, f., Festigkeit, f.

some, einige, plu.

something, etwas.

son, Sohn, m., -s, -öhne.

song, Lied, n., -s, -er.

soon, bald.

soothsaying, Weissagung, f., Spruch, m., -s, -üche.
sordid, karg.
sore, empfindlich (in, dat., über, acc.).
sort, Sorte, Klasse, Art, f.
soul, Seele, f.
sound, Geräusch, n., -es, -e, Lärm, m., -s, Laut, m., -s, -e, Schall, m., -s, -e.
sound, klingen, blasen.
sour, sauer, bitter.
source, Quelle, f.
southern, südlich, Süd-.
southward, südwärts, nach Süden, m., südlich.
space, Raum, m., -s, -äume.
spare, schonen; sparen, übrig haben.
sparkle, Perlen, n., -s.
sparkle, sprudeln.
spasm, with a s., krampfhaft.
speak, sprechen.
specially, hauptsächlich, besonders.
specimen, Exemplar, n., -s, Beispiel, n., -s, Muster, n., -s, Vertreter, m., -s.
speckled, fleckig, bunt.
speculate, spekulieren, sich wundern, berechnen.
speed, at s., at top s., in vollem Laufe (m., -s), im vollen Galopp, or Fluge, (m., -s).
spend, verbringen, zubringen, spenden, ausgeben.
spire, Turmspitze, f.
spirit, Geist, m., -s, -er, Seele, f.; spirits, Gefühle, n. plu., Stimmung, f.
spiritual, geistig.
spite, in s. of, trotz (dat.).
splendid, prächtig, herrlich.

sport, Spass, m., -s, -ässe, some s., etwas Lustiges; for s., zum Scherz (m., -s).
spot, Stelle, f., Ort, m., -e and Örter.
spotless, fleckenlos.
spring, Frühling, m., -s, -e, Frühjahr, n., -s; Quelle, f.
spring, springen, s. up, aufspringen.
spry, flink, lebhaft.
spur, Sporn, m., -s, -oren.
spur, spornen; spurred, gespornt.
spurn, verhöhnen.
square, breit.
square, Platz, m., -es, -ätze.
staffage, (environment), f.
stagger, stolpern; erschüttern.
stain, Flecken, m., -s, —; s. of blood, Blutschuld, f.
stain, beflecken.
stalk, schreiten.
stand, stehen, dastehen.
star, Stern, m., -s, -e; stars and stripes, das Stern(en)banner.
stare, angaffen, anstarren, drohen.
start, Vorsprung, m., -s, -ünge.
start, aufbrecken, fortreiten, sich auf dem Weg machen.
startled, erstaunt, überrascht.
state, Zustand, m., -s, Stellung, f.; Staats-.
state, aussprechen, berichten, melden.
stately, stattlich.
station, Bahnhof, m., -s, -öfe, Station, f.
statue, Standbild, n., -s, -er, Bildsäule, f.
stature, Gestalt, f.
stay, Aufenthalt, m., -s, -e.
steadily, stets, immer.
steady, ruhig.

steady, festhalten.
steal, schleichen, gleiten (über, acc.), s. through, durchwandeln.
steam, Dampf-.
steamer, Dampfer, m., -s, —.
steep, steil.
Stendal, n.
step, Schritt, m., -s, -e, Stufe, f., Gang, m., -s.
step, wandeln.
stern, streng, ernst.
Stettiner.
stick, rücken (auf, acc.).
still, noch.
stimulus, Erregung, f., Antrieb, m., -s, -e.
sting, Stachel, m., -s, -n.
stipulation, Bedingung, f.
stir, Lärm, m., -s.
stitch, sticken.
stock, Geschlecht, n., -s, -er, Familie, f.
stone, Stein, m., -s, -e; stones, Gerölle, n., -s.
stone, steinern.
stool, Stuhl, m., -s, -ühle.
stoop, sich bücken, sich neigen (über, dat.).
stop, halt!
stop, innehalten, einhalten, aufhören.
storm, Gewitter, n., -s, —.
stormy, stürmisch.
story, Geschichte, f., Lebenslauf, m., -s.
stout, dick, stramm, stark.
stove, Ofen, m., -s, Öfen.
stove-pipe hat, Cylinder, m., -s, —, Cylinderhut, m., -s.
St. Petersburg, Petersburg, n., -s.
straight, gerade, stracks.
straight-way, ein gerader Weg.

strain, anspannen.
strait, Strasse, f., Meerenge, f.
strange, eigentümlich, seltsam.
stranger, Fremde, m., -n, -n.
Strasburg, Strassburg, n., -s, Strassburger.
stray, sich zerstreuen.
stream, strömen, streben.
street, Strasse, f.
strength, Stärke, f., Kraft, f.; to gain s., erstarken.
stretch, Strecke, f., Stück, n., -s, -ücke.
stretch, s. forth, ausstrecken.
stride, Schritt, m., -s, -e.
strike, schlagen, anstossen, treffen, niederschlagen, fallen.
string, Reihe, f., Menge, f.
strip, Streife, f.
stripe, Streife, f.
strive, eifern (gegen, acc.).
stroll, Spaziergang, m., -s, -änge.
strong, stark, kräftig, gross.
strongly, ernst, nachdrücklich, dringend.
struggle, Kampf, m., -s, -ämpfe, Anstrengung, f.
struggle, sich bemühen; s. onward, weiter strebend.
student, Studént, m., -en, -en.
studio, Werkstätte, f., Arbeitszimmer, n., -s.
study, studieren, arbeiten.
stupid, dumm, Dummkopf, m., -s, -öpfe.
style, Stil, m., -s, -e, Schreibart, f., Weise, f.
Suabian, schwäbisch.
suavity, s. of, sanft, gewinnend.
subdivide, sich einteilen, sich abfachen.
sublime, erhaben.
subject, Gegenstand, m., -s, -ände.

subsequently, nachher.
subside, abnehmen, sich legen.
- succeed, glücklich sein, Erfolg haben.
succeeding, folgend.
success, Glück, n., -s, Erfolg, m., -s, -e.
succession, in quick s., rasch hinter einander.
successive, verschieden, auf einander folgend.
such, solch, das.
suddenly, plötzlich, jäh.
suffering, Leiden, n., -s, —.
sufficient, genug ; to be s., genügen.
suggest, andeuten, empfehlen.
suit, Anzug, m., -s, -üge.
suitable, passend, schicklich, anständig.
sullen, trübe, traurig, grämlich.
sum, Summe, f.
summit, Gipfel, m., -s, —, Spitze, f.
sun, Sonne, f.
sunbeam, Sonnenstrahl, m., -s, -en.
Sunday, Sonntag, m., -s,
sunlight, Sonnenlicht, n., -s.
sunny, sonnig.
sunshine, Sonnenschein, m., -s.
superb, prächtig, prachtvoll.
superiority, Vornehmheit, f., Überlegenheit, f.
supreme, höchst, grosst.
supper, Abendessen, n., -s.
suppliant, der or die Bittende.
support, helfen (dat.), eine Stütze sein.
suppress, unterdrücken.
sure, sicher, recht.
surface, Oberfläche, f.
surprise, Überraschung, f.

surprised, überrascht, erstaunt.
surtout, Surtout, m., -s, -s, Überrock, m., -s, -öcke.
sustain, unterstützen, erhalten.
swagger, s. about, einherstolzieren.
swear, fluchen.
sweat, schwitzen.
sweet, süss.
swell, anschwellen.
swift, schnell.
switch cane, Spazierstöckchen, n., -s.
Switzerland, Schweiz, f.
sword, Klinge, f., Schwert, n., -s, -er, Degen, m., -s, —.
sylvan, Wald-.
symmetry, Ebenmass, n., -es.
sympathy, Sympathie, f., Gefühl, n., -es, -e.
Syne, Auld Lang S., die gute alte Zeit.
system, System, n., -s, -e.

T.

table-talk, Tischreden, f. plu.
tablets, i. e. Heiligtum, n., -s.
Tacitus, m.
take, (hin)führen, ergreifen, nehmen, halten ; t. away, wegnehmen ; t. fire, feurig werden, in Feuer gesetzt werden, Feuer fangen.
talent, Talént, n., -s, -e.
talk, sprechen, (von ; über, acc.).
talk, Spötteln, n., -s, Worte, n. plu.
tall, gross, lang.
tallow, Talg-.
Tannhäuser, m., -s.
task, Aufgabe, f.
taste, Geschmack, m., -s.

tavern, Wirtshaus, n., -es, -äuser.
tea, Thee, m., -s.
teach, lehren.
tear, t. down, hinabjagen.
tear, Thräne, f.
teeth, Zahn, m., -s, -ähne.
telegram, Depesche, f.
telegraph, Telegraph, m., -en, -en.
tell, sagen, erzählen; zahlen, bezahlen; gelten, wirken, wichtig sein.
temper, geschmeidig machen, temperieren, stählen.
tempt, versuchen, verlocken or reizen (zu).
temptation, Versuchung, f.
tend, beitragen, darauf abzielen.
tendency, Richtung, f., Neigung, f., Hang, m., -s.
tenderly, zärtlich.
tense, gespannt, toll.
tent, Zelt, n., -s, -e.
term, Semester, n., -s, —.
terms, Bedingungen, f. pl.
terrace, Terrasse, f.
terraced, abgestuft.
terrible, schrecklich, furchtbar.
Testament, Testament, n., -s.
testimony, t. of respect, Ehrenbezeugung, f.
thank, t. Heaven, dem Himmel (Gott) sei Dank!
thanks, Danksagung, f., Dank, m., -s.
thankful, dankbar.
thaw, t. towards, auftauen (gegenüber, bei).
their, ihr.
then, dann, denn, now and t., hie und da.
theology, Theologie, f.
theorem, Lehrsatz, m., -es, -ätze.
there, da, es.

thereabouts, rings umher, dortig.
therefrom, daraus.
thick, dick, dicht, gross.
Thiers, m.
thin, mager.
thing, Ding, n., -s, -e(r), Sache, f.;
these t., dergleichen.
think, glauben, denken (an, acc.), meinen.
third, dritt.
thirteen hundred, dreizehnhundert.
thirty, dreissig.
thong, Riemen, m., -s.
thorn, Dorn, m., -s, -e, -en and -örner.
thoroughfare, i. e. Strasse, f.
thoroughly, gründlich, gänzlich.
though, obgleich.
thought, Gedanke, m., -ns, -n.
thousand, tausend.
three, drei.
thrice, dreimal.
thrifty, sparsam.
thrill, schlagen, klopfen, zittern;
t. towards, (dat.), entgegen etc.
thrill, Gefühl, n., -s, -e.
throat, Gurgel, f., Kehle, f., Hals, m., -s, -älse.
through, durch.
throw, werfen (auf, acc.); t. into, hineinwerfen; t. open, aufreissen.
thunderbolt, Donnerschlag, m., -s, -äge; Blitz, m., -es, -e.
thus, so, also.
tie, Verbindung, f., Freundschaft, f.
tight, knapp, eng.
tighten, zusammenziehen, eng ziehen.
till, bis.
tilt, stemmen (gegen).

time, Zeit, f., -en; at such times, dann, da; t. enough, früh genug.

time-smoothed, verwittert.

timid, furchtsam.

tip, schicken, kritzeln.

tire, müde werden.

tireless, unermüdlich, unermüdet.

tobacco, Tábak, m., -s.

tobacco-pipe, Tabakspfeife, f.

together, zusammen, gemeinschaftlich, gleich; t. with, nebst.

toil, Arbeit, f.

toil, arbeiten.

toilsome, mühevoll.

token, Zeichen, n., -s.

tolerate, leiden.

tomb, Grab, n., -s, -äber.

to-morrow, morgen.

tone, Ton, m., -s, -öne.

top, Höhe, f., oben.

topic, Thema, n., -s, -ta, -men and -s.

torchlight procession, Fackelzug, m., -s, -üge.

torments, i. e. Höllenpein, f.

torrent, Strom, m., -s, -öme.

toss-up, Glückswurf, m., -s, Würfelspiel, n., -s, Lotterie, f., Zufall, m., -s.

total, Summe, f.

touch, berühren.

toward, gegen, gen, nach.

towards, nach (. . . zu).

tower, Turm, m., -s, -ürme.

tower, hervorragen; t. above, überragen.

town, Stadt, f.

trace, t. out, verfolgen, ausspüren.

track, Spur, f., Weg, m., -s, -e.

tract, Strecke, f.

tragically, tragisch.

trail, Fährte, f., Landstrasse, f.

trait, Zug, m., -s, -üge.

traitor, Verräter, m., -s, —.

tramp, treten, t. over, hinweg fahren (über, dat.).

tramp, Getrampel, n., -s.

trample, zertreten, t. down, niederstampfen.

tranquil, ruhig.

translate, übersétzen.

translation, Übersetzung, f.

transplant, verpflanzen.

transport, versetzen (nach), verlegen (in, acc.).

travel, reisen, gehen.

traveller, Reisende, m., -n, -n, Wanderer, m., -s, —; t.'s register, Fremdenbuch, n., -s, -ücher.

tread-mill, (as adj.) abgedroschen, eintönig.

treasure, Schatz, m., -es, -ätze.

treat, behandeln.

tree, Baum, m, -s, -äume.

tremble, zittern.

tremendous, fürchterlich, erstaunlich, inhaltschwer.

trifling, unbedeutend.

triumph, Sieg, m., -s, -e, Erfolg, m., -s, -e.

triumph, siegen; t. over, überwinden.

triumphant, siegend, Sieges —.

trodden, zertreten.

trouble, belästigen.

true, wahr, treu (dat.).

truly, wahrhaft, wirklich.

trumpet, Trompete, f., t. sounding, trömpetenblasend.

trunk, Stamm, m., -s, ämme; Koffer, m. and n., -s, —.

trust, glauben (dat.) sich verlassen (auf, acc.).

trusty, treu, zuverlässig.

truth, Wahrheit, f.
try, suchen, versuchen.
tuft, Büschel, m. and n., -s, —.
tumult, Lärm, m., -s, Skandál,
m., -s.
tun, Fass, n., -es.
tunnel, Trichter, m., -s, —.
turbulent, unruhig, rastlos.
turn, in t., zur Abwechslung, zum
Ablösen.
turn, einschlagen or einlenken
(in, acc.); sich abwenden (von);
sich zuwenden (dat.); sich wen-
den (nach); t. round, úmdrehen.
tutor, Lehrer, m., -s, —.
twain, die Beiden.
twenty, zwanzig.
twenty-second, zweiundzwan-
zigst.
twenty-sixth, sechsundzwanzigst.
twice, zweimal, doppelt.
twilight, Zwielicht, n., -s.
twined, t. with ivy, epheuum-
schlungen.
twist, t. into, flechten (in, acc.).
two, zwei.
two-by-two, paarweise, je zwei
und zwei.
type, Bild, n., -s, -er.

U.

ultimo, vorig.
unable, nicht können, nicht im
Stande sein.
unadorned, schmucklos.
unaffected, ungezwungen, unbefangen.
un-American, unamerikanisch.
uncled, geonkelt, Onkel genannt.
unconscious, stumm, bewusstlos.
unconsumed, unversehrt.
uncontrollable, unaufhaltsam.

under, unter. •
underneath, unten.
understand, verstehen.
unearthly, unheimlich.
unerring, sicher, unfehlbar.
unfortunate, unglücklich.
unfortunately, unglücklicher-
weise.
ungrateful, undankbar.
uniform, Uniform, f.
unimpassioned, leidenschaftslos.
Union Jack, m.
unite, einstimmen (mit), sich
vereinigen (mit), sich vereinen;
u. with, unterstützen.
United States, Vereinigte Staa-
ten.
unity, Einheit, f.
universally, allgemein.
university, Universität, f.
unkempt, ungepflegt.
unknown, unbekannt.
unlearn, unzulernen, eine Meinung, or Vorstellung, ändern,
verlernen.
unless, wenn nicht, es wäre denn.
unlike, unähnlich (dat.).
unmistakable, unverkennbar.
unnecessary, unnötig.
unrelieved, nicht erleichtert.
unsaddle, absatteln.
unsophisticated, i. e. einfach, un-
verdorben.
until, bis, bis zu.
unwary, nachlässig, unvorsichtig.
up, hinauf, auf.
upon, auf.
upper, Ober —.
uproar, Geräusch, n., -es; of u.,
lärmig.
upset, úmwerfen.
urge, dringen (in, acc.), darauf
bestehen.

use, pflegen; verbrauchen; gewöhnlich (with verb).
use, Gebrauch, m., -s.
usher, führen, weisen.
usual, gewöhnlich.
usurer, Wucherer, m., -s.
utter, aussprechen.
utterly, äusserst, höchst, gänzlich.

V.

vacant, leer.
valley, Thal, n., -s, -äler.
valor, Tapferkeit, f.
value, schätzen.
value, Nutzen, m., -s, —.
varnish, schwinden, verschwinden.
vary, úmschlagen, umspringen, sich ändern or drehen.
vast, grossartig, ungeheuer, weit, gross.
veil, Schleier, m., -s, —.
vein, Ader, f., -n.
vellum-binding, i. e. Pergamentbände, m. plu.
venerate, verehren.
vengeance, Rache, f.
Venus, f.
verge, Rand, m., -s, Grenze, f.; to be on the v., auf dem Punkte stehen.
veriest, eigentlichst, niedrigst.
versify, in Verse bringen.
very, sehr, ganz, höchst.
Vesuvius, Vesúv, m., -s.
vexed, to be v., sich ärgern.
Vice-Consul, Vice-Kónsul, m., -s, -n.
Vicksburg, n., -s.
victim, Opfer, n., -s, —.
victorious, siegreich; to be v., siegen.

victory, Sieg, m., -s, -e.
Vienna, Wien, n., -s.
view, Aussicht, f., -en; Anschauung, f., Ansicht, f.
vigor, Eifer, m., -s.
vigorous, tüchtig.
village, Dorf, n., -örfer.
vindicate, rechtfertigen, verteidigen, loben.
vineyard, Weingarten, m., -s, -ärten.
Virgíl, m., -s.
virgin, jungfraülich.
Virginia, —.
Virorum, the same.
virtue, Tugend, f.-en, Unschuld, f.
visible, sichtbar.
visit, Besuch, m., -s, -e.
visit, besuchen.
Visp, n., -s.
voice, Stimme, f.
volcanic, vulkanisch.
voluntarily, freiwillig.
Vosges, Vogesen, plu.
vouchsafe, vergönnen (dat.).

W.

wagon, Wagen, m., -s, —.
waist, Leib, m., -s, -er.
wait, warten, aushalten, ausdauern, w. on, aufwarten (dat.).
waiter, Kellner, m., -s, —.
waiting-room, Wartezimmer, n., -s, —.
wake, wecken.
walk, Weg, m., -s, -e, Spaziergang, m., -s, -änge.
walk, gehen, spazieren.
wall, Mauer, f., -n, Wand, f., -ände.
wander, wandern, umherwandeln.
wanderer, Wanderer, m., -s, —.

wandering way, Wanderweg, m , ·s, ·e.
wane, vergehen, verrinnen.
want, wollen, wünschen ; fehlen (an, dat); nötig haben (acc.), bedürfen (acc. or gen.); brauchen, verlangen.
wanton, mutwillig.
wantonness, Übermut, m., ·s.
war, Krieg, m , ·s, ·e.
ward, verhindern ; **w. away,** abwehren.
warm, warm.
warmly, herzlich.
warrant, dafür stehen, wetten.
warring, entgegengesetzt.
waste, verschwenden, vergeuden.
watch, Wache, f.
watchfire, Wachfeuer, n., -s, —.
water, Wasser, n., -s.
watering-place, Bad, n., -s, äder; **trip to a w.,** Badereise, f.
wave, wehen, schweben; **w. aside,** abweisen (mit der Hand), zurückwinken; **w. off,** zurückweisen, zurückwinken , schwenken, winken or grüssen (mit).
way, Weg, m., -s, -e ; Weise, f. ; **w. homeward,** Rückweg.
way-bill, Personenliste, f., Frachtbrief, m , ·s, ·e.
wayward, w. track, Irrfahrt, f., ·en.
weakness, Schwäche, f.
weapon, Waffe, f., ·n.
wear, tragen, zeigen; **wearing** etc., mit etc.
weary, müde.
weather, Wetter, n., ·s.
weather-beaten, verwittert, gebräunt.
Wednesday, Mittwoch, m., -s, -e.
week, Woche, f.

weep, weinen.
weight, Wucht, f., Gewicht, n., -s, Bürde, f.
Weimar, n., .s.
welcome, willkommen.
welcome, begrüssen.
well, gut, wohl.
well-behaved, wohlgesittet, höflich, artig.
well-conducted, wohlerzogen.
well-known, wohlbekannt.
well-nigh, beinahe.
well-worn, abgetragen.
west, Westen, m., -s.
when, wenn, als, da
whence, von wo.
where, wo, dahin wo.
wherever, überall wo.
whether, ob.
while, während, so lange.
while, Weile, f.
whip, peitschen.
whisper, flüstern.
whistle, zupfeifen (dat).
white, weiss, blass.
white-haired, weisshaarig.
Whitehall, the same.
whole, ganz
wholesome, heilsam, gesund.
wide, weit, breit, ganz.
widow, Wittwe, f., -n.
width, w. of, weit or breit.
wife, Weib, n., -s, ·er, Frau, f., -en
wigwam, m. and n., -s.
wild, wild.
wild-fowl, wildes Geflügel.
wildly, heiss.
wild-sage, Salbei·.
will, wollen, wünschen.
will, Wunsch, m., es, ·ünsche.
willing, to be w., wollen, willens sein.
William, Wilhelm, m., ·s.

win, erringen.

wind, Wind, m., -s, -e.

winding, krumm, schlängelnd, gewunden.

window, Fenster, n., -s, —

wine, Wein, m., -s, -e.

wings, Schwingen, f. plu Flügel, m. plu.

wisdom, Weisheit, f.

wise, klug.

wish, Wunsch, m., -es, -ünsche.

wit, Witz, m., -es.

witchery, Hexenwesen, n., -s, Zauberspiel, n., -s.

with, mit, nebst.

withhold, vorenthalten (dat.), zurückhalten

within, innerhalb (gen.), in.

without, ohne, ohne dass.

witness, Zeuge, m., -n, -n.

witticism, Witz, m., -es, -e.

witty, witzig.

woe, Schmerz, m., -es, -en, Leiden, n., -s, —.

woman, Weib, n., -es, -er ; weiblich.

wonder, Wunder, n., -s, —.

wonderful, wunderbar, wunderschön.

wondrous, wunderbar.

wondrously, wunderbar, merk würdig, sehr.

woo, huldigen (dat.), freien, anbeten.

woods, Wälder, plu. (Wald, m., -s).

word, Wort, n., -s, -e and örter.

work, arbeiten, machen ; sich Mühe geben ; w. out, erwirken.

work, Werk, n., -s, -e ; Arbeit, f.

world, Welt, f.

worldly, Welt-

worry, Sorge, f., Plage, f.

worth, gelten, wert sein (gen.).

worthless, unwürdig, nichtswürdig.

worst, schlimmst.

would-be, the same, or : der gern sein möchte.

wreath, Kranz, m., -es, -änze.

wretched, erbärmlich, elend.

wring, erpressen (dat.), abzwingen (dat., or von).

wrist, Handgelenk, n., -s.

wristlet, i. e. Rand, m., -s.

write, schreiben.

writer, Schriftsteller, m, -s, —.

writing, w. agony of speed, fieberhaftes Vorwärtsstreben.

writings, Schriften, f. plu.

wrong, Unrecht, n., -s

wrong, unrichtig.

Würtemberg, n., -s.

Y.

yard, Hof, m., -s, -öfe, Schritt, m., -s, -e.

yea, ja, auch.

year, Jahr, n., -s, -e.

yell, Ruf, m, s, -e.

yellow, gelb.

Yellowplush, Yellowplush.

yesterday, gestern.

yet, doch, noch.

you, Sie, du, man.

young, jung.

your, Ihr, dein.

youth, Jüngling, m., -s, -e, junger Mensch, m., -en, -en ; Jugend, f

Z.

zigzag, Zickzack-.

Zobel, m., -s, —.

NOTES.

INTRODUCTORY.

THE following bibliographical notes may be of some benefit to teachers.

DICTIONARIES.

I. [In German only.]

GRIMM, J. und W. Deutsches Wörterbuch. Fortgesetzt von M. Heyne, R. Hildebrand, M. Lexer, K. Weigand und E. Wülcker. Leipzig, 1854–91. [Incomplete, — A–Geriesel; H–Roman; T–verleihen, — costing about $40,00.]

SANDERS, D. Wörterbuch der deutschen Sprache. Mit Belegen von Luther bis auf die Gegenwart. 3 Bde. Leipzig, 1860–65. 80 marks. As a supplementary volume: Ergänzungswörterbuch. Berlin, 1885. [50 marks.]

SANDERS, D. Wörterbuch der Zeitwörter. Berlin, 1882. 2 Aufl. [50 pfennigs].

CAMPE, J. H. Wörterbuch der deutschen Sprache. 5 Theile. Braunschweig, 1807–11. [About 20 marks.]

ADELUNG, J. CH. Versuch eines vollständigen grammatisch-kritischen Wörterbuches der hochdeutschen Mundart. 5 Theile. Leipzig, 1774–86. [About 10 marks.]

WEIGAND, FR. L. K. Deutsches Wörterbuch. 2 Bde. Giessen, 1881–82. 4. Aufl. [34 marks.]

KLUGE, FR. Etymologisches Wörterbuch der deutschen Sprache. Strassburg, 1889. 4. Aufl. [10 marks.]

[THE SAME.] An Etymological Dictionary of the German Language by FR. KLUGE. Translated from the 4th German edition by J. F. DAVIS. London and New York. Macmillan, 1891. [$3.00.]

ANDRESEN, K. G. Über deutsche Volksetymologie. Heilbronn, 1890. 6. Aufl. [5 50 marks.]

HEYNE, M. Deutsches Wörterbuch. Leipzig, 1889–. [Incomplete. Erster Band, A–Gyps. 1889–90. About 30 marks when finished.]

WENIG, CHR. Handwörterbuch der deutschen Sprache, Neubearbeitet von G. Schumann. Köln, 1885. 7. Aufl. [9 marks.]

KAPFF, R. Deutsche Vornamen mit den von ihnen abstammenden Geschlechtsnamen, sprachlich erläutert. Nürtingen am Neckar, 1889. [1 mark.]

PETRI, FR. E. Handbuch der Fremdwörter in der deutschen Schrift- und Umgangssprache. Neubearbeitet von E. Samostz. Leipzig, 1879. 13. Aufl. [6 marks.]

HEYSE, T. CH. A. Allgemeines Fremdwörterbuch. Neubearbeitet von G. Heyse. Hannover, 1879. 16. Aufl. Berliner Ausgabe, 14. Ster.- Aufl. Berlin, 1889. [5.50 marks.]

SANDERS, D. Fremdwörterbuch. Leipzig, 1879. [10.50 marks.] 2. Aufl., 1891–.

WEBER. J. Fremdwörterbuch enthaltend über 14,000 fremde Wörter und Redensarten welche in Zeitungen etc. vorkommen. Leipzig, 1883. [1.25 marks.]

SANDERS, D. Verdeutschungswörterbuch. Leipzig, 1884. [5 marks.]

SARRAZIN, O. Verdeutschungswörterbuch. Berlin, 1886. [4.60 marks.]

LYON, O. Zeichensetzung und Fremdwörterverdeutschung. Dresden, 1889. [30 pfennigs.]

DUDEN, K. Vollständiges orthographisches Wörterbuch der deutschen Sprache mit etymologischen Angaben, kurzen Sacherklärungen und Verdeutschungen der Fremdwörter. Nach den neuen amtlichen Regeln. 3. Aufl. Leipzig, 1887. [1.60 marks.]

RÖHRIG, E. Technologisches Wörterbuch. Deutsch-Englisch-Französisch. 3. Aufl. Wiesbaden, 1887. [32 marks.]

ACADEMICA JUVENTUS. ˙ Die deutschen Studenten nach Sprache und Sitte. Celle und Leipzig, 1887. [1 mark.]

BURSCHIKOSES WÖRTERBUCH, oder Studentensprache. München, 1878. [50 pfennigs.]

NEUES WÖRTERBUCH DER STUDENTENSPRACHE. 2. Aufl. Wien, 1888. [50 pfennigs.]

EBERHARD. J. A. Synonymisches Handwörterbuch der deutschen Sprache. 14. Aufl. Umgearbeitet von O Lyon. Leipzig, 1889. [11 marks.]

SANDERS, D. Wörterbuch der deutschen Synonymen. Hamburg, 1882. 2. Aufl. [10 marks.]

WANDER, K. F. W. Deutsches Sprichwörterlexikon. 5 Bde. Leipzig, 1867–80. [150 marks. May be found second hand for about 100 marks.]

SANDERS, D. Wörterbuch der Hauptschwierigkeiten in der deutschen Sprache. Grosse Ausgabe. 19. Aufl. Berlin, 1889. [3 marks.]

WESSELY, I. E. Grammatisch-stilistisches Wörterbuch der deutschen Sprache. Leipzig, 1883. [2 marks.]

II. [German and English.]

LUCAS, N. I. A Dictionary of the English and German and German and English Language. 2 vols. Bremen and London, 1854. [Out of print. About $50.00 ?]

HILPERT, J. L. A Dictionary of the German and English Languages. 3 vols. Karlsruhe and London, 1828-57. [About £3, new. Out of print.]

GRIEB, C. F. A Dictionary of the German and English Languages. 2 vols. 9. Ster.- Aufl. 1885. [17 marks.]

THIEME–PREUSSER. New and Complete Critical Dictionary of the German and English Languages. Revised by I. E. Wessely. Hamburg and New York. (Westermann.) Neue reich-vermehrte Stereotypausgabe, 1890.

CASSELL. New German Dictionary in two parts : German-English and English-German. By Elizabeth Weir. Boston, Heath & Co. [N. D., recent, $1.35.]

WHITNEY, W. D. A compendious German and English Dictionary, with notation of correspondencies and brief etymologies. New
York. [N. D., after 1877, $3.25.]

LONGMAN, F. W. Pocket Dictionary of the German and English
Languages. London and New York, 5th edition, 1889. [$ 0.90.]

HOPPE, A. Englisch-Deutsches Supplementlexikon. Erste Abtei-
lung : A-Close. Berlin, 1888. [32 marks when complete.]

FLÜGEL, F. A Universal English-German and German-English
Dictionary. First part, A-Bok. Braunschweig, 1890. [At present,
as far as I. 36 marks when finished.]

SACHS, K. Encyclopädisches Wörterbuch der französischen und
deutschen Sprache. *Grosse Ausgabe.* 2 Thle. Berlin, 1887-88. [5.
Aufl. 74 marks.] Hand- und Schulausgabe. 2 Thle. Berlin, 1889.
[50. Aufl. 13.50 marks, bound.]

VISTOR, W. German Pronunciation : Practice and Theory. Heilbronn, 1885. New York, Westermann. [2 marks.]

HUSS, H. Lehre vom Accent der deutschen Sprache. Alten-
burg, 1877. [1.20 marks.]

GRAMMARS.

I. [In German.]

GRIMM, J. Deutsche Grammatik. 2. Ausgabe. Neuer ver-
mehrter Abdruck. Besorgt durch W. Scherer. 2. Bde. Berlin,
1870-78. [36 marks.] 3. Bd. [Von E. Schroeder.] 1. Th. 1889.
[15 marks.]

HEYSE, J. CH. A. Deutsche Schulgrammatik oder Lehrbuch
der deutschen Sprache. Neubearbeitet von O. Lyon. 24. Aufl.
Hannover, 1886. [4 marks.]

BECKER, K. F. Handbuch der deutschen Sprache. Neubearbeitet von Th. Becker. 11. Aufl. Prag, 1876. [6 marks.]

BLATZ, FR. Neuhochdeutsche Grammatik mit Berücksichtigung
der historischen Entwickelung der deutschen Sprache. Tauberbi-
schofsheim. 2. Aufl. 1880. [12 marks.]

WILMANNS, W. Deutsche Grammatik für die Unter- und Mittel-
klassen höherer Lehranstalten. Nebst Regeln und Wörterverzeichnis
für die deutsche Orthographie. 8. Aufl. Berlin, 1891. [2 marks.]

JAHNS, J. CH. Lehrbuch der deutschen Sprache. 10. Aufl.
Hannover, 1886.

VERNALEKEN, TH. Deutsche Schulgrammatik. Mit Berücksichtigung des Mittelhochdeutschen und mit Einschluss der deutschen
Verslehre. 2. Aufl. Wien, 1872. [2.80 marks.]

II. [In English.]

BRANDT, H. C. G. A Grammar of the German Language for
High Schools and Colleges. 4th ed. Boston: Allyn and Bacon,
1888. [$1.25.]

JOYNES, E. S. A German Grammar for Schools and Colleges.
(Based on A. L. Meissner's.) Boston: Heath, 1888. [Revised
edition, $1.25.]

WHITNEY, W. D. A Compendious German Grammar. New
York: Holt, 1869. [Revised edition in 1888. $1.50.]

SHELDON, E. S. A Short German Grammar for High Schools
and Colleges. Boston: Heath, 1879. [$0.65.]

Syntax and Style.

VERNALEKEN, TH. Deutsche Syntax. 2 Thle. Wien, 1861-63.
[16 marks.]

BECKER, K. F. Der deutsche Stil. Neubearbeitet von O. Lyon.
3. Aufl. Prag, 1883. [6.50 marks.]

ANDRESEN, K. G. Sprachgebrauch und Sprachrichtigkeit im
Deutschen. 6. Aufl. Heilbronn, 1890. [5 marks.]

SANDERS, D. Deutsches Stil-Musterbuch mit Erläuterungen und
Anmerkungen. Berlin, 1886. [6 marks.]

ZEITSCHRIFT FÜR DEN DEUTSCHEN UNTERRICHT. Herausgegeben von O. Lyon. Leipzig, 1887-. [Six numbers annually, 10
marks.]

ZEITSCHRIFT FÜR DEUTSCHE SPRACHE. Herausgegeben von D. Sanders. Hamburg, 1887–. [Monthly, 12 marks.]

---

v. BAHDER, K. Die deutsche Philologie im Grundriss. Paderborn, 1883. [6 marks.]

NOTE. — The dictionaries of *Grimm* (incomplete) and *Sanders* are the best for definitions of German words. They supersede *Campe* and *Adelung*, which however are still valuable historically, and occasionally supply some additional information. *Weigand*, whose articles should be compared with Kluge's for verification, and *Kluge* afford chiefly etymologies rather than definitions. *Andresen* presents the best summary of "popular" etymologies. *Heyne* (incomplete) is planned to be a German "Webster," without illustrations or appendices. *Wenig* is a useful hand dictionary, with indication of the pronunciation. *Kapff* treats succinctly of a subject to which little attention is given in the ordinary lexicons. Either *Petri's*, *Heyse's*, or *Sanders's Fremdwörterbuch* would be adequate for ordinary needs. The *Verdeutschungswörterbücher* give German equivalents for foreign words rather than definitions. *Lyon's* treatise is useful for details of punctuation. *Duden* is valuable for identifying the revised orthography. *Röhrig*, the well-known work of Rumpf, Mothes, etc., is essential for the study of scientific or technical German. The *Academica Juventus*, etc., are rather light-weight collections of student slang. *Eberhard* (in the last edition) is the best authority on German synonyms. *Wander's* collection of proverbial sayings is a mine of erudition, invaluable for reference. *Sanders's* and *Wessely's* works, throwing light on many obscure and difficult points of grammatical usage, are indispensable for thorough teaching.

Of the German and English dictionaries, *Lucas* is a useful and bulky jumble of definition, expensive and scarce. *Hilpert* is voluminous, but rare and out of date. *Grieb* is more modern, but also no longer to be recommended in view of later productions in the same field. The best work for students is either *Thieme-Preusser* or *Cassell*. The former is more detailed; the latter, for its size, remarkably comprehensive and fresh. *Whitney* suggests etymologies, but by comparison is somewhat meagre in definition, and inadequate in the German-English portion. *Longman's* is a truly admirable pocket dictionary. *Hoppe* (incomplete) is to be an elaborate English-German lexicon. *Flügel*, when finished, (in 1892?) is likely to supplant all other works in the same field, (excepting possibly the work of Muret just announced?) and must be in the hands of every teacher. *Sachs*, through the medium of the French, will not infrequently prove of much service. *Vietor* and *Huss* formulate conveniently the common usage in pronunciation.

Of the grammars, *Grimm*, revised, is of course the standard authority for the subjects which it covers. *Heyse*, on which Whitney's is based, or *Becker*, affords a comprehensive treatment of the whole field ; while *Blatz* is specially to be recommended for a lucid and detailed treatment, including the syntax, from the modern historical standpoint. Shorter and convenient compendiums among the many school grammars are those of *Wilmanns, Vernaleken* and *Jahns*, the last-named containing a number of excellent practical exercises. In English, *Brandt* may be mentioned as the only grammar containing any adequate account of the recent results of the investigations of scientific German grammarians. *Joynes* and *Whitney*, as well as *Brandt*, with their accompanying exercises and readers, are excellent working grammars for ordinary classes in German composition ; and Sheldon's grammar affords a brief but clear outline of grammatical principles.

On points of syntax and style, *Vernaleken, Becker*, and *Andresen* are authoritative. Cp. *Sanders* and *Wessely* above. *Sanders's Stil-Musterbuch* contains extracts from German authors from Lessing to Heine, with comments on points of grammatical and linguistic usage.

The periodicals edited by *Lyon* and by *Sanders* are interesting and practical, and best for the teacher.

K. v. Bahder's manual includes exhaustive bibliographical lists on the subjects above mentioned.

N O T E S.

————◆————

I.

HEIDELBERG.

Page 3, l. 1: "if you come to Heidelberg, you will never want to go away," conditional inversion, *so* in conclusion. Or, *wenn Du nach Heidelberg kommst, wirst Du gar nicht wieder fort wollen.* (Kr., i. e. Krummacher.) l. 2: "is," *heisst.* l. 3: "out of which," *aus welchen.* l. 5: "there is no sense of imprisonment," *man fühlt sich gar nicht eingeschränkt.* l. 5: "the view is always wide open to the great plains," *man hat beständig die freie Aussicht auf die weite Ebene.* l. 7: "goes," *hinfliesst.* l. 8: *lachend* rather than *lächelnd.* l. 9: "without a desire to go farther, nor any wish," *ohne Lust weiter zu gehen, und ohne allen Wunsch.* l. 12: "what the students can find to fight their little duels about," *was für Gründe die Studenten für ihre kleinen Duelle finden können.* (Kr.) l. 13: "but fight they do," *aber sie fechten doch.* l. 15: "many of them," *von denen viele.* "stuck so far on the forehead," *so weit auf die Stirn gerückt.* l. 17: "like that worn by ladies," *wie bei Damen.*

Page 4, l. 2: "across the breast," *quer über die Brust.* l. 5: "some like to," *einigen gefällt es.* l. 9: "below ... below ... farther down," *unten ... darunter ... weiter unten.* l. 11: "beyond," *dahinter.* l. 13: "beyond that," *jenseit (der Brücke).* l. 14: "along which I see peasant women walking," *auf welcher ich Bauernweiber entlang gehen sehe.* l. 16: "down the river," *flussabwärts;* "above it," *über ihr* or *droben.* l. 18: "which runs along," *welcher sich hinzieht.* l. 24: "and the Neckar flowing out of it," *und den Neckar, wie er aus derselben in die Ebene fliesst.*

l. 26: "to the northward," *nach Norden zu.* l. 29: "purple in the last distance," *bläulich in weiter Ferne.* l. 30: " throw a stone into them," *einen Stein hineinwerfen.*

Page 5, l. 5: "goes down into the town," *geht (führt) in die Stadt hinab.* l. 6: " along which little houses cling to the hillside," *an welchem entlang eine Reihe Häuschen (sich) an den (or dem) Bergeshang nisten.* l. 7: "whence," *von wo.* l. 10: "I have only to go a few steps up a street," *ich brauche nur ein paar Schritte weit eine Strasse hinaufzugehen.* l. 15: "and seldom do go where I intend when I set forth," *und gehe selten wohin ich beim Ausgehen mich hinwenden wollte.* l. 18: "nor scarcely anything," *und kaum irgend etwas.* l. 22: "that lead to winding walks of the terraced hill," *die zu gewundenen Wandelgängen (Wegen) den abgestuften Berg hinaufführen, bis herum zu.* l. 23: " overlooking, etc.," *mit dem Blick auf den N.* l. 25: "if we do," *wenn wir dies thun.* l. 30: "cut to resemble, etc.," *die* (nom.) *epheubewachsenen Baumstämmen nachgemeisselt sind.*

Page 6, l. 1: "or rather go through," *oder lieber durch . . . gehen.* l. 2: "and under the teeth of the portcullis," *und unter den Zähnen des Fallgatters durch, in den Schlosshof.* l. 8: "and from here we pass out upon," *und von hier treten wir heraus auf die.* l. 10: "its base," *den Unterbau* (accusative absolute) *mit eine Fassade als* l. 11: "below the town . . . and beyond the plain," *unter sich . . . den Fluss . . . und drüben die Ebene.* l. 12: "sit and dream," *sitzen und träumen* (infinitives). l. 15: "and the sun over Heiligenberg goes down upon his purpose," *und die Sonne über dem Heiligenberg geht über unserm Vorhaben unter.* (Cp. Ephesians iv. 26: "let not the sun go down upon your wrath," *lasset die Sonne nicht über eurem Zorn untergehen.*)

II.

A BEER SCANDAL.

Page 7, l. 1: "on their way homeward," *auf ihrem Rückwege,* or *beim Nachhausegehen.* l. 5: "he was a student," *er war Student.* l. 17: "you are a baron," *Sie sind ein Baron.* l. 18: "what you

and I do," *was Sie (Du) und ich thun,* or, *was wir Beide thun.*
l. 19: "urging him," *als er in ihn drang.*

Page 8, l. 7: "unless it were a Scandinavian heaven," *es wäre denn ein skandinavischer Himmel.*   l. 14: "Mossy-Head," (*bemoostes Haupt*), i. e. *ein Student in hohen Semestern,* an "old boy." — "Prince of Twilight," i. e. a "night-owl (?)." — "Pomatum-Stallion" (*Pomadenhengst*), i. e. *der nach Pomade riechende,* "gay buck." Cp. Tennyson's "oiled and curled Assyrian bull" in *Maud.*   l. 16: "Broad-Stone," formerly a sort of footpath composed of big round paving stones in the middle of the road (at least at Halle), though it may elsewhere have been near the gutter. When two students met, each tried to keep the footpath and oblige the other to step aside. (Kr.) l. 18: "Besens" and "Zobels," student slang for servant girls or other women. "Poussades," sweethearts, love-affairs. (The latter more properly, although it may also be used as a "concretum." Kr.)

Page 9, l. 6: "Foxes," *Fuchs* is the name applied to a German University student in his first semester.   l. 10: "made an enormous pair of mustaches," *malten einen ungeheuren Schnurrbart auf die,* etc. ·
l. 12: "beneath," *unter* (dat.) . . . *hindurch gehen.*   l. 25: "on entering life," *bei ihrem Eintritt ins Leben.*

Page 10, l. 16: "to the brim," *bis an den Rand.*   l. 22: "like the crossing of swords," *wie wenn (als ob) sich Schwerter kreuzten.* l. 29: "hardly a long breath drawn between," *kaum dass sie dazwischen einen tiefen Atemzug thaten* (Kr.), or, *indem sie sich kaum Zeit liessen, Atem zu holen.*

Page 11, l. 1: "he was the first to drain," *er leerte zuerst.* l. 5: "hit," *gelungen (getroffen).*   l. 15: "his coat was off, etc.," "*ohne Rock, im blossen Halse, fliegenden Haares, die Augen weit geöffnet.*" (Note the interchangeable variety in construction of these phrases.)   l. 20: use infinitive (with *ohne*), or clause with *während,* or independent sentence.   l. 22: "crushing," *indem er zertrat.* l. 23: "at his approach," *bei seinem Anzug.*

Page 12, l. 2: "on his hands," *auf dem Halse.*

III.

THE MAN WHO SPEAKS ENGLISH.

Page 13, l. 6: "going on . . . on their way over the Simplon," *und . . . über den Simplon weiter reisen wollten.* l. 10 : "seemed to expect," *schien zu erwarten, dass man ihn verstehen müsse.* l. 12 : "as he always did," *wie er immer that.* l. 17 : "scarcely . . . when," *kaum . . . als.*

Page 14, l. 4 : "suggested . . . as," *schlug vor . . . als.* l. 11 : *mit seinem Mondscheingesicht oben auf dem Kopfe.* (Kr.) l. 27, etc.: translate the participial phrases by subordinate clauses introduced by *wie.*

Page 15, l. 5: "perched behind," *der hinten angebracht war.* l. 19 : translate by a clause introduced by *da ;* "lost on the official," *für den Beamten verloren.*

Page 16, l. 10: "gone to them," *hinein,* or, *hinaufgegangen.* l. 11 : "to show me to my room," *mir mein Zimmer anzuweisen.* l. 15 : "rolling his face about on the top of his head violently," *indem er sein Gesicht oben auf dem Kopf heftig herumdrehte.* (Kr.) l. 26 : "who cried out in indignation at being disturbed," *die sich über die Störung laut beschwerte,* or, *die bei der Störung entrüstet ausrief.*

Page 17, l. 16: "unite with us in," *mit uns einstimmen um.*

IV.

MARTIN LUTHER.

Page 18, l. 17 : "at heart," *innerlich.* l. 20 : "whether his act be glorified or condemned, etc.," *man mag seine That verherrlichen oder verdammen: dass sein Volk hinter ihm stand kann niemand leugnen.* l. 21 : "regions," *Landschaften.*

Page 19, l. 1 : "for a long time," *für lange Zeit.* l. 19 : "the after-effects of the might of his spirit," *die nachwirkende Macht seines Geistes.*

V.

LESSING.

Page 20, l. 1 : "without," *ohne dass.*   l. 7 : "but in, etc.," *sondern indem er.*   l. 18 : "as," need not be translated.
Page 21, l. 2 : "there is nothing like," *nichts gleicht.*   l. 4 : "except lie for it," *nur nicht lügen.*   l. 8 : "with," *bei.*   l. 15 : translate the participial phrases by relative clauses.

VI.

GOETHE.

Page 22, l. 1 : "what most interested our travellers," *was unsre Wanderer am meisten interessierte.*
Page 23, l. 4 : Claudian (c. 400, A. D.), i. e. in his poem *Gigantomachia,* vss. 23–24 :

Hinc Atlantis apex flammantia pondera fulcit,
Et per canitiem glacies asperrima durat.

l. 10 : "hews into him lustily," *haut tüchtig auf ihn los.*   l. 14 : "for . . . being," *deshalb . . . weil.*   l. 23 : "he certainly was," *das war er gewiss.*   l. 29 : "nothing more than," *nichts weiter* (or *anders*) *als.*
Page 24, l. 12 : "there was not wanting," *es fehlte nicht an* (dat.). l. 27 : "for the very reason that," *eben weil.*   l. 29 : "while its branches streaming magnificently toward heaven, etc.," *weil seine Zweige so prachtvoll bis in den Himmel ragten, so dass es aussah, als seien die Sterne,* etc.
Page 25, l. 6 : "drive the hens out of the garden without trampling down the beds," *die Hühner aus dem Garten treiben, ohne die Beete zu zertreten.*
Page 26, l. 11 : "the great I," *das grosse Ich.*   l. 12 : "it is both," *Beides.*   l. 13 : "that flings out before and behind," *das vorn und hinten ausschlägt.*   l. 18 : "looked . . . on," *blickten . . . auf* (acc.).   l. 22 : "were near," *lagen neben* (dat.).

VII.

COLLEGE.

Page 27, l. 4: "with nothing of your fellow . . . but the name," *die* (i. e. *Bekanntschaft*) *mit deinem Kameraden . . . nur den Namen gemein hat.* l. **10**: "but with . . . it is different," *anders aber ist es mit.* l. **22**: "you fall to thinking how," *du sinnst darüber nach, warum ;* or, *du fängst an, nachzudenken, wie.*

Page 28, l. 6: "a giant of remorse," *wie ein riesenhafter Vorwurf.* (*riesengross und reuevoll.*) l. **9**: "the great *Now*," *das grosse Jetzt.* l. **11**: "the temper of Life is to be made good by big honest blows," *das Leben muss man mit grossen tüchtigen Schlägen geschmeidig machen.* l. **14**: "success rides on every hour," *das Glück fährt mit jeder Stunde vorbei ;* or, *jede Stunde kann dir Glück bringen.* l. **18**: "there were some seventy of us," *es waren unser etwa siebzig.* l. **23**: "met wandering," *traf wandernd* (not *wandern*), or, *als er wanderte.* l. **27**: "and ran on to talk of our lives," *und gingen dann zu unserm Leben über.* l. **28**: translate, "we sat down and told." l. **29**: "looking off upon that blue sea," *der* (i. e. *der Felsenvorsprung*) *einen Blick über das graue Meer gewährte.* l. **30**: "and told each other our respective stories," *und erzählten uns gegenseitig unsern Lebenslauf.*

Page 29, l. 2: "that was reflected from the walls," *welcher von den Mauern . . . zurückgestrahlt wurde.* l. **4**: "he to wander, . . . and I," *und er wanderte . . . während ich.* l. **14**: "in our wayward tracks," *auf unsern Irrfahrten.* l. **16**: "tire of comparing," *müde werden zu vergleichen.* l. **25**: "envied him the possession of his wife," *beneidete ihn um seine Frau.* l. **30**: "were leaning back upon the rail after the old fashion," *lehnten sich noch nach alter Weise an die Wandleiste zurück.*

Page 30, l. 14: "but as he went on with his rusty and polemic vigor, etc.," *aber wie er in seiner eingerosteten Streitbarkeit fortfuhr, erwärmte die Poesie seines Innern dann und wann seine Seele in einem Erguss glühender* (or, *feuriger*) *Beredsamkeit, und sein Antlitz strahlte* (or, *glühte*), *seine Hand zitterte,* etc. (Kr.)

Page 31, l. 1: "of tightening his cloak about his nether limbs,"

den Mantel um die Beine eng zu ziehen.   l. 2 : "nor," *auch nicht.*
l. 3 : "to catch at the handle of some witticism," *nach irgend einem
Witze zu haschen.*   l. 27 : "would have chosen for a scholar," *als
Modell zu einem Gelehrten gewählt hätte.*

Page 32, l. 1 : "with all his polish of mind," *bei all seiner feinen
Bildung war er auch* (not *doch!*).   l. 4 : "that used to be ranged
below," *die sich einst dort unten reihten.*

VIII.

THE YOUNG AMERICAN.

Page 33, l. 3 : translate "born," "bred," etc., either as partici-
ples, or by relative clauses, i. e. *der von guter Familie ist,* etc.   l. 3 :
"bred in good principles," *in guten Grundsätzen erzogen.*   l. 16 :
"their elegantly set heads, column-like necks," *ihre vornehm aufgesetz-
ten Köpfe, säulengleichen Hälse.*   l. 17 : "firm chins, deep chests,"
das feste Kinn, die geräumige Brust.   l. 19 : "it may well be questioned," *es lässt sich wohl fragen.*   l. 21 : "local, not planetary,"
engumgrenzt nicht erdumspannend.

Page 34, l. 5 : "above all things, if he aspired to know as well as
to enjoy," *vor allem : wenn er ebensowohl nach Erkenntnis als nach
Genuss strebte, fan der,* etc. (Kr.)   l. 10 : "to be sought for only as
gold is sought," *so dass man es wie Gold . . . suchen musste.*   l. 11 :
"never was there anything like the condition," *nie gab es irgend etwas
wie den Zustand.*   l. 14 : "having in possession or in prospect," *im
gegenwärtigen oder künftigen Besitz.*   l. 15 : "with all its climates to
choose from," *mit der freien Auswahl aller ihrer Klimate.*   l. 20 :
"with huge leviathans always ready," *indem riesige Leviathane immer
bereit sind.*   l. 28 : "knit into the most absolute solidarity with
mankind," *zur unbedingtesten Solidarität (Einheit) mit der Menschheit
verknüpft durch,* etc. (Kr.)   l. 30 : "free to form his opinions,"
ungehindert seine Meinungen zu bilden.

Page 35, l. 3 : "that of stating the laws, etc," *nämlich die (i. e. die
Freiheit) : die Gesetze . . . auszusprechen.*   l. 4 : "without hindrance
except from," *ohne ein Hindernis ausser durch.*   l. 5 : "he seems,"

scheint er (or, *so scheint er*, or even, *er scheint*, i. e. the normal order
may be followed in such a conclusion, although earlier not so com-
monly employed), *nichts zu entbehren, was zu einem . . . Leben gehört.*
l. 7 : "is that he will think," *ist die* (i. e. *Gefahr*) *dass er glauben
könnte.* l. 7 : "is made for him," *sei für ihn da.* l. 13 : "society
has subdivided itself enough to have a place," *die Gesellschaft hat sich
genug eingeteilt* (*abgefacht*) *um für jede Form des Talentes einen Platz
zu haben. Wenn zum Beispiel ein Mann auch nur eine Spur von
Begabung zum Bildhauer oder Maler verrät.* (Kr.) l. 22 : "belongs
where he is wanted," *gehört dahin, wo man ihn braucht.* l. 25 :
"head," *Haupt.*

IX.

A GALLOP OF THREE.

Page 36, Ein Galopp zu Dreien.—l. 1 : "we were off, we three,
on our gallop to save and to slay," *fort sprengten wir drei auf unserm
Ritt zu retten und zu rächen.* l. 3 : "they were ready to burst into ·
their top speed," *sie wollten im vollen Laufe lossprengen* (*in vollen
Lauf kommen*), *und wütend fortjagen* (*in rasendem Laufe dahinstür-
men*). l. 5 : "this long easy lope," *diesen langen, leichten Schritt
(gestreckte bequeme Gangart*). l. 12 : "the sound of galloping hoofs,"
das Geräusch des Hufschlags (Kr.), or, *das Getöse der stampfenden
Pferde* (*der Pferde Getrampel*). l. 22 : "they have terrible hours
the start," *sie sind uns um schreckliche Stunden voraus.* (Kr.)

Page 37, l. 6 : "it is long odds of a start," *sie sind uns um eine
weite Strecke* (*einen weiten Weg*) *voraus.* l. 18 : "I made a good
omen of this remembrance," *ich liess diese Erinnerung für ein gutes
Zeichen gelten.* l. 23 : "brave enough for," *tapfer genug für.* l. 24 :
"led off by a neck, we ranging up instantly," *kam wieder um eine
Halslänge voraus, aber wir holten ihn gleich wieder ein.*

Page 38, l. 1 : "we rode side by side, taking our strides together.
It was a waiting race," *wir ritten nebeneinander mit gleichem Schritte.
Es war ein aushaltendes Wettrennen* (*ein Rennen mit Abwarten.*
Kr.). l. 5 : "spend, but waste not," *spenden aber nichts verspenden*
(*verschwenden*). l. 9 : "make the most of," *aufs beste benutzen* (*ver-*

werten). 1. 11 : "came and sang in my ears to the flinging cadence, etc.," *klang mir in die Ohren zu dem brausenden Takt der stampfenden Hufe, die über hohlen Gewölben . . . und über grossen leeren Gründen (Klüften) hinwegfuhren.* 1. 17 : "but nearing now and lifting step by step," *die aber mit jedem Schritte immer näher und höher sich zeigten.* 1. 25 : "drew down," *zug herunter.* 1. 27 : "were lifted anew to their work," *und legten sich wieder mit neuer Kraft (gestärkt) daran.*

Page 39, 1. 3 : "as a lane rifts in the press of hurrying legions 'mid the crush of a city thoroughfare," *wie eine Gasse sich mitten im Gedränge von eilenden Tausenden auf einer wimmelnden Strasse der Stadt aufthut.* 1. 12 : "they sprang toward me," *sie sprengten zu mir hin.* 1. 15 : "still going at speed and holding by one leg alone, after the Indian fashion for sport or for shelter against an arrow or a shot," *noch im vollen Fluge, und sich nur mit einem Beine festhaltend, wie die Indianer entweder zum Scherz oder zum Schutz gegen einen Pfeil oder einen Schuss (eine Kugel) es thun.*

Page 40, 1. 20 : "stooped forward and hung over us as we rode," *bogen sich vor und hingen über uns wie wir hinritten.* 1. 22 : "where it dipped suddenly down upon the plain," *wo sie plötzlich in die Ebene sich senkte.*

Page 41, 1. 7 : "by the force of a purpose alone," *nur vermöge seines Entschlusses.* 1. 28 : "noon's packing of hot air had been dislodged by a mountain breeze drawing through," "*die drückende Hitze des Mittags war durch einen Luftzug vom Gebirge vertrieben worden.*"

Page 42, 1. 11 : "it had made its way as water does, not straightway, etc.," *er hatte sich, wie das Wasser thut, keinen geraden Weg gebahnt, sondern war nach der wirksamen Art der Weiber der düstern Stirne jedes Hindernisses ausgewichen und hatte, ins Thal hinabgleitend, den starren Fels stehen lassen, der das wilde Geschöpf gern hätte anhalten mögen.* 1. 25 : "lifted him at a leap," *trieb ihn zu einem Sprunge.* 1. 27 : "he fell short," *er trat zu kurz.*

Page 43, 1. 2 : "at the knee," *am Kniegelenk.* 1. 5 : "the scream went echoing high up the cliffs," "*der Schrei wand sich im Echo die Klippen hinauf*" (*hallte wieder gegen die hohen Felsen*).

l. **17**: "rising up and swelling in a flood of thick uproar," *der (Wieder-hall) sich erhob und zu einer grossen lärmenden Flut anschwoll, bis er über den Gipfel stieg.*

Page 44, l. 3: "macheers" (?), probably for Spanish *machete*, a sword-like knife about three feet long, usually a part of the horseman's kit. l. **7**: "was upon us," *lag auf uns.* l. **8**: "for," *für, im Verhältnis zu* (or, *trotz*) *meiner Grösse.* l. **14**: "striking true as a thunderbolt," *der sicher wie ein Donnerschlag traf.* l. **15**: "that writhing agony of speed," "*das fieberhafte Vorwärtsstreben.*" l. **17**: "thrilling to mine, etc.," *schlug* (or *klopfte*) *mir entgegen und der herrliche Körper gehorchte dem klopfenden Herzen.* l. **27**: "could have held with the black," "*hätte es mit dem Rappen aufnehmen können.*"

Page 45, l. 4: "between the ring of the hoofs," *zwischen dem Klingen der Hufe.*

Page 46, l. 1: "blindly," *in blinder Eile.*

X.

THE LADY OF LYONS.

Page 47, l. 2: "two years and a half from the date," *zwei (und) ein halb* (or, *drittehalb*) *Jahre,* or, *zwei und ein halbes Jahr, nach der Zeit,* etc., i. e. May 10, 1797 (cf. 48, 7 and 49, 17). l. **4**: "enter left," *treten (von) links ein.* l. **7**: "it is just two years and a half since I," *vor gerade zwei und einem halben Jahre,* or, *es ist grade dritthalb Jahre her seit ich,* etc. l. **11**: "now the war in Italy is over," *nun (dass) der Krieg in Italien vorbei ist,* or, *da der Krieg nun,* etc.

Page 48, l. 3: "I shall make the best use of my time," *ich werde meine Zeit aufs beste verwerten (den besten Gebrauch von . . . machen).* l. **6**: "a professional cicerone," *Cicerone von Beruf.* — "by the way," *beiläufig (gesagt).* l. **20**: "sore upon this point," *empfindlich in diesem Punkt.* l. **23**: "exeunt right," *gehen rechts ab.* l. **26**: "say (of) interest rather," *sagen Sie vielmehr der Teilnahme.* l. **30**: "all tend," *das alles trägt bei.* — "as much . . . as," *so wohl . . . als,* or, *ebenso sehr . . . wie.*

Page 49, 1. 10: "no sooner did he enter Lyons than he waved his hand to me," *kaum war er in Lyon* (*angekommen*), *da* (or *so*) *winkte er mir* (or, *als er mir winkte*) *mit der Hand.*   1. **12** : "I warrant," *wett' ich.*   1. **15**: "success to him," *ich wünsche ihm Glück.*   1. **26**: a humorous reference to the memorial verses in the Eton Latin Grammar:

> "Propria quae maribus tribuuntur, mascula dicas ;
> Ut sunt divorum Mars, Bacchus, Apollo ; virorum
> Ut Cato, Virgilius etc."

Page 50, 1. 19: "heiress to what," *Erbin — wovon !* or, *was wird sie von mir erben ?*   1. **21** : "six pairs of white leather inexpressibles," *sechs Paar weisse* (better than *weisser*) *Hosen.* "*Unaussprechliche*", is sometimes heard, but is rare, and quite ludicrous. (Kr.) 1. **27** : "all a toss up," *das ist alles die reine Lotterie.*   1. **30** : "not like the rest of us soldiers," *und nicht wie wir andern Soldaten.*

Page 51, 1. 11 : "that is to make her mine," *der sie zu der Meinigen macht* (or, *wodurch sie die Meinige* (or *mein*) *wird*), *binnen einer Woche nach dem Tage an welchem*, etc.   1. **18** : "well met," *seien Sie mir willkommen*, or, *gut, dass ich Sie treffe.*

Page 52, 1. 20 : "who sets his heart upon a woman," *der sein Herz an ein Weib hängt.*   1. **25** : "just as the gale varies from north to south, from heat to cold," *wie der Wind von Nord nach Süd, von Hitze zu Kälte umspringt* (*umschlägt*), or, *warm wird oder kalt.* 1. **28** : "thou art the author of such a book of follies in a man, that it would need the tears of all the angels to blot the record out."

> *Es ist dein Werk*
> *Im Manne solch ein Buch voll arger Thorheit,*
> *Dass aller Engel Thränen kaum genügten,*
> *Die Schrift zu löschen.* (Kr.)

Page 53, 1. 5: "crosses left," *geht über die Bühne nach links.* 1. **10**: "sate in my heart," *besass mein Herz.*   1. **12** : "that did not wear her shape," *die ihre Gestalt nicht hegte.*   1. **18** : "I went but by the rumor of the town," *ich liess mich nur von Stadtgespräch bestimmen* (or, *ging nach dem Stadtgespräch*).

Page 54, l. 1: "why should she keep, through years and silent absence, the holy tablets of her virgin faith true to a traitor's name," *warum sollte sie während der Jahre meiner stummen Abwesenheit den Namen des Verräters im Heiligtum ihrer iungfräulichen Treue aufbewahren?* l. 5. "than to be what I am," *als (das) zu sein, was ich nun bin.* l. 6: "so wildly welcomed," *so lebhaft* (or *heiss*) *begrüsst.* l. 7: "singled out of time and marked for bliss," *aus der Zeit herausgelesen und zur Glückseligkeit gestempelt.* l. 11: "the bronzed hues of time and toil," *dein Gesicht durch Zeit und Arbeit gebräunt* (or, *verändert*). l. 12: "belief in your absence," *der Glaube an deine Abwesenheit* (or, *dass du in der Fremde bist*). l. 22: "the veriest slave that ever crawled from danger," *der elendeste Sklave der jemals vor der Gefahr verkroch.* l. 27: "that ever smiled destruction on brave hearts," *die lächelnd edle Herzen je gemordet,* or, *deren Lächeln je tapfern Herzen Verderben brachte* (Kr.), or, *die je mit verderblichem Lächeln tapfre Herzen bedrohten.*

Page 55, l. 15: "have I lived to pray, etc.," *muss ichs erleben, dass ich bitten möchte, du könntest,* etc. l. 23: "that prouder wealth," *den edlern Schatz.* l. 27: "is there no hope? no hope but this," *bleibt keine Hoffnung mehr? keine als nur diese?*

Page 56, l. 3: "sinks to the west," *nach Westen sinkt.* l. 5: the reading is *insolvent,* or *insolent.* l. 7: "how pride has fallen," *wie ist der Stolz erniedrigt!* l. 14: "love has no thought of self," *die Liebe denkt nicht an sich selbst.* — "love buys not with the ruthless usurer's gold, etc.," *die Liebe kauft mit Wuchergolde nicht die ekle Unzucht einer Hand, vergeben ohne das Herz.* (Kr.) l. 25: "my sand is well-nigh run," *mein Stundenglas ist beinahe abgelaufen.* l. 28: "are laid," *liegen.* l. 30: "that lays the beggar by the side of kings," *die den König wie den Bettler zu Boden streckt.*

Page 57, l. 3: "whose lips never knew one harsh word," *von dessen Lippen ich nie ein hartes Wort vernahm.* l. 10: "thy state will rank first 'mid the dames of Lyons," *du wirst im Range die erste Stelle einnehmen unter den Damen von Lyon.* l. 11: "shelter," *schützen.* l. 17: "shed the light," *lass leuchten.* l. 18: "lost evermore to me," *auf ihn, den ich für immer verloren.* l. 19: "centre, left," *links durch die Mitte.* l. 24 · "we had once looked higher," *einst machten wir höhere Ansprüche.*   l. 29 : " have two considerations," *zwei Rücksichten haben.*

Page 58, l. 3 : " left centre," *links von der Mitte.*   l. 14 : " you ask from me what I have not the sublime virtue to grant," *Sie verlangen von mir, was ich nicht die erhabene Tugend habe, zuzugeben.* l. 20 : " retires to left of table," *zieht sich an die linke Seite* (or, *zur Linken*) *des Tisches zurück.*   l. 22 : " enter centre left," *treten durch die Mitte links ein.*   l. 27 : " crosses," *geht hinüber.*   l. 28 : " throws himself into a chair, left upper entrance," *wirft sich auf einen Stuhl am oberen Eingang links.*

Page 59, l. 2 : " you are going to be divorced from poor Melnotte," *Sie wollen sich von dem armen Melnotte scheiden lassen.* l. 26 : " the last plank to which I clung is shivered," *das letzte Bret, an welches ich mich geklammert, ist zerscheitert,* or, *so ist mir der letzte Halt genommen.*

Page 60, l. 2 : " left centre," *links in der Mitte.*   l. 7 : " one word, I beseech you," *auf ein Wort, ich bitte Sie.*   l. 8 : " how the old time comes o'er me," *wie die alte Zeit mich ergreift.*   l. 14 : " in the dumb show," *mit Geberdenspiel.*   l. 21 " myself and misery know the man," *ich und das Unglück, wir kennen ihn.*   l. 23 : " and you will see him, and you will bear to him, etc.," *und Sie werden ihn sehen, und Sie werden ihm alles sagen, — ja Wort für Wort — was dies Herz, welches, wenn es von ihm scheidet, bricht, ihm sagen möchte.* l. 28 : " never nursed a thought that was not his ; — that on his wandering way, daily and nightly pour'd a mourner's prayers," *keinen Gedanken gehegt, der nicht von ihm* (or, *nur an ihn gedacht*), *dass Tag und Nacht auf seinen Wanderpfad sich einer Trauernden Gebet ergoss.* (Kr.)

Page 61, l. 4 : " live upon the light of one kind smile from him," (*ich möchte*) *im Lichte seines Lächelns lieber leben.*   l. 11 : " read," *durchschauen,* or, *in meinem Herzen lesen.*   l. 15 : " he calls his child to save him," " *er ruft sein Kind, damit es ihn errette.*"   l. 20 : " who is left," *der links steht.*   l. 26 : " were but your duty with your faith united," " *wäre aber Ihre Pflicht vereint mit Ihrer Treue.*" l. 28 : " Ah better death with, etc.," *ach, lieber den Tod* (sc. *möchte ich wählen*) or, *lieber tot, mit,* etc.

Page 62, l. 5: "the instant she has signed," *sobald sie unter-schreibt,* or, *den Augenblick wo sie unterzeichnet.* **l. 5** "you are still the great House of Lyons," *Ihr Haus bleibt noch immer gross in Lyon.* **l. 25:** "the stain is blotted from my name," *der Flecken an meinem Namen ist ausgelöscht.*

Page 63, l. 1: "thus have heard the beating of thy heart against my own," *das Klopfen deines Herzens an meinem so vernommen.* **l. 3** "places Pauline in a chair," *drückt Pauline in einen Stuhl.* — "goes off, centre left," *geht durch die Mitte links ab.* **l. 7:** "grow sour and blackened into hate," *bitter, schwarz und hässlich werden,* **l. 11:** "curses are like young chickens, and still come home to roost," *Flüche sind wie Küchlein — sie kommen stets zur Hühnersteige heim.* (Kr.) Note the German sayings: *der Fluch klebt an Niemand denn am Flucher;* and, *wie man in den Wald ruft, so ruft es wieder.* **l. 18:** "right centre," *rechts in der Mitte.*

Page 64, l. 6: "Heaven smiled on conscience! As the soldier rose from rank to rank," *der Himmel lächelte der Tugend zu* (Kr.), or, *der Himmel war mir wegen meiner Reue* (or *Rechtschaffenheit*) *günstig. Als der Soldat von Rang zu Rang sich hob.* **l. 11:** "crosses to him," *geht zu ihm über.* **l. 13:** "Ah! the same love that tempts us into sin, if it be true love, works out its redemption," *ach dieselbe Liebe, die uns zur Sünde reizt* (or, *verlockt*), *kann, wenn sie wahr ist, sich selbst erlösen* (or, *ihre eigne Erlösung erwirken*). — "he who seeks repentance for the past should woo the Angel Virtue in the future," *wer Busse für Vergangenes will thun, muss mit der Tugend Engel sich vereinen* (Kr.), or, *muss dem Engel "Tugend" huldigen,* or, "*Wer für die Vergangenheit Busse thun will, muss es für die Zukunft mit dem Engel ' Tugend' halten.*"

XI.

FROM MOTLEY'S CORRESPONDENCE.

Page 65. I. Bismarck's own English. **l. 2:** "May 23, 1864," *den* (*am* not so common) 23. Mai. Also: d. 23. Mai; 23. Mai; 23. v. 64; ²³/₅ 64. **l. 3:** "where the devil are you," *wo den* (or, *zum*)

Henker steckst du?   1. 6: "as well as looking on your feet tilted against the wall of God knows what a dreary color," *als deine Füsse ansehen, die gegen eine Wand von Gott weiss welcher traurigen Farbe gestemmt sind.*   1. 14: "the sweet restorer, sleep," *den süssen "Erneuerer" Schlaf.*   1. 15: "Auld Lang Syne," use the same words, or, *die gute alte Zeit.*   1. 19: "make out the time," *Zeit gewinnen.*

Page 66, 1. 3: "let politics be hanged," *lass die Politik zum Henker fahren.*   1. 5: "pour damnation upon the rebels," *Verdammis über die Rebellen giessen.*   1. 13: "haunted by the song, 'In good old Colony Times,'" *verfolgt vom Lied:* (English title, or,) "*In guten alten Kolonialzeiten.*"   1. 22: "this is all the commentary I shall make to-day," *heute mache ich keine Bemerkung mehr über die Geschichte.*   1. 23: "to me the most interesting part of the Conferences was," *was mich an diesen Konferenzen am meisten interessierte, war.*

Page 67, 1. 4: "there is nothing of the shabby-genteel, the would-be-but-could n't-be fine gentleman," *an ihm ist nichts Schäbig-Vornehmes, nichts von dem möchte-wohl-kann-nicht feinen Herrn* (Kr.), or, *der ein feiner Herr gern sein möchte, aber es nicht vermag.*   Platen says: "*was kannst du mögen, das du nicht vermagst.*"   Cp. Zimmermann: *keine Tugend kommt neben dem schäbichten Flitterstaat schmutziger und buntscheckiger Bettler vom Stande in Vergleichung* (Sanders's *Wörterbuch,* III., 876).   1. 7: "blundering occasionally, but through blunders struggling onward towards what he believes the right," *dann und wann Fehler machend, aber durch seine Fehler vorandringend zu dem, was er für Recht hält.* (Kr.)   1. 16: "I am delighted to hear of you as improving in health and spirits," *ich bin sehr froh zu hören, dass deine Gesundheit und Stimmung sich bessert.* (Kr.)   1. 24: "date August 6," "*datiert vom 6. Aug.*"

Page 68, 1. 1: "since the days of Fort Donelson, few attacks made in front upon entrenchments by either belligerent have succeeded," *seit den Tagen von Fort Donelson haben wenig Front-Angriffe auf Verschanzungen seitens einer der kriegführenden Parteien Erfolg gehabt.* (Kr.)   1. 6: "which I always thought would be his game," *was ich immer für sein Spiel gehalten.*   1. 8: "the only ripple we have had on our surface is when, etc.," *der einzige Wellenschlag auf* *unserer Wasserfläche entstand als.* (Kr.) l. **15**: "can tolerate any remaining at table after the finger-bowls," *kann das Verweilen bei Tafel nach den Fingerbecken (Fingergläsern, Mundgläsern,) leiden.* l. **24**: "a dinner of a dozen," *ein Diner von zwölf Gedecken.*

Page 69, l. **3**: "your writing to me," *dass du mir schreibst.* l. **13**: "doubt, etc." *Hamlet,* II., 2. l. **14**: "for three weeks my paper has been lying ready to write to you in London," "*seit drei Wochen lag das Papier fertig, um dir nach London zu schreiben.*" l. **16**: "to make up for your secret flight across the ocean," "*zur Genugthuung für deine heimliche Flucht über See.*"

Page 70, l. **1**: "otherwise I would come and find you and bring you to the backwoods here," "*sonst suchte ich dich auf, um dich hier in die Backwoods abzuholen.*" l. **24**: *Banhoff,* an apparent misprint for *Bahnhof.* l. **28**: "just in time for the dinner-bell," *zur rechten Zeit für das Mittagsessen.*

Page 71. V. This extract is Bismarck's own English. l. **4**: "from the waggon to the wagen," i. e. from the car to the coach, *aus dem Waggon in den Wagen.* l. **14**: "your name is familiar to her lips, and never came forth without a friendly smile," *dein Namen ist ihren Lippen vertraut, und ist niemals ohne ein freundliches Lächeln ausgesprochen* (or, *genannt*). l. **21**: "give my most sincere regards to her," *ich bitte um meine aufrichtigen Empfehlungen an sie* (Kr.), or, *ich lasse mich ihr aufrichtigst empfehlen.*

Page 72, l. **4**: "with the Bancrofts," *bei Bancrofts* (plural). l. **25**: "and made to sit down and go on with the dinner which was about half through," *und uns gleich setzen und am Essen teilnehmen mussten, obgleich sie damit schon halb fertig waren, weil wir,* etc.

Page 73, l. **4**: "so full of *laissez-aller,*" *lässt sich so ganz gehen.* (Kr.) l. **10**: "that it is the regular thing to be," *dass es das Gewöhnliche ist, einer zu sein* (Kr.), or, *als ob es alles ganz in der Ordnung wäre.* l. **13**: "who cast a far more chilling shade over those about them than Bismarck does," *welche einen viel kühleren Schatten über ihre Umgebung werfen als Bismarck.* (Kr.) l. **28**: "he is the least of a *poseur* of any man I ever saw, little or big," *er hat am wenigsten vom Poseur* (or, *Wichtigthuer*) *an sich von allen Menschen, klein oder gross, die ich je gesehen habe.* (Kr.)

Page 74, l. 1: "I wish there could always be attached to his button-hole," *ich wollte, es könnte an sein Knopfloch immer angehängt sein.*   l. 6: "the military opinion was bent on going to Vienna after Sadowa," *nach Sadowa ging die Meinung der Militärs* (or, *der Generäle ?*) *dahin, auf Wien zu marschieren.* (Kr.)   l. 17: "crossed the room," *ging durch das ganze Zimmer.*   l. 23: "as wise, etc.," translate: *weil er klug,* etc., or, *wegen seiner Klugheit,* etc.

Page 75, l. 7: "until," *bis* or *vor.*   l. 10: "entirely at leisure," *der gänzlich frei ist.*   l. 19: "he talks away right and left about anything and everything," *er redet hin und her über alles und jedes.* l. 21: "than for," *als wenn.*   l. 23: "as to Holland," *in Betreff Hollands.*   l. 25: "it had never occurred to him or to anybody," *es wäre weder ihm noch sonst jemand jemals eingefallen.* (Kr.)   l. 26: "as to Belgium," *was Belgien betrifft.*

Page 76, l. 4: "for," *zu.*   l. 5: "and he was perfectly hardened against eloquence of any kind," *und er wäre völlig abgehärtet gegen Beredsamkeit aller Art.*   l. 7: "as" to be omitted in translating. l. 11: "to commit this letter to the bag," *um diesen Brief dem Postbeutel zu übergeben.*   l. 14: "so don't be frightened at getting one," *daher erschrick nicht wenn du eins bekommt.* (Kr.)

XII.

FROM TAYLOR'S CORRESPONDENCE.

Page 77, l. 2: see note to p. 65, l. 2.   l. 6: "that one day has only repeated the impression left by the previous one. We went out on the smoothest of oceans that day, and carried calm weather with us," *dass jeder Tag nur den Eindruck seines Vorgängers wiederholt hat. Wir fuhren bei ganz ruhiger See ab und nahmen das ruhige Wetter mit.* (Kr.)

Page 78, l. 1: "as if we had gone from New York to dine in Brooklyn," *als wenn wir von New-York zum Mittagsessen nach Brooklyn gekommen wären.*   l. 6: "I breathe an atmosphere," *ich atme eine Atmosphäre.*   l. 11: "a good broad stretch of sky," *ein guter breiter Streifen Himmel.*   l. 12: "invite my soul to whatever sort of banquet she may prefer," *meine Seele einladen zu jeglichem Schmaus den.* 1. 14: "to get away from the grooves in which one's life must run," *aus den alten Geleisen loszukommen, in welchen unser Leben verläuft.* (Kr.) 1. 16: "you walk further away from your canvas, and see the truer relations," *du trittst von deiner Leinwand weiter zurück und kannst richtiger sehen,* etc.

Page 79, 1. 1: "our ties, now, have the light and sparkle and strength and smoothness of ripe old wine," *unsere Freundschaften* (or, *Verbindungen*) *haben jetzt den Glanz und das Perlen, die Kraft und Milde des reifen alten Weines.* (Kr.) 1. 7: "I have done nothing except to read a few books," *ich habe nichts gethan als ein paar Bücher durchgelesen* (or, *durchzulesen*). 1. 21: "by," *auf.*

Page 80, 1. 4: "this on account of 'Faust,'" *das geschah wegen meines "Faust."* 1. 9: "is a good thing for," *befördert.* 1. 13: "which," *was.* 1. 14: "I work half the day compiling for Scribners," *ich arbeite die eine Hälfte des Tages an Sammelwerken für Scribners.* 1. 16: "and of such is not the kingdom of Heaven," *und solcher* (genitive) *ist nicht das Himmelreich.* 1. 22: omit *that* in translating. 1. 23: "is," *wäre* or *sei.* "led," *verleitete* (or the passive may be used). 1. 26: "showed so much interest in Longfellow," *fragten mit solchem Anteil nach Longfellow.* 1. 27: "I forgot ceremony, and felt quite at home," *ich·vergass völlig die Etikette* (or, *ich machte keine Umstände*), *und fühlte mich ganz heimisch.*

Page 81, 1. 3: "so much was crowded into my two months' sojourn," *so viel drängte sich in meinem zweimonatlichen Aufenthalt zusammen.* 1. 4: "where to begin to tell you about it,"·*wo ich bei meiner Erzählung anfangen soll.* 1. 5: "I had not been there many days, before," *nicht viele Tage hatte ich dort zugebracht, als* (or *da* with inversion). 1. 18: "thawed toward me," *taute mir gegenüber gänzlich auf.*

Page 82, 1. 10: "I was at once placed in the very relation to all which I wished to have established," *da wurde ich sogleich in eben die Beziehungen zu Allen gebracht, die ich mir gewünscht hatte.*

Page 83, 1. 12: "after knowing Weimar," *nachdem ich Weimar gesehen.* 1. 15: I wish I had space to tell you more of what I learned, and how immensely I have been encouraged," *ich möchte* *gern mehr Raum haben* (or, *hätte ich nur Raum*), *so könnte ich dir mehr erzählen von alledem, was* (or, *über alles, was*) *ich gelernt* (or, *erfahren*) *und wie man mich so unendlich ermuntert hat.* l. 23 : "with a mock reproach," *mit scheinbarem Tadel* (Kr.), or, *in scheinbar* (or, *scherzhaft*) *vorwurfsvollem Tone.* l. 26: "which I did," "*das that ich denn auch.*" l. 28 : "otherwise only the family," *sonst war nur die Familie dabei* (or, *anwesend*). "it gave me a thrill of pride," *es kam ein Gefühl des Stolzes über mich* (or, *es überkam mich ein Gefühl*, etc.). **Page 84**, l. 2 : "I lashed properly," *ich geisselte gehörig.* l. 5 : Stedman, Stoddard, Aldrich, Howells. l. 9 : "for," *auf* (with accusative). l. 12 : "which will give me," *so kann ich zusammenbringen.* l. 16 : "done," *fertig.* "even allowing," *selbst wenn ich einrechne.* l. 20 : "intending this letter to be read by all," *mit der Absicht, dass der Brief von Allen gelesen wird* (or, *der Brief soll aber von Allen gelesen werden*). l. 21 : "we are very busy just now getting settled," *augenblicklich* (or, *in diesem Augenblick*) *sind wir sehr damit beschäftigt, alles einzurichten.* l. 25 : "yesterday week," *gestern vor acht Tagen.*

Page 85, l. 6 : "M. and L. nearly saw the attempt," *beinahe hätten M. und L.* (or, *es fehlte nicht viel und M. und L. hätten*) *den Angriff gesehen.* l. 12 : "we are busy looking out for a residence," *wir suchen fleissig eine* (*nach einer*) *Wohnung.* l. 14 : "adding, etc.," translate by the accusative absolute. l. 15 : "I think," *wahrscheinlich.* l. 18 : "by," *bis zum.* "to buy all that is necessary," *um damit alles Nötige zu kaufen.* l. 19 : "so far as I can judge, the expenses will be just about what I calculated," *so weit ich urteilen kann, werden unsere Ausgaben so ungefähr meiner Berechnung entsprechen.* l. 22 : "gorgeous in his gold-banded stove-pipe hat," *prangend in seinem goldbetressten Cylinderhut.* (Kr.) l. 24 : "adds immensely to our respectability," *erhöht unsere Achtbarkeit unermesslich,* or, *ganz bedeutend.* (Kr.) l. 26 : "we know what to do, and people are rather surprised to find that we know it," *wir wissen uns zu benehmen und die Leute sind ziemlich erstaunt bei der Erfahrung* (or, *wenn sie finden*), *dass wir es wissen.* l. 29 : "take all the bother off my hands, etc.," *befreien mich von der ganzen Quälerei, und ich bin in Betreff meiner literarischen Arbeit ganz heiter gestimmt.*

Page 86, l. 1: "full summer," *Hochsommer.*   l. 8 : "to," *bei.*
l. 12 : "he being accompanied," *er wurde . . . begleitet,* etc., or translate "he" by the accusative and "dog" as nominative.   l. 17 :
"an effect only a little less profound than the murder of Lincoln,"
eine Wirkung die kaum minder tief ist, als beim Morde Lincolns.
Page 87, l. 6: "my first intimation of his coming," *die erste
Anzeige, die ich erhielt.*   l. 14: "to arrange in advance for such
interviews and honors, etc.," *im voraus Vorkehrungen zu treffen,
damit solche Besuche und Ehrenbezeigungen ihnen zu teil werden sollten,
die zu bewirken wären in einer Zeit, wo allen solchen eine ausserordentliche Bedeutung beigelegt werden konnte.*   l. 19 : "to maintain her
privacy in the palace," *im Palais zurückgezogen zu bleiben.*   l. 24 :
"the number of prearranged dinners and social assemblages arising
therefrom, etc.," *die Menge der damit zusammenhängenden und vorausbestimmten Diners und Gesellschaften verhinderte, "dass dem Ex-
Präsidenten diejenige Aufmerksamkeit zu teil wurde, welche er zu jeder
andern Zeit* (or, *sonst*) *in vollem Masse hier gefunden (genossen) haben
würde."*   l. 28 : "after having arranged for a reception," *nachdem
ich mit . . . einen Empfang verabredet hatte.*

Page 88, l. 15: "invited to dine at the new palace in Potsdam the
next evening," "*lud auf den nächsten Tag nach Potsdam zum Diner
im neuen Palais (ein)."*   l. 18: "I was surprised to find," *fand ich zu
meiner Überraschung.*   l. 22 : "on reaching the palace," *bei meiner
Ankunft im Palais.*   l. 25 : "the Emperor's interest in General
Grant's history," "*Interesse welches der Kaiser an dem Lebensgang
von General Grant nehme."*   l. 28 : "implied an authorization,"
schien mich zu berechtigen, or, *mir die Ermächtigung zu geben.*

Page 89, l. 4: "he has the peace of the world at heart," *der
allgemeine Weltfrieden liegt ihm am Herzen.*   l. 5: "nothing so
much," *nichts so sehr.*   l. 6 : "to make it your task," *zu Ihrer Aufgabe zu machen.*   l. 9 : "this is the Emperor's message to you, and
he asked me to give it to you in his name as well as my own," "*dieses
ist der Auftrag, den mir der Kaiser für Sie gab, den ich Ihnen, wie
er mich bat, in seinem so wie in meinem Namen ausdrücken solle."*
l. 18 : "on reaching the station," *bei unserer Ankunft* (or, *als wir
ankamen) am Bahnhof.*   l. 20 : "to," *bis zum.*   l. 21 : "on reaching Potsdam," *bei der Ankunft in Potsdam.*

Page 90, l. 1 : " both being the places of honor," "*da dies die bei-den Ehrenplätze waren.*"   l. 2. "I did not consider it consistent with the dignity of the government I represent, etc.," *ich hielt es nicht für vereinbar mit der Würde der Regierung welche ich vertrete* (Kr.), *im voraus irgend welche Bedingungen betreffend* (or, *in Betreff der*) *die Etikette zu machen, noch irgend eine Frage darüber zu thun.* l. 7 : " during the return to another station, by a longer drive through the park, General Grant received every mark of respect from the people, who crowded the streets to see him pass," *während der Rückkehr nach einer andern Station auf einer längeren Fahrt durch den Park erhielt General Grant jeden Beweis der Achtung von der Bevölkerung, welche die Strassen füllten, um ihn vorbeifahren zu sehen.*

Brandt's German Reader.

WITH NOTES

AND VOCABULARY.

12mo. Half leather.

420 pages. $1.25.

The aim of the editor has been to prepare a book, which, first of all, shall be <u>practical</u>, supplying sufficient material to enable the pupil to read with ease ordinary German prose.

It is <u>progressive</u>, leading step by step from the simplest prose and poetry to matter of usual difficulty.

It is <u>interesting</u>, containing a large variety of selections, none of them trivial, and many of permanent value.

It is <u>attractive in appearance</u>, the generous space between the lines enabling the student to read the German text with ease.

The extracts are divided into six sections:

Section I. EASY PROSE. 31 pages.

„ II. EASY POETRY. 16 pages.

„ III. LEGENDS AND TALES. 75 pages.

„ IV. SONGS AND LYRICS. 39 pages.

„ V. A COMEDY. 21 pages.

„ VI. HISTORICAL PROSE. 47 pages.

Brandt's German Reader.

Prof. W. T. Hewett, *Cornell University, New York.* — The selections have been made with admirable judgment; every separate division is in itself a contribution to the whole. The notes are extremely instructive, and only such as an experienced and skilful teacher could prepare. The vocabulary is worthy of high praise, and will facilitate a thorough knowledge of the German language. No German reader meets more clearly my views of what such a book should contain.

The Independent, *New York.* — The first impression one is likely to receive from the book, beyond that from the very handsome make-up, is that it excels in the variety of its contents. To obtain this variety, and at the same time avoid making a collection of mere scraps, is no easy task. A good reading book must contain matter which is mainly simple in thought, and direct in expression. Poetry should be mingled with prose, but the latter should be more in quantity. Prof. Brandt has made admirable selections. Of the two hundred and thirty pages of text, there are fifteen pages of easy poems, about forty of songs and ballads, and the rest is devoted to prose of excellent variety. The vocabulary is an especially good feature. The whole book is marked by good taste, and the author has given to it a thorough German character. You feel the spirit of loyalty to Fatherland, and to the best and noblest of its traditions and memories. This spirit, which pupils must to some extent come to feel themselves, if they will understand German literature, meets them here from the outset. Its presence gives a value which could not otherwise be obtained by any amount of learning or of labor.

Allyn & Bacon . . . . Boston.

Prof. Albert S. Cook, *Yale University.* — The matter in Brandt's Reader is interesting and skilfully arranged; the notes are judicious in selection and composition; the vocabulary is convenient and exceptionally clear.

Prof. F. B. Gummere, *Haverford College, Pa.* — I like its plan and contents. It is a great mistake to keep young students working on nothing but prose. German poetry of the simple character selected by Professor Brandt attracts every scholar, and lessens his labor by turning a task into a pleasure.

Prof. H. B. Richardson, *Amherst College.* — It pleases me at every point, — a beautiful text, judicious and scholarly notes, and a good, legible vocabulary.

Prof. H. C. O. Huss, *College of New Jersey, Princeton.* — I do not hesitate to say that it has uncommon excellences, and I intend to adopt it next year.

Prof. O. Seidensticker, *University of Pennsylvania.* — Brandt's Reader answers all the requirements that can be made of a book of that description; it certainly is what it claims to be, practical, progressive, interesting, and attractive. As there is no Reader which so faithfully comes up to this program, it will be put in the hands of our Freshman Class.

Modern Language Notes, *Baltimore.* — The most attractive collection of easy prose and poetry published for a long time. The discretion in the matter of notes is a happy change from the methods employed by the editors of other recent Readers. The typography and general appearance of the book are uncommonly attractive.

Brandt's German Reader.

Adopted for use at

Phillips Andover Academy, Mass. ;
Wesleyan Academy, Wilbraham, Mass. ;
Groton School, Groton, Mass. ;
Friends' Central School, Philadelphia ;
Germantown Academy, Germantown, Pa. ;
Sewickley Academy, Sewickley, Pa. ;
Stern's School of Languages, New York ;
Episcopal Academy, Alexandria, Va. ;
Female Seminary, Kalamazoo, Mich.

In the High Schools at

Boston and Malden, Mass. ; Auburn, Attica,
Binghamton, Canandaigua, Elmira,
Jamestown, Hornellsville, Mexico,
Medina, Warsaw, Westport, N. Y.
Newark, N. J. ; Burlington, Ia. ;
New Haven, Conn. ;   Denver, Colorado.

And at

Bowdoin College, Me. ; Middlebury College, Vt. ;
Williams College and Tufts College, Mass. ;
Yale University Scientific School, Conn. ;
Cornell University and Hamilton College, N. Y. ;
Princeton College and Rutgers College, N. J. ;
University of Pa. and Dickinson College, Pa.
Bucknell University and Curry University, Pa. ;
Adelbert College and Miami University, Ohio ;
Wesleyan and Wooster Universities, Ohio ;
Illinois Wesleyan University, Bloomington ;
Olivet College, Mich. ; Coe College, Iowa ;
Hampden-Sidney and Roanoke Colleges, Va. ;
University of Georgia, Athens, Georgia.

Schiller's Der Neffe als Onkel.

With Notes and Vocabulary by Prof. C. F. RADDATZ, Baltimore City College. 16mo. Cloth. 50 cents.

This comedy is so well adapted to the wants of beginners that it is surprising that no adequate edition of it has hitherto been published in this country. By a careful revision of the text, ample notes, and a complete vocabulary, the editor has tried to meet this want.

Prof. Edwin F. Bacon, *State Normal School, Oneonta, N. Y.* — I am using with much satisfaction your recently published edition of *Der Neffe als Onkel,* and find it the clearest, neatest, and best printed German text that I have ever seen in a book of its class ; and, as the notes and vocabulary are also excellent, I beg to express the hope that, in the interest of human eyes, you may go on to issue other German classics in the same style. Why should this be the only one of Schiller's works printed in this country with notes and vocabulary? Blessings on you for giving us one German text as good as human skill could make it !

Prof. A. Guyot Cameron, *Miami University, Ohio.* — I am delighted with your choice of the text, the charming appearance of the book, and the clear, concise, idiomatic notes, free from grammatical over-loading. The play is bright and lively, and I shall use it as an introduction to the longer dramatic works of Schiller.

Allyn & Bacon . . . . Boston.

MODERN LANGUAGES.

Brandt.   First German Book $1.00

German Grammar 1.25

German Reader 1.25

Chardenal. First French Course 60

Second French Course 60

Complete French Course . . 1.00

Advanced Exercises 90

Lodeman. German Exercises 50

Raddatz. Schiller's Neffe als Onkel 50

Super. *Readings from French History* 1.00

White. *German Composition* 0.00

HISTORY AND PHILOSOPHY.

Bowen. Hamilton's Metaphysics $1.50

Treatise on Logic 1.25

Champlin. Constitution of the United States . .80

Pennell. History of Greece 60

History of Rome 60

De Tocqueville. American Institutions . . . 1.20

Democracy in America. 2 vols. 4.00